True Love

Books by Millie Criswell

Wild Heather
Sweet Laurel
Prim Rose
Desperate
Dangerous
Defiant

Published by Warner Books

MILLIE CRISWELL

True Love

WARNER BOOKS

A Time Warner Company

WARNER BOOKS EDITION

Copyright © 1999 by Millie Criswell
All rights reserved.

Cover design by Diane Luger
Cover illustration by Franco Accornero
Hand lettering by David Gatti

Warner Books, Inc.
1271 Avenue of the Americas
New York, NY 10020

Visit our Web site at
www.warnerbooks.com

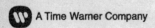 A Time Warner Company

Printed in the United States of America

First Paperback Printing: June, 1999

10 9 8 7 6 5 4 3 2 1

To Larry, my own true love, whose love and unwavering support has been a constant in my life these past thirty years.

And to Jesse, who keeps me company while I write, gives unconditional love, and who requires only an occassional pat on the head and a dog biscuit in return.

True Love

Chapter One

New York City, Summer 1889

"WE'RE IN A WORLD OF TROUBLE, EMILY JEAN." Maxwell Wise paused before Emily Jean Bartlett's desk, waiting impatiently for her to finish writing her sentence.

When Max cleared his throat for the third time, Emily finally looked up, and the chastisement teetering on the tip of her tongue died suddenly at the ashen look on her publisher's face. Max was not a man given to hysteria or theatrics, so it was obvious that something was terribly wrong.

After setting down her ink pen, she gathered up the sheets of her latest dime novel, *The Montana Kid*, and pushed them aside, intending to transcribe them later on the typewriting machine, as was her practice.

She hadn't decided yet whether or not the Kid was going to kill off the determined sheriff anyway, so it was probably just as well that she had more time to think the scene through. Fight scenes were always the most difficult for her to write; she absolutely abhorred violence. That was a bit ironic, considering the type of lurid novels she wrote.

"What's wrong? You look like you've lost your last friend."

"More like my business." He waved a piece of paper at her. "I've just received another dunning notice. The third in as many days." Heaving a dispirited sigh, he eased himself into the oak chair fronting her desk, looking far older than his fifty-eight years. His kind gray eyes were troubled, and the deep frown he wore only added to the numerous wrinkles etched across his forehead.

"Wise Publishing is failing, Emily Jean. I don't know what we're going to do. I've got stacks of bills and little money to pay them."

His words were leaden and laced with defeat, alarming the young novelist. Max Wise had excellent business instincts. He was not one to turn tail and run from a problem. He thrived on a good fight. In the three years Emily had worked for him, he had waged many a battle on behalf of his publishing house, and her.

Unlike novelists who wrote a completed manuscript, then sold it to a publisher for a sum of money, Emily was a work-for-hire writer. Max planned the books he wanted written, hired authors to pen them, then packaged them up and sold them to the public.

The job didn't pay a great deal, but what she'd learned from Max about writing and the publishing business in the last three years couldn't be measured monetarily.

"I've got a little money put aside—"

"No!" Insulted by the offer, Max shook his head.

"You should know me better than that by now. I would never take your money."

Emily did know better, but she had to try just the same. Max was like a father to her. He had hired her to work for him when no one else would, had saved her from becoming destitute after her own parents had cut her off both financially and emotionally. She owed him. And if her meager savings could help him out of his present predicament, then she wanted him to have it.

"Don't be so proud and stubborn," she scolded gently. "You helped me when I needed it. I want you to take the money. It's the least I can do to repay you for your many kindnesses."

His affectionate smile held a great deal of sadness. "You have a good heart, Emily, and it's always in the right place. But I'm afraid that your hard-earned funds won't be enough to pay off my creditors."

"But I thought you said that my last book had sold very well." Though *Blood on the Moon* had received some rather scathing reviews, it had sold nearly sixty-four thousand copies. Not bad for a book that was said to have "set the publishing world back a hundred years with its lurid prose and insipid characters." Emily still had the newspaper clipping. She kept it tucked in the bottom of her reticule and read it aloud whenever her determination to succeed began to waver. *The New York Times*'s reviewer might not have believed that E. J. Bartlett had any talent, but she knew better. And one day the world would know it, too.

"We've been losing money these past two years, despite the modest success of your dime novels." Max's admission made Emily's eyes widen in surprise. "But even the works of E. J. Bartlett can't help me compete with the larger publishing houses like Beadles and Adams or Frank Leslie, who are putting out these books in much greater quantities and have far more authors than I to crank out the stories."

Emily frowned at the mention of the two publishers who had turned down her repeated requests for employment. They hadn't wanted to take a chance on a woman writing pulp fiction. Even if that woman had ability. They were short-sighted men with no eye for competence and talent, both possessing a definite lack of taste, in her humble opinion.

"There must be something we can do to turn things around. Wise Publishing has been part of the New York literary scene for years. You've a wonderful reputation for honesty and integrity. Surely a bank or private lender will—"

"Your naiveté is showing, Emily Jean." Max hated to poison the young woman's optimistic attitude with a heavy dose of reality. Emily's unfailing optimism was one of the many things he loved about her. There was nothing that Emily Jean Bartlett thought she couldn't accomplish if she put her mind to it. Her eager, fearless determination to succeed was one of the reasons he'd hired her. In her he'd glimpsed a small piece of himself thirty years before.

"I've already been that route, and they all say the same thing: Wise Publishing needs a commercial or literary success to get back on top, to become a viable risk. And we're not cranking out literary masterpieces, if you get my meaning."

"But—"

"The way it stands now, I figure we've got six months,

eight tops, to get the house back on firm financial footing before creditors shut us down for good. In that time I've got to figure out a way to sell more books."

Emily drummed ink-stained fingers on the desktop, contemplating the situation. Six months didn't afford her a great deal of time to implement a plan whereby she could write a commercially appealing book.

True, dime novels weren't literary masterpieces, but she ventured a guess that they outsold literary fiction two to one. At least one dime novel was listed in each issue of *The Bookman* literary magazine's "Books on Demand" column, which featured the country's best-selling books. The list was compiled from bookstore sales in sixteen cities across the nation. And if a book appeared on the list it usually sold even more copies.

The key to commercial success, aside from making *The Bookman*'s best-seller list, was the subject matter. Something provocative and bold that would grab the public's attention, like the Buffalo Bill books that were currently so popular.

Legendary buffalo hunter and Indian scout William F. Cody had had numerous dime novels written about him. Readers couldn't get enough of his daring exploits. He, along with Wild Bill Hickock, had given rise to the success of the dime novel industry.

Aimed at the working class, the books were sold at newspaper stands, in retail establishments, and by mail order, their covers purposely provocative to entice the buying public to plunk down their hard-earned money. Though the books took a great deal of literary license with the truth, readers didn't seem to mind, for they were eager to gain insight into the West of the 1800s. They clamored for more thrills, more derring-do, insatiable in their appetite for western heroes and heroines.

Authors and publishers who wanted to succeed gave the readers what they wanted, often going to great lengths to get those stories written. Wise Publishing could do no less.

After a moment Emily said, "What we need isn't just one book, but a series of books on the same subject. A series that will enthrall the buying audience and have them clamoring for more." She ignored the older man's skeptical look and continued.

"I attended a production of Buffalo Bill Cody's Wild West Show some months back, and—"

"Writing a successful series is a feat easier said than done, I'm afraid," Max interrupted on a sigh. "Beadles and Adams have pretty much cornered the market on Buffalo Bill Cody and his escapades. The books are selling faster than hotcakes. I don't think—"

"I'm not talking about doing another series on Cody, Max. I'm talking about someone else—someone who's never been written about, but who's a legend in his own time. I saw the man perform when Cody's show came to New York last January. He was"—*tall, handsome, and quite unforgettable*—"larger than life."

She remembered the moment she had first laid eyes on Jess Murdock. In a blaze of gunfire, he had ridden his white stallion into the arena. It had been a glorious sight, theatrical in the extreme. The man was the stuff dashing heroes were made of, and she had not been unaffected.

Even now when she thought of the handsome cowboy her palms started to sweat.

With a perplexed look, Max scratched his head. "Who is this so-called legend, then? And why haven't we written about him before now?"

"Because Jess Murdock has purposely chosen to keep a low profile." An incongruous idea, considering his present profession and the fact that he performed before thousands of people every year.

A shrill whistle flew from Max's lips. "Jess Murdock. I've heard of him. He was married for a time, but his wife deserted him. Big scandal. Nasty stuff. There was a child, I believe." The excitement in the astute publisher's eyes started to burn.

Emily couldn't comprehend why any mother would willingly give up her child, and she wondered what had prompted Jess Murdock's wife to run off. As intriguing as the mystery was, she dismissed it with a wave of her hand. "As interesting as that tidbit of news may be, that's not what's going to sell books. The fact that Jess Murdock's performed with the Wild West show, is rumored to have killed fifty-seven men while marshal of Abilene, busted broncs, distinguished himself at the Battle of the Little Big Horn, and led a hell-raising kind of life is what's going to sell books. He's done enough in his lifetime to warrant a whole series of books about his adventures, like the series done on Cody that's selling like there's no tomorrow."

Max rubbed his chin in contemplation. "What you say may be true. But I don't have many writers left on the payroll to do a series. Those who remain are already committed to other projects. Who am I going to get to write it?"

Emily smiled confidently and poked herself in the chest. "Me. I write fast. You know I'm good. And I already have a fairly large reading audience."

"Now, Emily . . ."

Before he could protest, she added quickly, "Normally we sell about sixty thousand copies of one of our dime novels. Isn't that right?"

"Yes, but—"

"I think we could double, even triple, that amount with the cowboy's story. By placing ads in large newspapers, printing handouts ahead of the publication date that could be distributed through the mail, in bookstores, public libraries, and elsewhere, we could reserve, even sell, copies of the book before it hits the street.

"If we garner enough enthusiasm, attract enough attention, the series on Jess Murdock could very well be the salvation of Wise Publishing."

Max tempered Emily's eagerness with a dose of common sense. "If the man doesn't seek the limelight, Emily Jean, what makes you think he'll agree to be interviewed? Jess Murdock's probably had lucrative offers before, and we cannot afford to pay him."

"Leave that to me," she replied, undaunted. "I can be very persuasive when I put my mind to it."

Still extremely skeptical, Max worried at the confidence shining brightly on the young woman's face. Impulsiveness was one of Emily's greatest faults. She tended to leap before she looked, and he couldn't afford any missteps at this time. Not when the future of Wise Publishing hung in the balance.

And though Emily's creative business plan to make money off of Jess Murdock's fame was tempting, Max had certain scruples about invading people's privacy. "I'm not a vulture, Emily Jean, so if the man doesn't want his story written—"

"Not want!" Astonishment touched her face, her eyes growing round as saucers, as if such a thing were totally incomprehensible. "Of course Jess Murdock will want his story written. The man's been in the public eye for years. Obviously he'll want the attention. Who wouldn't want to be glorified like Hickock or Cody? We're offering him the chance of a lifetime."

Max was still not convinced. "I don't know. . . ."

Reaching out, Emily squeezed his hand. "Trust me, Max. When *Jess Murdock: Legend of the West* hits the streets, it's going to be a sensation. The biggest thing since the invention of the telephone. You can fire me if that isn't so."

Rolling his eyes heavenward, he held up his hands in surrender. "And who will drive me nuts if I do?"

Smiling confidently, Emily reached for a fresh sheet of paper and proceeded to write Jess Murdock a letter.

Clutching the telegram to her breast, Emily gazed at the open valise on her bed and grinned from ear to ear. After months of waiting, she had finally discovered the whereabouts of Jess Murdock. And not from the man himself.

All of the letters she had sent to him in care of the Wild West show had been returned unopened. Then, one day a few weeks back, she had received a note from someone named Belle Starling, self-proclaimed "Queen of the Western Plains," who had written to say that Jess Murdock was no longer performing with the show.

Devastated by the setback, but by no means defeated, and certainly not as upset as Max when he'd heard the disappointing news, she had used a portion of her meager savings and enlisted the aid of the Pinkerton Detective Agency. The missive she now held was from them, informing her that Jess Murdock had been found living on the outskirts of True Love, Montana, on a cattle ranch, of all things.

Although the man had begun his illustrious career as a cowboy, Emily couldn't believe that a popular Wild West show performer, a man as legendary as Jess Murdock, would be content to live on a cattle ranch among smelly cows out in the middle of nowhere. Not after everything he had experienced in his lifetime.

She had pictured him doing something far more exciting, like sailing on a steamship to some exotic port of call or living in a mansion high atop a hill in San Francisco surrounded by luxurious things. But she had not pictured him rusticating in True Love, Montana.

True Love. It was a romantic name for a town, she mused, tucking it away in her vast repertoire of useless but often used knowledge. An author never knew when a name would find its way between the pages of a book. True Love might just make a wonderful addition to the romantic novel she was planning to write one day.

A big fan of Jane Austen and Charlotte Brontë, Emily intended to follow in their footsteps and write a heartwarming and poignant tale of love conquering all. She considered the penny dreadfuls she was presently composing to be stepping-stones to the kind of literature she was truly interested in pursuing. Her ultimate career goal was to pen the best, most widely read romantic novel of all time.

She hadn't told Max her plan as yet. The publisher viewed romantic novels as fluffy costume dramas and wouldn't be at all pleased to learn that she intended to write one.

The idea of costumes diverted Emily's attention back to the pile of clothing littering the bed. What was one wearing in True Love, Montana, these days? She had no earthly idea how big the town was, where it was situated in the vast state, or how on earth she was going to get there.

"First things first, Emily Jean," she told herself, fingering the expensive but out-of-date fashions. She hadn't had the money to buy anything new since leaving her parents' opulent brick mansion over three years before.

Clothing was something she'd never really given much thought to, anyway. Her mother had been the one who loved to shop and had always kept Emily's wardrobe closet full of the latest creations from New York and Paris. But that had been before the falling-out she'd had with her parents over her refusal to wed her father's business associate, Thomas Neely, and her plan to pursue a career as a novelist.

Marian and Louis Bartlett had had Emily's future all planned out for her, which included marriage to Mr. Neely, a half dozen grandchildren, and Emily's transformation to a proper pillar of New York society.

They had been appalled at the idea that one of their children wanted to work for wages as a "hack," a writer. Especially when that child was female—a socially elite female from New York's East Side.

"It's a woman's role to marry and have children," her mother had said.

"Women do not work for a living," Louis Bartlett thundered on numerous occasions.

Though Emily had tried to explain that she didn't love Thomas Neely, had no plan to marry anyone at this time in her life, and desired a writing career above all else, they would hear none of it, stating that a career in publishing was foolish, impractical, and totally out of the question.

Her heartfelt pleas had fallen on deaf ears. In the end, she had packed her bags and moved out and had not laid eyes on her parents since that day three years ago.

Fortunately her younger sister, Elaine, and brothers Herbert and Harry had sought her out at the publishing house from time to time, and she'd been able to stay abreast of all the latest developments in their lives, much to her relief. She missed them dreadfully.

Truth be told, she missed her parents, too, but she was too proud and still smarting over their rejection to take the first step toward reconciliation, though Max had encouraged her to do so numerous times.

"You'll be sorry someday, Emily Jean, if you don't make amends with your parents. They're the only family you've got, and I know deep in their hearts that they love you.

"I wish I hadn't been as stubborn or strict with my own daughter."

Max's daughter had run away when he had refused to allow her to marry a man outside their religious persuasion. She died later in childbirth, and Max had never laid eyes on her again. Ten years had passed and he still grieved deeply, blaming himself for what he considered to be his "proud stupidity."

Emily sighed. "Maybe someday," she whispered, then refocused her attention on the problem of what to pack.

After casting a thoughtful eye on a gray foulard silk gown, she tossed it into the valise along with a jaunty green tam-o'-shanter and several other articles of clothing that she deemed absolutely necessary to take with her.

She might be traveling to the wilds of Montana, but there was no reason not to look her best when she encountered Jess Murdock for the first time.

"Jess Murdock actually invited you to come to his ranch in Montana?" Max continued pacing back and forth across the confines of his smoke-filled office, the disbelief on his face clearly evident, his searching gaze growing more intent as he stared at the young woman before him.

Emily detested cigarettes and moved to open a window, grateful she didn't have to look Max squarely in the eye as she added more embellishments to her tale. "I received his letter late last evening. I'm leaving for Montana first thing tomorrow morning. I've already purchased a train ticket as far west as Billings. I'll have to take a stage from there to True Love."

"True Love? He lives in a place called True Love?" Max rolled his eyes, then shook his head. "You're leaving tomorrow? I don't know how I let you talk me into this, Emily Jean. I'm not comfortable with the idea of you traveling clear across the country to interview some hell-raising cowboy you've never met. It could be dangerous, and—"

She scoffed at the idea of danger. This was 1889 after all. There were no Indians on the warpath, no herds of buffalo to impede train travel—greedy people like Bill Cody had killed them all. Emily expected her journey to True Love would prove quite boring, which was most unfortunate. She craved a little excitement in her life.

Though she enjoyed her work as a dime novelist, writing other people's adventures and living vicariously through them was no substitute for the real thing.

Her parents had sheltered her from the harsh realities of life while she was growing up. And even though she'd had a taste of hardship and hard work living in the real, unprivileged world these past three years, she still had experienced only a small measure of what life was truly about.

Now was the opportunity to see for herself, to experience life to the fullest. To visit the Wild West and see firsthand the places she had written about but never visited. To experience the thrill of the wide-open spaces, the adventure and excitement she could only imagine.

There was also the lure of Jess Murdock. Since her first encounter with the legend, she had dreamed of seeing him again, hungered to learn more about the man who had fueled the imagination of many, including her own.

She clutched her publisher's arm tightly, hoping she

could ease the tension and worry from his face. "Max, you know perfectly well that time is our enemy. I must move quickly if we are to stay ahead of the creditors. And we wouldn't want Mr. Murdock to change his mind, now, would we?" She held her breath and hoped she sounded convincing enough, believing that Jess Murdock was their only hope.

His frown deepened as he held out his hand. "Let me see Murdock's letter."

She swallowed. "It's . . . it's in my room, packed with all my other things. But let me assure you that Mr. Murdock is quite excited about the possibility of having me write a series of novels based on his exploits." Though she hated lying to Max, she knew it couldn't be helped. He would never have agreed to let her go if he discovered that Jess Murdock hadn't consented to her visit. Her publisher was far more principled than she and far too proud to do what she considered to be for his own good. And her own.

Max had been trained as a journalist and had taught her that getting the story was the most important thing to a writer. She was only following his tutelage.

And it wouldn't be a lie if she succeeded, she told herself.

Convinced that what she was about to do was the right thing, and the only recourse Wise Publishing had left if they were to remain in business, Emily kissed Max on the cheek, made her farewells, and barreled out of the office before the older man could form any further protestations about her imminent journey west.

Chapter Two

En Route to True Love, Montana, Autumn 1889

As THE STAGECOACH ROCKED AND BUCKED LIKE A WILD mustang, careening down the rocky incline toward True Love, Emily's bottom refused to stay put on the leather-covered seat, and she knew she'd be black and blue by the time she arrived at her destination. The bustle she had fool-ishly donned beneath her charcoal gray traveling suit was likely to catapult her clear through the roof, and landing on the damn wire cage again was not an experience she'd care to repeat any time soon.

Her traveling companion seated directly across from her had boarded the coach in Judith Gap. Elderly, with thinning white hair parted straight down the middle and slicked down on both sides, he was as wrinkled and shriv-eled as an apple left out in the sun to dry, and not much taller than Emily herself. He'd been asleep for much of the trip. A blessing, since she didn't feel particularly talkative at the moment.

The journey from New York on the Northern Pacific Railroad had been tiring, unbearably monotonous, and without incident. There were times when she'd actually longed for the sight of those all-but-extinct stampeding buffalo. Even a marauding Indian or two would have been welcome, offering respite from the mind-numbing tedium of crossing the plains. So far nothing about the Wild West had been anything like what she'd imagined or written about.

The danger Max had worried himself over had been conspicuously absent, unless one counted the awful food and sleeping conditions. She only hoped True Love had better accommodations, but she wasn't holding her breath. From what she'd gleaned from the folks back at the train station in Billings, True Love was a small ranching community without a great deal of amenities.

Emily longed for a hot bath, a decent meal, and a good night's sleep, preferably on clean, sweet-smelling sheets, and she prayed fervently that the town had, at the very least, a respectable hotel.

"Haw! Haw!" the driver shouted, cracking his whip as he urged the team to gallop faster. The horses' pace increased. The stagecoach seemed to be flying through the air when all of a sudden one of the wheels hit a rut in the road and landed with a jolt, nearly propelling the startled passengers skyward.

Emily screeched, gripped the edge of the seat with both hands, and shut her eyes, praying silently for deliverance. A gravelly sound alerted her to the fact that her snoring companion was now wide awake. She opened her eyes to discover that the old geezer was laughing at her.

"First time riding a stage, young woman?" Though he was shouting at her, Emily could barely hear what he was saying above the incessant wind howling through the windows.

She nodded. "Yes. I'm on my way to True Love. And I don't care if I never have the pleasure of riding in one of these contraptions again. It's caused me a great deal of consternation."

Cupping his ear, he leaned forward. "Eh? What'd you say? You're suffering from constipation? Eat prunes, young woman. That's what I do. Works wonders for the bowels. At my age you've got to do something about the plumbing. Tends to get backed up, if you know what I mean."

Nearly choking on her embarrassment, Emily blushed, but if the man noticed that he'd offended her by his outrageous comments, he gave no indication. "I'm not used to traveling by stage," she said, hoping to clear up the humiliating miscommunication.

"Sage is good for seasoning meat. But for constipation prunes is the only thing that gives relief. Mark my words, you'll be much happier if you take my advice."

It was painfully obvious that the elderly gentleman had a hearing problem, and Emily decided that it would not be worth the effort or further embarrassment to try to make herself understood. She had more pressing problems at the moment, like not being catapulted into the heavens.

"Oh!" she exclaimed when the stage listed dangerously to the left and she was tossed in that direction.

"Name's Woolsey. Hiram Woolsey," the man continued, seemingly unfazed by the motion of the coach. "I'm on my way to True Love to attend my granddaughter's wedding.

"Lori's a pretty little thing—reminds me of my Hester, now dead these past six years—but she's stubborn as a herd of mules about to cross a river. Told her not to marry Gus Meadows. Pig farming just ain't as lucrative as it once was. 'Course, Gus ain't that smart to do much else."

Emily had always heard that westerners were prone to keep their own counsel and not ask too many questions. She guessed Mr. Woolsey had never heard of that particular idiom. He seemed to be waiting for a reply, and she didn't want to appear rude, so she said finally, "I see."

"You from back east? I noticed you was dressed mighty fancy when I boarded the stagecoach in Judith Gap. That's where I live, you know. My daughter's been after me to move in with her and that no-good husband of hers since the wife died, but I said no. I ain't so old that I can't take care of myself."

"Independence is a good thing." Emily certainly cherished hers, though there were times when she got a bit lonely. There hadn't been many men in New York City who had sparked her interest, certainly not Thomas Neely, who was at least twenty years her senior and forty pounds overweight.

Those men with whom she worked looked upon her as a competitor; she thought of them as business associates, not love interests. The few times she had dated, the pairing had left her cold. None of the men she met could compare with the fictional heroes in her books.

She was waiting for the man who would sweep her off of her feet, lay down his life for her, if need be, cherish and love her for time and all eternity. Unfortunately she had yet to meet the man who fit the bill, so she remained single.

Mr. Woolsey glanced down at her hand, and Emily fought the urge to pull it back, wishing she hadn't taken off her gloves. But she hadn't been able to get a decent grip on the seat with them on and had totally disregarded her mother's admonition that a gently reared woman was not seen in public with her hands uncovered.

Unfortunately the fact that she wasn't wearing a wedding ring was all too apparent to her frowning companion. "You ain't married." The way he said it was almost accusing, and Emily felt her cheeks grow hot. "Marriage is a good thing, too," he declared. "At least I hope it'll be for Lori."

Emily breathed a sigh of relief when his thoughts turned back to his granddaughter again. "I'm grateful the stage got repaired. I'd have been in a real fix if I'd missed my granddaughter's wedding."

The stagecoach Emily had boarded in Billings had broken an axle just north of Harlowton. They'd been delayed several hours until the driver had managed to devise a temporary fix, and they'd literally limped into Judith Gap in the middle of the night like a three-legged dog.

The accommodations at the way station had been primitive to say the least, but she'd finally been able to secure a private bedchamber after the proprietor's wife discovered she was unmarried and traveling alone. She would always be grateful to that woman. Hiram Woolsey had arrived the following morning.

"I'm from New York City," she finally replied in a voice loud enough to wake the dead, hoping the older man would hear her this time.

Hiram Woolsey did and was apparently impressed. He attempted to whistle, but the absence of several of his front teeth prevented that particular action. A rush of hot, stale air came pouring out in its place. "Never been. Hear it's something to behold. Got a hankerin' to see that Statue of Liberty. Hope to go one day before I meet my Maker."

As frail as he appeared, that could be soon, Emily decided. "It's an exciting place to live. Lots of shops and restaurants. There's always something to do." Scouring the many museums was her favorite pastime, and often she could talk Max into accompanying her when he wasn't on a deadline of one sort or another. Max, she had quickly discovered, was always on a deadline.

"You'll find plenty to do here in Montana, but it'll be different from what you're used to, I expect. Ain't much in the way of entertainment, unless you count quilting bees and such. But we've got plenty of fresh air and some of the prettiest scenery you're ever going to lay eyes on."

Glancing out the window, Emily acknowledged the truth of his words. The sky was as blue as a robin's egg. Great granite mountains dotted with dark ponderosa pine and fragrant Douglas fir trees rose sharply from the plain on either side, imposing and majestic.

The vast stretches of land made one feel insignificant, as if God had decided to put heaven on earth and call it

Montana. It was the Spanish that had actually named the territory. Montana meant "Mountainous Region," though from what she'd observed that was a far more fitting description for the western region than the eastern, which was mostly high rolling prairie.

"Well, it's absolutely beaut—"

Gunshots suddenly rang out, and Emily screamed, swallowing whatever it was she was going to say. The driver shouted to the horses and slapped the reins against their rumps, urging them to run faster.

Terrified, Emily plastered herself against the back of the seat, wondering how much harder her heart could pound before it exploded.

"Hang on, folks!" the driver yelled down to them. "It appears we got company. I'm going to try to outrun them varmints."

Swallowing hard, Emily glanced at her companion, who had scrunched down low and looked paler than bleached muslin. "Don't worry, Mr. Woolsey, I'm sure the driver will be able to outrun them." He didn't reply, and she cautiously pulled back the leather curtain and peered out to find two men on horseback gaining on them.

"Dear Lord!" she cried, wondering what was to become of them. It appeared that outlaws were attempting to hold up the stage.

Despite the fact that she wrote about them in her books, outlaws were not something she had thought to encounter on her trek west. This was 1889, for heaven's sake! Towns were electrified with incandescent light bulbs, telephones connected people across the miles. And though it was true that New York City had its share of ruffians, they didn't chase people down the middle of the street and attempt to rob them.

More gunshots exploded, one hitting the side of the stage with a *zing*, then she heard one of the outlaws shout, "Hold up, or I'll shoot your fool head off!" Despite her best efforts to remain calm, she started to shake.

The driver must have believed their threats, for a moment later the coach slowed considerably. The outlaws caught up quickly and were riding alongside them now. When the stage pulled to a halt, the door was thrown open and a tall, dark-haired man wearing a blue bandanna across his face stood with his gun pointed at Emily's breast.

If the situation hadn't been so perilous, she would have taken notes for her next book. He looked awfully authentic. Vicious, even. Instead she wiped sweaty palms on the skirt of her dress.

"Get out and be quick about it," he ordered, waving his weapon at her. The gun was tooled silver with a pearl handle, and she doubted that she'd ever forget the sight. He had what Emily suspected was a Mexican accent.

Turning to help Mr. Woolsey, Emily discovered that the elderly man had fainted at the first sight of the outlaw's gun. Drawing a sigh, she wondered when the hero who was going to save her from this predicament would show up.

In her novels ladies were never manhandled; rather, they were cosseted and protected by handsome heroes who adored them. As a gloved hand reached in to yank her down to the ground, nearly causing her to stumble, she truly understood the meaning of the term "literary license." Apparently she had taken it with most of her books.

Mustering up the courage to speak, she said to the swarthy, foreign-accented outlaw, "You are a very rude individual," then moved to stand near the stagecoach driver, who flashed her a look of pure annoyance.

The outlaw's eyes narrowed as he sized Emily up from head to toe. "Did you hear that, *mi compadre?* The lovely *señorita* thinks we are rude. That is such a shame. I was hoping to get to know her much, much better."

Frightened, Emily took a step back.

"Just take what you want and leave us be," the driver insisted. "We don't want no trouble."

Emily watched as the man the Mexican called Slim moved to the boot of the coach and removed her and Hiram Woolsey's luggage. "Hope you got more in your valise than petticoats, lady," Slim said before he began rifling through her unmentionables.

Her face reddening in embarrassment and anger, Emily clenched her fists and was about to say something more when the driver cautioned in a low voice, "Just let them have their way, ma'am. Whatever you got in that bag ain't worth dying for. And I got me a wife and two young'ns to think about."

Emily nodded, knowing that all the money she had in the world—$114.37—was lying beneath her underclothing. If they found it, she'd be penniless.

The brigand gave a warlike yelp just then, indicating that he had discovered her precious hoard. "We struck paydirt, El Lobo. This here little lady's rich. There's over a hundred dollars buried in her prim and propers. *Whooee! This is our lucky day."*

"El Lobo," his partner had called him. Emily fought the urge to roll her eyes. And *she'd* been accused of creating insipid characters. Never in a million years would she have named one of her outlaw characters El Lobo, the Wolf. But perhaps this wolf could be reasoned with. It was worth a try.

Throwing caution to the wind, she clasped the outlaw's forearm. "That's all the money I have in the world, my life savings. Please don't take it all."

Her plea fell on deaf ears. "You are *muy bonita, señorita,* and I am a man of discriminating taste." He stepped closer and reached out to caress her cheek. "I am tempted to see what you have beneath that intriguing bustle of yours. I can tell you are a woman of much passion."

He attempted to kiss her then, but Emily pulled back. His words left no doubt that he was talking about violation. Her stomach fisted into a knot of fear, and she swallowed, wondering how she was going to write herself out of this horrible predicament.

Where, oh where, was a hero when you needed one?

"We ain't got no time for any hanky-panky. There's a posse on our tail, remember?" Slim reminded his partner. "We'll be stretching a piece of hemp if we don't get the hell outta here."

The outlaw nodded, then smiled regretfully at Emily. "Another time, perhaps, *señorita.*" A moment later the two men mounted, $114.37 richer, and departed for parts unknown. Emily released the breath she didn't know she'd been holding.

It was then Hiram Woolsey managed to climb down from the coach, looking shaken and somewhat embarrassed as he mopped his perspiring forehead with a handkerchief. "Sorry to desert you in your hour of need, young woman, but I ain't much good at gunplay. My eyesight's poor, and my hands shake too bad to hold a gun. Not that I was ever good with one. Tailoring's my trade."

"That's all right, Mr. Woolsey. I doubt there was anything you could have done." Emily stooped to pick up her discarded clothing and put it back into her valise.

So much for making a good impression on Jess Murdock.

Suddenly she paled. How on earth was she going to get to Jess Murdock's ranch now? And where was she going to stay when she got to True Love? She had no money for a hotel, meals, or anything else.

Concerned by her distraught appearance, the driver clasped her arm. "You ain't going to faint, now, are you, ma'am? I ain't got no smelling salts or nothing."

She leveled a look of pure disgust at him. "Certainly not. I'm not that cowardly."

He stiffened. "If you're insinuating that I am because I didn't stop those men from—"

"I'm not insinuating anything, Mr. . . . Cooper, isn't it? But I'm out a great deal of money, and I've nowhere to stay when I get to True Love."

"Afraid I can't help you out," Hiram stated with a shake of his head. "My daughter ain't got no extra rooms, what with the wedding guests and all."

"I don't live in these parts," the driver added. "And I don't got no extra cash. But you can file a complaint with the stage line and hope they'll give you some of your money back."

"How long does that usually take?" A kernel of hope sprouted in Emily's breast, then died when he replied:

"Anywheres from six weeks to forever. The home office is in Independence, Missouri, and they ain't real fast at processing claims." He held open the stage door and she climbed back in, fighting the urge to cry.

"Sorry I can't be of more help, ma'am."

"I am, too." Hiram took the seat across from her once again. "You seem to be in a real predicament, young woman. I don't mean to be indelicate . . ." He paused, and Emily rolled her eyes, thinking about his prune dissertation. "But the whorehouse is likely to have extra rooms. You could—"

She gasped, clutching her throat. "Thank you for your suggestion, Mr. Woolsey, but I'm not *that* desperate. I will think of something by the time I get to True Love. It's what I do for a living."

He scratched his head. "You're a tinker? Never would have taken you for that."

Emily leaned back against the seat and closed her eyes, unable to decide which was worse: being robbed of her $114.37 or her naiveté where the Wild West was concerned.

True Love, Montana, Autumn 1889

"Fester! Fester, come back here!"

Screeching at the top of her lungs, Emily jumped out of the way just in time to avoid tripping over a two-hundred-pound pig that had come careening around the corner toward her. Its owner, a boy of about thirteen, smiled apologetically, then continued running after the errant swine, shouting obscenities at him.

Emily could think of a few that she'd like to impart as well. Pigs running loose! Whoever heard of such a thing!

Catching her breath, she clutched her valise tightly and continued down the sidewalk. Her visit to the sheriff's office had proven futile. True Love had no officer of the law at the moment, so she was unable to report the incident of the stagecoach robbery and her loss of funds.

A weaker, less determined person would have grown discouraged and fled—True Love was a world apart from New York City—but Max was counting on her, and if she wanted to save Wise Publishing and her own job, she had to succeed in her mission to write Jess Murdock's story, no matter what she had to do . . . including pig wrestling, if necessary.

Raucous music and laughter poured from the many saloons and brothels she passed, an indication that at least one type of business was thriving in the rural community. This came as no surprise. New York had its share of prostitutes as well.

Recalling the old man's suggestion that she try one of the houses of ill repute to obtain a night's lodging, Emily felt her cheeks heat anew. Staying at a bordello would have given her an excellent opportunity to do some research into the life of a prostitute, but she just wasn't brazen enough to consider it.

Mr. Woolsey had meant well. And when she'd said good-bye to him at the stage depot, she had felt almost sad, for she realized that she was saying farewell to the only person she knew in Montana, or in the West, for that matter.

Continuing on, she noted that the false-fronted buildings lining the main street needed a fresh coat of paint and some repair. The sign hanging over the physician's office, depicting a mortar and pestle, was hanging lopsided from only one rusted hook. The enticing odor of frying chicken from a nearby restaurant had her mouth watering, but she hadn't the funds to procure a meal or anything to drink. And she was both hungry and thirsty.

Friendly passersby continued to smile and nod in greeting at her, so she thought perhaps there might be someone in the town, some generous good Samaritan, who might be willing to help a stranger in need of a place to stay for the night.

When she came to the end of the wooden sidewalk, Emily encountered what she considered to be the hand of divine providence. A small whitewashed church stood at the end of the main thoroughfare, glistening in the afternoon sun like a beacon of hope, and she knew immediately who could be counted on to lend her some assistance.

Gazing up at the cloudless sky, she gave silent thanks to the Almighty and proceeded to the sanctuary. The sign in front read "Holy Redeemer Methodist Church, Reverend Phinneas Higgbotham, Pastor." The inscription below stated "No burden is too heavy for the Lord to shoulder. Come, sinners, and be saved."

"Amen to that," Emily muttered, making her way up the front steps and opening the door. The Lord helps those who help themselves, she reminded herself, grateful that most churches were never locked.

The church was dark when she entered, only a few tapers had been left burning, and Emily squinted as she tried to bring everything into focus. Suddenly a large rotund man stepped forth from the shadows, startling her, and she yelped.

His kind face held a great deal of apology. "May I help you, miss?" He was dressed all in black, his white clerical collar the only relief from the somberness of his attire, and she surmised him to be Reverend Higgbotham, her soon-to-be savior.

Breathing a deep sigh of relief, she held out her hand, hoping it wasn't shaking too badly. Her morning's encounter with the outlaws had left her nerves on edge. "I'm Emily Jean Bartlett, recently arrived from New York City."

His brow shot up, then he smiled warmly. "You don't say? Come in and shut the door behind you, Miss Bartlett. Keeping the house of the Lord warm is no easy feat in these parts. That wind'll blow right through you, if you let it."

Emily followed the cleric to the front of the church and took a seat in one of the pews he offered. "You look troubled, miss. I hope nothing's wrong. Confession is always good for the soul, if that's why you've come." He had an eager look on his face that said he hoped she'd be willing to impart some juicy transgressions.

Emily was sorry to disappoint the good reverend, but confession was the farthest thing from her mind at the moment. Fabrication, however, was an entirely different matter. She'd have to tell a few white lies to gain assistance with her dire circumstances and entrance into Jess Murdock's life, for there was no telling how protective the townsfolk might be of their resident hero.

"As I said, I've recently arrived from New York City. I've come west to visit an . . . an acquaintance by the name of Jess Murdock. Perhaps you know him?"

"You've come to visit Jess Murdock?" The man's bushy eyebrows lifted nearly to his balding pate. "Of course I know him. But I wasn't aware that he was expecting any visitors, especially any *female* visitors."

Emily filed his comment away for future reference.

"Well, then." He patted his chubby knees. "So you're here to see Jess? I fail to see what could possibly have you looking so distraught, then, young woman. I can assure you that Jess Murdock is a very upstanding member of this community. Well respected and admired, a pillar, in fact."

That description didn't coincide with the Jess Murdock she'd always heard about. Pillars of the community didn't make for very interesting reading. She forced a smile. "Mr. Murdock has so many admirable qualities, Reverend.

"My mother, bless her soul, was always saying how fond she was of Mr. Murdock. Mother always hoped to see him again one day, but—" Heaving a sigh of mock despair, she shook her head, prompting the man to pat her hand in a consoling fashion.

"I'm so sorry to hear about your mother, my dear. I hope her passing was peaceful. She sounded like a delightful woman."

"She is . . . was, I mean. Anyway, I was on my way here to see Mr. Murdock when my stagecoach was held up by two vicious outlaws. I was robbed of all my money, as was Mr. Hiram Woolsey." She added the older man's name, lest the cleric think she was lying about the holdup. "Mr. Woolsey, being quite elderly, was most distraught. We both were."

He clucked his tongue several times. "That is just dreadful."

"I've nowhere to stay the night. Since the hour is getting late, and I don't want to make the trip out to Mr. Murdock's ranch until tomorrow—I'm quite frightened of brigands since my ordeal, you see—I was wondering if you could possibly put me up for the night? I'd be ever so grateful. And I'm sure Mr. Murdock would be most appreciative that you took me in, in my hour of need, so to speak."

The reverend seemed totally taken aback by her suggestion. "Why—why, I don't know. I'd have to ask Mrs. Higgbotham. See what she has to say." He rubbed one of his double chins, contemplating the matter. "We don't usually put folks up in the rectory. It's just the two of us, but we have only the one bedroom."

"I'd be perfectly willing to spend the night in the church on one of the pews, Reverend Higgbotham, if that would make it easier."

He seemed aghast at her suggestion and shook his head. "Spend the night in here? In the house of the Lord? Young woman, that is out of the question."

Removing a handkerchief from her pocket, Emily dabbed at her eyes. "The sign outside said the Lord could shoulder my burdens, but if He can't—if you can't—" Her voice faded to a whisper. "I understand. I don't want to be any trouble to you."

Reverend Higgbotham's wife always claimed he was a soft touch when it came to pretty girls and puppy dogs. This time proved no exception. He rose to his feet. "Wait right here, young woman. I'll go speak to Mrs. Higgbotham. I'm sure she'd love to have you stay with us."

He smiled kindly. "After all, it wouldn't do to throw an acquaintance of Jess Murdock's out in the street, now, would it? And tomorrow I will drive you out to the ranch myself, make sure you get there safely."

Forcing a small smile, Emily watched him walk out the door, then breathed a sigh of relief. Though she knew that she'd probably be struck down for lying to a man of the cloth, she didn't see that she had a whole lot of choice. She needed a place to stay, and Reverend Higgbotham would be the perfect person to introduce her to the legendary cowboy.

And who was to say that she and Jess Murdock wouldn't soon be the very best of friends?

Chapter Three

As the buggy bumped along the Montana countryside the following morning, Emily's apprehension began to grow by leaps and bounds. She didn't know what to expect when she reached Jess Murdock's ranch.

Would she be tossed out on her ear? Would Jess Murdock be mean and hateful when he discovered why she had come to see him and bring charges against her for trespassing?

She swallowed, wondering what would become of her if the worst happened. She wouldn't be able to count on the Reverend and Mrs. Higgbotham to rescue her again, not after the way she had deceived them. And Max certainly didn't have the extra funds to bail her out of her predicament. She was definitely on her own.

"I'm sure Jess is going to be very happy to renew your acquaintance, Emily Jean," Reverend Higgbotham remarked. "How long did you say it had been since you'd seen him? A year, was it?"

She inclined her head, continuing to look straight ahead.

"Well, I do hope you'll come back to visit me and Mrs. Higgbotham. Clara has been singing your praises all morning. Imagine you being involved in all that charity work back east." He shook his head in wonder. "You surely did make an impression on my Clara. I can tell you that. And Clara's not an easy woman to impress."

Emily fought to keep her face perfectly impassive. Clara Higgbotham had been a hard nut to crack, that was for certain. But with a little buttering up, and those outrageous lies she had told about the good deeds she'd performed at the orphanage, the woman's dour mood toward her had softened. By the end of dinner, which had proven to be a delicious meal of ham, green beans, and sweet potatoes, they had formed a friendship of sorts. Of course, it was a friendship based on half-truths and deceit, much to Emily's great regret.

Prevarication was becoming a tad too easy, Emily decided. True, she and Max had always joked about how in their line of work they were forced to lie for a living, but this was different. She didn't feel good about returning the Higgbothams' kindness with deception.

"You and Mrs. Higgbotham have been very kind, Reverend. I don't know how I can ever repay you."

"You just keep doing good deeds, young woman. That's all the repayment Mrs. Higgbotham, the good Lord, or I require."

Smiling weakly, she changed the subject. "What size ranch does Mr. Murdock own? I saw a sign quite a ways back depicting the 'Bar JM' brand. I'm assuming that we've been on Murdock property for quite a while now." And if that was the case, then Jess Murdock was very well situated and might not require payment for his life story. An important consideration, given her present state of poverty and Max's dire financial situation.

Phinneas clucked to the horses, urging them to pick up their pace. "So you know about brands and such? I didn't expect an eastern woman to know of such things."

He was absolutely right. Most women, east or west, wouldn't know much about brands. Unless, of course, they lived on a ranch or wrote dime novels for a living. She thought quickly, realizing that she'd have to be more careful about what she said in the future. "I have two younger brothers who are always reading dime novels." That was the truth. Herbert and Harry were wild about her books, which pleased her greatly. "Guess I just picked up the information from them."

"Those books are mostly inaccurate," the reverend said. "But I confess to enjoying them. They really help while away the hours on a cold winter's night. And we get plenty of cold nights here in Montana. So cold, in fact, that I doubt the Devil himself would be able to keep warm." He chuckled at his witticism.

Pleased that the reverend was so open-minded about his choice of reading matter, Emily smiled and made a mental note to send him an autographed copy of her latest book when she returned to New York. "I confess to having read one or two of them myself, Reverend. I was curious as to what had intrigued my brothers so. I found the books to be very entertaining."

He nodded in agreement, then said, "To answer your earlier question about Jess's ranch, I'd say he's got about two thousand acres of prime range land and runs between five hundred and a thousand head of Hereford.

"He bought the place years ago when land was relatively cheap, but almost lost it during that awful winter we had back in '87. Many ranchers suffered terrible losses that year, including their herds and life savings."

"How awful. I recall reading about the Montana ranching situation in the New York newspapers. They called it 'the Great Die-Up,' if I recall." A terrible drought had consumed the land in the spring and summer of 1886. The parched range and stunted grass provided little nutrition for the grazing herds of cattle, which numbered in the hundreds of thousands. Autumn was little better, and when winter came with its relentless blizzards and bitter cold temperatures, the ranchers were doomed.

"There's not much a body can do when nature chooses to dump foot after foot of snow on the ground." The reverend shook his head, obviously saddened by the situation. "Cattlemen had been free ranging their cows back then, letting them forage for what grass and water they could find. But that harsh winter changed things. Those stockmen that survived don't have such large herds now as they once did, and they've got their grazing lands fenced off into smaller, more manageable sections."

Emily thought it sad that the West was changing so dramatically. Soon it would become just as crowded and civilized as the East. She was glad she'd been able to see it before that happened. "The Wild West is growing more tame, I guess," she said, adding as an afterthought, "Except for some persistent outlaws." The thought of the two men who had robbed her of her life savings, almost thwarting her plans to save Wise Publishing, brought a deep frown to her face.

"Probably just as well. It was hellish back when the Indians were running loose. Of course, we took everything they had, so I can't say that I blame them for wanting to avenge themselves against the white man. Still, I sleep much easier now knowing that most are on the reservation.

"As for outlaws . . . well, there's always going to be those who think nothing of taking what's not theirs, whether that be money, cattle, or someone else's life.

"Don't be fooled into thinking that things are the same here as back east, young lady. We've got cattle rustlers aplenty. Sadly, you've already experienced the outlaw vermin that still exist. Montana's not as tame as you might think."

Pondering the cleric's words, Emily wondered how tame Jess Murdock was likely to be. From the little she knew, he'd been quite the wild cowboy in his day, hard drinking, two-fisted, and mean as all get-out with a gun.

He'd also had the most devastatingly handsome smile. She remembered quite clearly the day that smile had been cast in her direction. Of course, it hadn't been flashing at her alone. She was only one of hundreds of attendees of the Wild West show who had come to see Jess Murdock perform.

But she'd never forget how the sight of his smile had made her heart race, how the blue of his eyes had dazzled brightly in contrast with the deep tan of his complexion.

She sighed. *I can hardly wait to see him again.*

"You'd best take care, young woman," the reverend said, interrupting her reverie. "There are many lost souls here in Montana."

"Guess you should be grateful for those men and women who still need saving, Reverend."

"How so?" He turned to look at her questioningly.

"Without sinners you'd be out of a job," she said with a rueful smile. And she was lumping herself in that category.

A short time later they reached the ranch proper. Located near Ford Creek in the fertile Judith Basin in central Montana, it was a little piece of heaven. Emily could certainly understand why Jess Murdock had chosen it for himself.

It was well grassed and watered and had an abundance of yellow pine, which had been used for the corrals and fencing. The large log house stood in an open meadow, an imposing fir tree gracing the front yard.

Emily couldn't help but fantasize about what the tree would look like decorated for Christmas, with strings of cranberries and popcorn attached and a silver star at the top. The Christmas trees she'd purchased in the city had been small and puny, not tall or magnificent like this one.

Outlying cabins stood at the rear of the house, and on either side of the horse corral were the blacksmith shop and bunkhouse. Beyond that was the recently constructed barn.

In the adjoining pasture, fat, contented Herefords grazed. Emily envied them for living in such a beautiful, sweet-smelling place. "It's wonderful here," she said in an awe-filled voice. "So wide open and incredibly breathtaking. I just love it." The vast blue sky seemed to reach down to the earth, and it was almost as if she could raise up her hand and touch the sun.

The reverend smiled, pulling the horses to a halt in front of the handsome residence. "I thought you might. Jess takes great pride in his ranch, in most everything that belongs to him. It's his way."

He jumped down from the buggy and came around to help her alight, and Emily's stomach sprouted nervous butterflies. The moment of truth was at hand. In a matter of minutes she would be face-to-face with Jess Murdock. Suddenly she felt like retching up the breakfast of pancakes and eggs that Mrs. Higgbotham had insisted on making for her.

The reverend knocked several times, and Emily held her breath, releasing it a short time later when the door was pulled open and a large, rawboned woman answered. She had red hair sprinkled with gray, which had been pulled back in a bun at the nape of her neck, and a splattering of freckles across her cheeks. The reverend introduced her as Frances Ferguson, Jess Murdock's housekeeper.

"Mrs. Ferguson, meet Emily Jean Bartlett. Emily's come all the way from New York City to visit with Jess. Is he here?"

The housekeeper's eyes widened in surprise, then she shook her head, staring intently at Emily. "No, Reverend. Mr. Murdock 'tisna at home. He's riding herd wie the rest o' the lads and willna return for several more days." Mrs. Ferguson's Scottish brogue was as thick as her waist.

Emily didn't know whether to feel elated or devastated at the news that Jess Murdock was not at home. She'd been given a short reprieve, but she still didn't know what to expect when the cowboy finally did arrive. And if Mrs. Ferguson turned her away . . .

Emily was not about to let that happen. Holding out her hand, she smiled warmly. "As the reverend explained, Mrs. Ferguson, I'm Emily Jean Bartlett, an acquaintance of Mr. Murdock's from New York City."

The woman's red brows shot up, but she said nothing to contradict the statement and ushered everyone into the front room. "Mr. Murdock dinna say anyone was expected, but any friend o' his is welcome here just the same."

Emily breathed a sigh of relief. Phinneas Higgbotham seemed relieved as well, no doubt grateful that he wouldn't have to ask Mrs. Higgbotham for any more favors.

"Got any of that pecan pie, Mrs. Ferguson?" he asked. "I sure am fond of your pecan pie." The reverend turned to Emily. "Not even Mrs. Higgbotham can make pies as good as Mrs. Ferguson, but don't tell her I said that." He chuckled.

The housekeeper looked at the reverend's protruding stomach, which was bouncing like gelatin, and shook her head. "I think ye're fond of more than pie, Reverend. I think ye like all food tae much." Never one to mince words, Frances Ferguson smiled at his indignant expression, then disappeared into the kitchen to fetch the pie and coffee.

When she returned a few minutes later, a small child was tugging at her skirts. "Zach, say hello tae the reverend and yer father's friend, Miss Bartlett," the housekeeper instructed.

The child hesitated for only a moment, then hurried toward Emily, a big grin on his impish face. "Hello, Miss Bartlett. Are you going to stay here a while? Gran said you was probably going to stay until Papa returns." The words came out in a rush.

Emily's heart melted at the sight of the boy. He was adorable and made her realize just how much she missed her sister and brothers. "Why, yes, I am. I've traveled all the way across the country to see your father." That was the truth, at least. She didn't want to lie to the child.

"Do you like to read stories and play cowboys and Indians? Because I do." His look was hopeful as he seated himself on the dark green leather sofa between Emily and Reverend Higgbotham.

Smiling, she brushed back a shock of reddish brown hair that had fallen across his brow. "I love doing both, Zach. But I haven't played much lately. I hope you'll be willing to show me how. And I hope you'll call me Emily."

His face lit with anticipation, his bright blue eyes sparkling with joy, and Emily wondered if Jess Murdock's eyes were of a similar color.

"Gran, did you hear?" Zach shouted. "Emily wants to play with me."

"Yes, lad, I heard. Now run along. Ye'll get a chance tae talk tae yer friend later. Now ye must see tae yer chores like a good lad."

"Aw, shucks." Clearly disappointed, the child kicked the leg of the coffee table defiantly.

"Zachary James Murdock, ye better say ye're sorry and be quick about it, or ye'll be feeling the back of me hand."

Under Mrs. Ferguson's stern glare, the child apologized and stalked out. "He's a good lad, just a wee bit excited tae be having company," she explained, embarrassed by the child's outburst in front of a stranger.

Emily nodded, then turned her attention to something the reverend was saying, and Frances took the opportunity to study the lovely young woman seated across from her.

She was a comely lass, with her short curly black hair and deep blue eyes, sparkling with life and perhaps a bit of mischief. Emily Jean Bartlett laughed easily at something the reverend said, as if the action were as natural to her as the air she breathed.

Jess hardly ever laughed anymore, so maybe it was good that he would have someone lighthearted around who could lift his spirits and make him forget all his troubles. Lord knew that he needed a respite from worry and sadness.

The housekeeper thought of how good Emily had been with Zach and nodded approvingly to herself. The child had taken to her immediately, which was usually not the case. Zach tended to shy away from strangers. He was distrustful of them, just like his father.

There was something to be said for a woman who was good with children, Frances decided, though she was still curious as to the reason Emily Jean Bartlett had come to visit. Jess was not the type of man to invite passing acquaintances into his home. He hadn't mentioned a word about this young woman's visit. And if Miss Bartlett was a friend of Jess's, as she claimed, he would have confided as much to Frances.

Frances had been with Jess Murdock since Zach was born. Her husband, Ennis, had died of the influenza while sailing from Scotland to America, leaving her alone and frightened in her newly adopted country. Learning of Jess Murdock's urgent need for a housekeeper had been fortuitous and a turning point in her life.

They had grown close in the five years she had worked for him; she considered Jess to be the son she never had and Zach the grandchild she'd always wanted.

Still, it wasn't her place to question the why of things. And she'd find out soon enough, at any rate. Jess would be home in just a few days.

Emily entered the kitchen later that afternoon to find the housekeeper bent over the large wood-burning stove. Steam clouds rose from simmering kettles, and she was stirring something that smelled suspiciously like pot roast. Her stomach rumbled in response to the fact that she hadn't eaten since early that morning. As tempting as the pecan pie had looked, she'd been too nervous to partake of it.

"Do you need any help, Mrs. Ferguson? I'm fairly handy in the kitchen." Emily loved to cook, though she had little time for it these days. As a young woman, she was always pestering her mother's chef to teach her his recipes and culinary secrets. Fortunately the man had had the patience of Job and liked showing off his skills, and Emily had become quite adept in the kitchen.

The older woman shook her head and brushed back a few errant strands of hair from her face. "I'm used tae doing fer myself, lass. But thank ye just the same." Wiping her hands on her apron, she finally turned to face Emily, who was poised by the long maple table.

"I hope ye found yer room tae be satisfactory. I woulda spruced it up a bit, but like I said, I dinna know ye was coming."

"It's very nice, Mrs. Ferguson. Thank you." The room she'd been placed in was as sparsely decorated as the rest of the house. The log walls had not been plastered over as was usually the custom, nor had any pictures or decorative items been hung. Nothing that smacked of femininity could be found anywhere in the large dwelling.

Jess Murdock's home was functional, masculine, and not the least bit homey, and she suspected it was a reflection of the man himself.

"'Tis nice enough, I guess. Jess has little use fer pretties. Like most men, he's more concerned wie the practical side o' things."

"Have you been with him long, Mrs. Ferguson?" Emily seated herself at the table. Under the watchful eye of the housekeeper, she began peeling the potatoes in the blue splatterware bowl sitting there, hoping she could glean some tidbits of information about the man.

"Since Zachary was a bairn. His mother ran off, and I was hired tae take care o' the poor wee thing." She tsked several times, and her mouth tightened in disapproval. "'Twas a shame, her running out on a fine mon like Mr. Murdock."

"Yes, it was," Emily concurred, wondering again what had possessed the woman to leave her husband and child. Any woman would be proud to have a son like Zach. He was a very sweet, good-natured child. Of course, his father could very well be a different story.

"How long have ye known Jess, if ye don't mind me askin', Miss Bartlett?"

"Please, call me Emily." She stared down at the potato in her hand, unable to look the woman in the eye. "I believe it was about a year ago, when Mr. Murdock was touring with the Wild West show. It was a passing acquaintance, really. He said if I was ever in Montana that I should look him up. I doubt he'll even remember me." That, at least, was the truth.

"The mon has a mind like a steel trap. He'll remember ye, if he met ye. There ain't much that gets by Jess Murdock. Funny ye should want tae visit a mon who might nae remember ye, though."

The housekeeper's gaze was intent, almost suspicious, and Emily felt her cheeks warm under the scrutiny. "Yes, well . . . I . . . I have a business proposition to discuss with him, and I thought it best that I do it in person."

"A business proposition, is it? Don't know that Jess will be wanting tae do business wie a woman, but I guess that's fer ye tae find out fer yerself."

"Yes, well, it shouldn't be too much longer now. You did say he'd be home in a few days."

Mrs. Ferguson nodded. "I did. But I was wrong. Jess'll be home tomorrow, in fact. I've had word from one o' the hands who rode back a day early wie the news."

Emily felt the color drain from her face. *Tomorrow!* She swallowed, trying to keep the panic she felt from showing. "How exciting," she said finally, though she was too nervous to muster up much enthusiasm.

Mrs. Ferguson smiled knowingly. "That it will be, lass. I'm sure o' it."

"Emily, come sit back down on the floor and play with me. My soldiers are whopping the heck out of your Indians." Zach moved the wooden figurines around in mock battle, making shooting noises as his soldiers defeated the Comanche warriors.

"I'll be there in just a second."

"How come you keep staring out the window, anyway? Are you waiting for Papa?"

Dropping the tanned cowhide that served as a window covering back in place, Emily seated herself near Zach in front of the large stone fireplace. The fire in the grate burned low, but it was enough heat to keep them comfortably warm while they played atop the green-and-gold braided rug—the floor covering a concession to practicality rather than decor, she was certain.

"I was just wondering if it was going to rain," she replied not quite truthfully, still anxious over Jess Murdock's impending arrival.

"Naw. It's not. You can hear the thunder coming off the mountains when it's going to rain. I don't like thunder much."

"How come?" She clasped her arms around her knees, enjoying the child's openness and innocence.

"I guess it scares me. Papa says I should be brave, but I still get scared sometimes. Do you think that makes me a baby?"

It was easy for a man like Jess Murdock to counsel bravery. The man fairly oozed with it. But Emily, who knew what it was like to be afraid of thunder, the dark, and numerous other childhood horrors, could empathize with Zach's fear. "No, I don't. And the next time it thunders, you just pretend that your cavalry are shooting off some cannon. Make a game out of it, then you won't be nearly so frightened."

The child brightened instantly at the suggestion. "Is that what you do when you're scared? Make a game out of it?"

"You know what I do to little boys who get scared?" she said. He shook his head, grinning. "I tickle them. I tickle them so hard that they forget all about being afraid." She proceeded to show him and soon had him rolling on the floor with laughter.

"Stop, Emily!" he screeched, laughing and screaming loudly enough to wake the dead.

Emily began giggling, too, chasing Zach around on all fours, growling ferociously, and pretending that she was the tickle monster that was going to eat him up.

It was at that moment that the front door banged open. Jess Murdock entered the room to find his son being pursued by a total stranger—a woman he had never laid eyes on before.

The sight of Zach rolling on the floor with an attractive grown woman, whose petticoats were up around her shapely calves and whose short dark hair was curling every which way in riotous fashion, had him staring open-mouthed.

They were tickling each other, laughing uproariously, and screeching at the tops of their lungs, totally oblivious of his presence. Covering his ears against the onslaught of noise, he waited.

A few moments later the hairs on the back of Emily's neck began to prickle. Out of the corner of her eye she caught sight of a pair of dust-covered boots. With a sinking heart, she allowed her gaze to rise up a long pair of denim-clad legs, past a silver belt buckle proclaiming the owner to be a rodeo rider, to a flat stomach covered by a faded blue cambric shirt, all the way up a massive chest to land on a scowling, bearded, blue-eyed visage. She swallowed.

Jess Murdock was home.

Chapter Four

THE WOMAN'S HORRIFIED EXPRESSION WAS ALMOST laughable. But Jess, who was hungry and dirty and had just discovered earlier that day that fifty head of his cattle had been rustled, was not in a laughing mood.

"Papa!" At the sight of his father, Zach jumped to his feet and scampered across the room, wrapping his arms about the tall man's legs and giving him an exuberant hug. "I've missed you so much."

Jess smiled affectionately at his son. "I've missed you, too, Zach." He picked up the boy and kissed him on the cheek before setting him back down again, his gaze never leaving the woman still seated on the floor.

"There ye are, Jess lad." Mrs. Ferguson barreled into the room, wiping her flour-covered hands on her apron in no-nonsense fashion. "Have ye met yer friend Emily, then? She's been waiting fer ye."

All eyes turned on Emily, who smiled weakly in response.

"Has she?" He shook his head. "No. I haven't had the pleasure."

Mrs. Ferguson gave Emily a measured, somewhat disappointed look, shook her head, then clasped the small boy's hand and said, "Come, lad. I've made yer favorite oatmeal cookies and ye can have some before dinner," leaving Emily and Jess Murdock all alone.

Stepping farther into the room, Jess stood before Emily and held out his hand to assist her up. "Mrs. Ferguson mentioned that we were friends, but I don't recall ever having had the pleasure, ma'am." And he would have remembered meeting someone as lovely as the woman sprawled at his feet, someone who had a penchant for rolling about the floor like a hoyden, someone whose smile could light up an entire room.

On her feet, Emily found that the cowboy's steely gaze wasn't much warmer than the cold silver buckle fastened at his belt. "It was really just a passing acquaintance, Mr. Murdock. I told your housekeeper it wasn't likely that you'd remember me."

He crossed his arms over his chest, wondering why she thought it necessary to lie. "Really? And here I've always been credited with having such an excellent memory."

There was a lot more to praise Jess Murdock about than just his memory. He was far more handsome and virile than Emily had remembered, though the memorable smile was conspicuously absent. His dark hair held a lot of gray for a man of thirty-six, but it didn't detract from his rugged good looks. Even through a week's growth of beard she detected the strong chiseled features, full lips, and small cleft in his chin. His legs and arms were rock hard with muscles, his chest wide and his hips slim.

He might be a legend in his own time, and larger than life, but Jess Murdock was one hundred percent man.

And that man was presently staring daggers at her.

The way Emily saw it, she had one of two choices: she could either brazen it out and pretend that they really did know each other, compounding lie upon lie, or she could confess all and state her business and reason for seeking him out.

The coldness in Jess Murdock's eyes made her want to choose the first, but the disappointment she'd seen in Mrs. Ferguson's made her select the second.

"We haven't really met, Mr. Murdock," she confessed, holding out her hand, which, to her total mortification, was shaking. "I'm Emily Jean Bartlett of New York City."

"New York City?" He dropped her hand immediately, as if she had some contagion. "I might have known. You're one of those nosy newspaper people come to dig up dirt, expose secrets, invade my privacy, aren't you?" And he had plenty of secrets to expose. None of which he wanted printed in a newspaper and made known to the public.

She shook her head. "Umm, not really. But I do work in the publishing business."

He headed straight for the decanter of whiskey on the side table and poured himself a stiff drink. "I'd invite you to join me, Miss Bartlett, but I doubt you'll be staying that long."

Panic set in and Emily held out her hands beseechingly. "Mr. Murdock, please! Just hear me out. I'm in desperate circumstances, and you're my only hope."

He plopped down on the sofa, studying the determination and apprehension on her face. She had guts, he'd give her that. "Can't rightly recall ever being anybody's only hope before." He sighed. "Go on, Miss Bartlett."

"I apologize for presuming on an acquaintance we didn't have, Mr. Murdock, but I feared what your reaction would be if you knew who I really was."

"I still don't know, Miss Bartlett, but I'd be overjoyed if you'd cut to the chase and tell me. I've had a long day. I could use a bath, a hot meal, and a good night's sleep." And smelling her lavender scent made him realize how long it had been since a night's sleep had included a warm, willing woman. The stirrings of awareness made him uncomfortable and more annoyed than ever.

"I'm a novelist, Mr. Murdock. I work for Wise Publishing in New York City. Perhaps you've heard of Maxwell Wise? He's been in business for years. Very reputable. A true gentleman in every sense of the—"

"Let me guess. You've come to write my life story? Am I getting close?" As her face paled, his registered disappointment. "Better men than you have tried. And failed miserably, I might add."

"I'm a very good writer, Mr. Murdock. Better than very good, actually. Perhaps you've read some of my books: *Blood on the Moon, Custer's Last Hurrah, Out-law's—*"

His mouth dropped open, disbelief etched clearly on his face. "Son of a bitch! You write dime novels?" He shook his head, as if he couldn't quite believe what he was hearing. "You mean to stand there and tell me that you're E. J. Bartlett? You? A woman?"

Emily's eyes widened, and she nodded, surprised that he would know of her. Jess Murdock didn't strike her as the type of man who would read dime novels. After all, he'd lived most of the adventures that had been written about. "You're familiar with my work?"

He'd read several of E. J. Bartlett's dime novels and was embarrassed to admit that he'd enjoyed the heck out of them. Emily Jean Bartlett was a good writer, though some of her portrayals and historical details were inaccurate. But as good as she might be, she wasn't going to write his life story. He had no intention of becoming another dimestore curiosity for eastern folks to gawk at. Bad enough his stint with Cody's Wild West show had turned him into a sideshow freak, of sorts.

"I've read a few. No offense, Miss Bartlett, but I'm not a fan of the genre."

"Mr. Murdock, Wise Publishing doesn't want to write just one book about your life, but a whole series of books. Along the lines of what Beadles and Adams has done for William F. Cody."

Jess screwed up his face in disgust. Bill Cody was a glory seeker. And though Jess counted him as a friend, he wanted no part of the glamour and notoriety that surrounded the showman. He'd had enough of that kind of life. Now all he wanted was peace and quiet and to be left alone to raise his child in relative obscurity.

"I realize I should be flattered, Miss Bartlett, but I like to keep my private life private. I've got a son to think about, and I don't want him believing that his father is more than he is." Or less, for that matter. "I'm a rancher, nothing more, despite what you have been led to believe."

The man was impossibly stubborn, and Emily was a hairbreadth away away from screaming out her frustration. But she didn't. Anyone who attempted to match wits with Jess Murdock would have to remain as cool and calmly collected as he was. She had an important mission to accomplish. Max was counting on her. She couldn't, wouldn't, let him down by losing her temper.

"I respect the fact that you have a son and would want to protect him. I wouldn't dream of dragging Zach into any of the stories or exploiting him. I like your son very much, Mr. Murdock. He's a delightful child."

Jess's lips twitched in what could almost be considered a smile. "He seemed quite taken with you as well, ma'am."

She blushed at the memory of her recent behavior. "But that doesn't mean you should just dismiss the opportunity I'm offering. I think you should allow yourself some time to think about it. I'm positive that once you've had time to consider my proposition, to get to know and trust me, you'll gladly consent to having me write the series." And if she remained on the ranch for a period of time, she might be able to ferret out enough information to write the

book without his help. There were people working at the
Bar JM, like Mrs. Ferguson, who knew of Jess's background and might be willing to talk. Interviewing was one
of her strong suits, along with determination.

"I admire your tenacity, Miss Bartlett, but I'm not
going to change my mind."

She dug in her heels, her expression mutinous. "I
think you will."

"I think you should leave."

"I can't."

He looked at her strangely. "What do you mean, you
can't?"

"I'm flat broke. I have no money, nowhere to stay, and
no way to return to New York." She told him about the
stagecoach holdup and how she had come to lose all of her
life savings. "So you see, you really are my only hope."

Jess plowed agitated fingers through his hair. He'd always considered himself a chivalrous sort of man, but this
woman was asking a lot more than he was willing to give.
He had no intention of allowing her to write about his exploits, but he couldn't just toss her out on her rear.

He continued to study her, noting the upturned nose,
the stubborn set of her chin, the intriguing depths of her
dazzling blue eyes, and he felt something stir that hadn't
been stirring in quite a while. "Damn!" he cursed, shaking
his head.

"Can you ride a horse?" he asked finally.

She was taken aback by the question. "A horse? No,"
she admitted, shaking her head. "But I'm sure I could
learn. I'm a very quick study. I once learned to make a

cheese soufflé on my very first try, and they're extremely difficult, I'll have you know."

"What the hell is a cheese—" He shook his head. "Never mind. Everyone at the Bar JM pulls their own weight, Miss Bartlett. It doesn't seem that you're qualified to do much except snoop into other people's affairs."

Not about to be dismissed so easily, Emily thought quickly. "Reverend Higgbotham mentioned that True Love has not yet acquired a schoolteacher. If that's the case, I can offer my services as teacher to Zach. Surely you want him to be educated, to learn to read and write and master his multiplication tables."

"I'm teaching Zach his letters." And doing a piss poor job of it. He didn't have the patience or the time to devote to educating his son. And Frances Ferguson was little help, not with her thick Scottish brogue and the fact that she herself couldn't read or write English.

"I'm college educated," Emily went on. "I know Latin, Greek, French, and I'm very well versed in the classics. I could teach Zach many important things that he wouldn't learn in a one-room schoolhouse."

Temptation loomed. Emily Bartlett had struck where Jess was the most vulnerable: his son. "And in exchange for your tutoring . . . ?"

"I would want to remain here and write your series."

"Dammit, woman! I told you I'm not interested in having my life story told."

"But you will be after we get to know each other better, Mr. Murdock. I'm positive of that."

He arched a brow. "And just how well are we going to get to know each other, Miss Bartlett?"

She stiffened at the implication. "I'm not a loose woman, Mr. Murdock. I came here in order to help my publisher sell books, not to sell myself."

"As delightful as that prospect might be, Miss Bartlett, I'm not interested in pursuing a personal relationship with you, or in having you write my book."

Emily didn't know whether to feel relieved or insulted.

Jess decided to try another tactic with the headstrong woman. "I noticed some errors in your research while reading your books, Miss Bartlett. It's obvious that you've never had any personal experience with horses, ranch life, or cowboys in general."

"That's true. But I fail to see—"

"I don't think you're qualified to write my life story. I wouldn't want it filled with inaccuracies."

Emily forced her temper down, and a smile rose to her lips. "You, Mr. Murdock, are obviously a man who's always up for a challenge, so I shall offer you one. Let's spend some time getting to know each other. During that time, I shall endeavor to convince you to let me write your life story, and at the same time I shall become familiar with the workings of the ranch and learn to ride a horse, so that I may be eminently qualified to write your series."

"You're going to learn to ride a horse?" He threw back his head and laughed. "You really are desperate, aren't you?"

"What's the matter, Mr. Murdock? Afraid to take the

challenge? After all, I'm only asking you to commit to a period of time, a few weeks. If after that time you're still not convinced to go ahead with the project, then I guess I'll have no recourse but to leave, provided I can beg, borrow, or steal the money to return to New York." She had absolutely no intention of leaving on those terms, but he didn't need to know that.

"There's not much in this life that I'm afraid of, Miss Bartlett. I've faced my demons and survived. And I'm certainly not afraid of a little bit of a thing like you." He shook his head. "I just find it hard to believe that you'd actually be willing to risk your hide and your pride to write a damn book."

"This series is extremely important to me, Mr. Murdock. I'd be willing to do almost anything to get it written." And the fact that he was so reluctant to cooperate sparked her curiosity even more. What was Jess Murdock so fearful of? The careful, somber man before her was in direct contrast with the dashing, carefree hero she remembered. Why had he changed so?

His brow shot up, and his manner grew teasing. "Anything, Miss Bartlett? Maybe I should reconsider—"

Her cheeks filled with color at the implication. "I said *almost* anything. And you mustn't flatter yourself, Mr. Murdock, into thinking that I'm any more attracted to you than you are to me. You are an assignment, nothing more.

"As a writer I've learned to become completely objective about my subjects. I never get personally or emotionally involved. So you may rest easy on that score.

I have no interest in pursuing a personal relationship with you, either." Well, she did lie for a living, Emily thought.

Jess should have felt relieved, but all he felt was annoyed. Emily Jean Bartlett had just bruised his male ego all to hell. So no one was more surprised than he when he said, "You may remain at the ranch for the time being, Miss Bartlett."

"Emily," she retorted, grinning, and Jess was grateful that he was still sitting down with his legs crossed. Her smile packed more of a wallop than a Colt .45 Peacemaker.

"Understand that I will not change my mind about the story."

The grin grew wider. "We'll see."

Jess grew more annoyed. "I'll expect you out at the horse barn at first light to begin your riding lessons."

Her smile faltered somewhat. Emily hated horses, was absolutely terrified of them, and had been since childhood, when a neighbor's pony had stepped on her foot and broken it. But she wouldn't give Jess Murdock the satisfaction of knowing her weakness. "I'm looking forward to it."

"Tutoring Zach will have to wait until the afternoon. He has chores in the morning. You can discuss with Mrs. Ferguson what time is best for his lessons."

"I'll do that." If the woman was still talking to her. She owed Mrs. Ferguson a huge apology for being untruthful with her.

Jess stood. "I think you're going to find that life on a ranch, life in the West, is far different from what you've been writing about. It's a life-and-death struggle out here, Miss Bartlett. I hope you're up to it. Somehow I doubt you will be."

"Then I'm not the only one with inaccurate preconceived notions, Mr. Murdock. And it's Emily," she reminded him.

Emily Jean Bartlett, who had one foot in the door.

Chapter Five

EMILY JEAN BARTLETT MIGHT HAVE HAD A FOOT IN the door, but she did not have one in the stirrup.

"You ornery, mule-headed, no-good varmint! Stand still, will you?" she admonished the stubborn bay gelding, lifting her foot as she tried once more to mount. But the horse only snorted and backed away, causing her to fall on her rear, much to her mortification. "He's not cooperating. I need another horse."

Jess fought his smile at the colorful westernisms spewing forth from her lips and helped her up. "We're running out of horses, Emily. This is the third one you've tried on for size this morning. Don't any of them fit?"

She shook her head. "They're all too big. Maybe if I had a ladder—"

"A ladder!"

"They don't stand still. I don't see how a body's supposed to get up and—"

He crossed his arms over his chest and leveled a challenging look at her. "*Tsk. Tsk.* Ready to give up already?

That's not what the characters do in your novels. Oh, I forgot. That stuff's just made up, isn't it?"

Her cheeks pinkened, and she bit her tongue, unwilling to play Jess's game. He'd love for her to pack it in, admit defeat, and be on her way back to New York. Obviously he didn't know her very well. "I am not ready to give—"

The horse whinnied loudly just then, and Emily screamed and jumped straight into the cowboy's arms. Wrapping herself about Jess's waist like an ivy vine, she buried her face in his shirtfront, shaking like a cottonwood leaf in a stiff wind. "He . . . he hates me. He's trying to . . . to kill me."

"Now, now," he said, patting her back to calm her down, the same way he gentled a skittish filly. "You have to make friends with him first. Caesar's as friendly as a lamb, once you get to know him. And it's important to show him who's boss. If he thinks you're afraid of him, he'll take advantage of you."

She glanced up, her look accusing. "Did you teach him that?"

Grinning, he set her at arm's length, though he was loath to do it. Jess hadn't held a woman in his arms in a very long time. Not a decent woman, anyway. He frequented the whorehouses from time to time, when the need became too strong. Whores were not demanding, and he wanted no entanglements, no personal relationship, with a woman. Not after Nora had ripped out his heart, lightened his bank account, and left without a word.

Five years and still the memories burned bitter. Not so much for what she'd done to him, but because she had run out on an innocent child. Their child. His child now.

He shook his head and the unpleasant memories with it. "No. I didn't teach him that. But I did teach him this. Caesar," he directed. "Count to five for the lady."

To Emily's astonishment the horse pawed the ground five times, then whinnied, obviously proud of his accomplishment.

"Play dead," Jess demanded, and the horse lowered himself to the ground and remained unmoving.

Before Emily had a chance to offer a compliment, the Bar JM's foreman walked up, grinning like a well-fed tomcat.

"You ain't showing off for the lady, now, are you, Jess?" He turned to Emily. "You must be that purty gal Fan told me about—the writer from back east." The man tipped his sweat-stained hat in greeting, revealing a shock of pure white hair.

Emily smiled back. "Yes. I'm Emily Jean Bartlett."

"This is my ramrod, Frosty Adams," Jess explained, and the novelist found herself irresistibly drawn to the older man's friendly, engaging smile. His skin was as tanned and leathery as a well-worn saddle, his eyes the most startling shade of green, reminding her of the lush lawn in New York's Central Park.

"How do, ma'am. It sure is nice to have a ceeelebrity here at the Bar JM. Me and the boys are tickled to sundown that you've come to write Jess's story. 'Bout time, I say."

Emily didn't dare look at Jess, for she was sure that he was scowling at the well-intentioned man. "Thank you, Mr. Adams. But if you don't mind my asking, who is this Fan you mentioned earlier? I don't believe—"

"Fan? That'd be Frances Ferguson." He chuckled. "Sometimes I call her Fanny, but she don't like it none. The old gal tells me I've overstepped my bounds. But at my age I sorta figure that iff'n I don't step over them bounds sprightly, I ain't never goin' to get nowheres."

Emily couldn't imagine anyone calling Mrs. Ferguson Fanny and getting away with it. She certainly hadn't gotten away with fibbing to the woman. Mrs. Ferguson had given her a blistering set-down shortly after dinner last evening for the story she had fabricated—which Emily felt she deserved—then had accepted her apology and gone off to put Zach to bed.

Emily still wasn't certain if she had been forgiven or not. She certainly hoped so. Frances Ferguson wasn't someone she wanted for an enemy. She could certainly use an ally at the Bar JM. And she truly liked the woman.

"Are you and Mrs. Ferguson courting, then?"

Scratching his whiskered chin, the old man shook his head, looking quite put out. "Heck, no. Fan won't have nothin' to do with me. Says I'm crude and that I smell bad. Well, there are days that I smell like three-day-old fish, I'll grant you that, but I got me a mess of manners when I put my mind to it. Not like that no-account cowboy Stinky Wallace."

"I think I should explain that Frosty and Stinky have a bit of a rivalry going on over Frances Ferguson," Jess said, unable to hide his amusement. "They'd both like to keep company with he, but she's got better sense than to let either of them near her."

"Hmph! Just 'cause you ain't got no use for women, boss, don't mean that they don't come in right handy on a cold winter's night. Beggin' your pardon, ma'am," Frosty added hurriedly, making Emily grin in spite of herself.

Jess, however, didn't find his foreman's comments the least bit amusing. "I don't pay you to stand around and jaw, Frosty. Don't you have something better to do, like check the fences to make sure they've not been cut again?"

"I've got some men on it now, Jess. We'll catch that no-good varmint who's been stealing them cows. Mark my words."

Emily's eyes widened at the revelation. "Your cattle are being rustled?" She couldn't keep the excitement out of her voice.

"Well I'm glad someone is fascinated by the prospect." Jess's voice dripped icicles. "I've just spent four days looking for the wily bastards who ran off with fifty head of my best stock. That means less money to me, and—"

"I'm sorry," Emily apologized quickly, hoping to avoid any further animosity between them. "I'm just not used to all of the problems associated with ranch life yet."

"Better get used to them, then, if you're going to continue writing books about the West."

"I—"

He didn't allow her to continue. "Riding lesson's over for today. I've got work to do. You'd best get back to the house and clean up." He wrinkled his nose in disgust. "And take a bath. That horse manure you're wearing isn't nearly as nice as that lavender scent you had on last night."

Emily counted to ten, trying her best not to let the cowboy's high-handed ways anger her. "How nice of you to notice, Mr. Murdock. I wasn't aware you were a connoisseur of women's fragrances."

Frosty chuckled at the woman's spunky remark. "That'd be Stinky, ma'am. He's the one who's fond of sweet-smelling parfumes. The man doses himself up with cologne instead of bathing regularly. That's how he got his nickname. Stinky sure does seem to fit."

And what nickname did they call Jess Murdock? she wanted to ask. Nasty? Rude? Hardheaded?

As if the imperious cowboy could read her mind, he said, "They call me boss, Emily. But you can call me Jess, unless you prefer the other." He stalked away, leaving Emily speechless for once.

Since her tutoring lessons with Zach wouldn't begin for another hour, Emily headed upstairs to her room to clean up and work on her book. Max expected *The Montana Kid* to be sent in on time despite her current assignment, and she was nowhere near completing it.

After slipping off the offending garments, she held them at arm's length and brushed them vigorously with a clothes brush, intending to borrow some baking soda from Mrs. Ferguson later to eradicate the smell. She didn't have many changes of clothes with her, and she certainly couldn't afford to buy any, so she'd have to be more careful in the future about what she wore to her riding lessons.

At the window, dressed only in her combination, she peered out, spotting Jess immediately standing by the horse corral, talking to a couple of his men. One had russet hair and an engaging grin, the other was a lad of about eighteen. He dwarfed them both by at least two inches, and it was easy to ascertain by his commanding presence who was the leader of the group—"the boss," as he'd informed her so smugly.

The younger of the two men handed Jess a rope, and after a moment's hesitation Jess began to twirl it above his head, spinning it like a halo; then he dropped it toward his feet and jumped in and out of the loop, earning a round of applause from the men.

Mesmerized by the sight of the impressive trick, Emily watched in awe.

As if he could sense her eyes upon him, Jess looked up and stared straight at the window, shading his eyes from the glare of the sun. Emily jumped back, mortified that he might have seen her in her undergarments, and wondered fleetingly what he would think of her if he had. No doubt he'd be disappointed. Her figure was far less impressive than her brain or her writing ability.

Moving to the washstand, she poured water from the enamel pitcher into the basin and cleansed herself as best she could, then dabbed cologne behind her ears and between her breasts. Remembering the remark Jess had made about her lavender scent, she flushed.

She seated herself at the mahogany desk—the only really fine piece of furniture in the room, next to the brass bedstead—and thumbed through the pages of her manuscript. Scanning what she'd already penned, she frowned deeply. *The Montana Kid* just wasn't coming together right. Something was definitely missing.

Deciding to start over, she reached for a fresh piece of

paper and a pencil. To begin with, she decided that the title was all wrong, so she wrote instead, "Montana Cowboy," then nodded in satisfaction and continued.

>   *Jake Molloy pointed his pearl-handled, sil-*
>   *ver-tooled six-shooter at the frightened, helpless*
>   *woman, his piercing blue gaze burning into her*
>   *like a branding iron.*
>   *The woman nearly swooned at the sight of*
>   *the virile outlaw. "Please, don't shoot me. I'll*
>   *willingly give you my money."*
>   *His grin was devilish and incredibly ap-*
>   *pealing. "It's not your money I'm interested in,*
>   *little lady. I'm thinking more of what's beneath*
>   *your bustle—"*

Emily gasped, felt heat rise to her cheeks as the images on the paper became all too familiar. Jake Molloy's handsome visage looked suspiciously like Jess Murdock's, down to the piercing blue gaze and rakish grin. The frightened woman bore a remarkable likeness to herself. And then there was that bustle remark, no doubt branded deep into her mind—thanks to that awful outlaw El Lobo.

Heaving a disgusted sigh, Emily crumpled the paper and reached for another, chewing the end of her pencil as she thought; but the words were not forthcoming, only images of Jess Murdock grinning at something she'd said, holding her close during her frightening experience with the horse, wielding that rope so expertly. Acting rude and overbearing.

The knock at the door was a welcome intrusion into her disquieting thoughts. "Yes?" she asked, reaching for her wrapper and donning it.

"It's Frances Ferguson. May I come in?"

Emily opened the door, smiling apologetically at the woman for her present state of undress. "I was just freshening up a bit before beginning my first tutoring lesson with Zach."

The foul-smelling clothes lay on the chair by the door, and the housekeeper picked them up, her distaste at the unpleasant odor quite apparent. "I'll clean these fer ye, lass. And we'll need tae get ye something else fer yer riding lessons. It would nae be good tae have ye ruining yer good clothes around them horses."

"Thank you, Mrs. Ferguson. You're very kind. After the way I behaved I don't deserve such thoughtful treatment."

The older woman brushed off the remark with an airy wave of her hand. "That's in the past now, lass. Ye've apologized and I've accepted. We willna speak o' it again, unless ye do somethin' tae hurt me boys. That I canna allow."

"I understand completely."

"Good. Now I'll be getting back tae the reason I came tae see ye. I want tae learn tae read and write English."

Emily's eyes widened. "You don't know how?"

The woman shook her head, her embarrassment evident by the reddening of her cheeks. "Me and Ennis, that's me departed husband, meant tae learn when we came tae America, but he died and I was tae busy learning to survive on me own. After I went tae work for Jess, I was always meaning tae learn, but I was tae embarrassed tae ask anyone fer help.

"There's no teacher in True Love, and I'd have been ashamed at any rate tae sit down wie a bunch of schoolchildren and expose me ignorance."

"But what about Mr. Murdock? Surely he would have taught you, had you asked." It was quite apparent that Jess held his housekeeper in very high regard. And with good reason: the kind woman was the only mother figure his son had ever known.

"The dear mon offered. But Jess is nae the type tae sit still fer great lengths o' time and fuss wie an old woman like me. He had his hands full, he did, trying tae teach the wee lad his letters. The mon's patience was tried on more than one occasion, and I jes couldna bring meself tae ask it of him."

"It must be difficult for you not knowing how to read." Emily reached for the woman's work-roughened hands and clasped them in her own. Mrs. Ferguson's plight touched her deeply. Reading was and always had been a great source of enjoyment to her, and she just couldn't imagine a life without books in it.

"I'd be happy to teach you, Mrs. Ferguson. You can sit down with Zach and me, or I can give you private lessons, whichever you prefer."

"I think it would be tae distracting fer Zach tae learn alongside me. Perhaps we can do our lessons after he's gone tae bed. I'll have the time tae concentrate then. It's said that ye canna teach an old dog new tricks, so I dinna know how quick I'll be tae learn, but I'll give it my best."

"I'm sure you'll do just fine," Emily reassured her with a smile.

Mrs. Ferguson fidgeted nervously with the folds of her apron. "I noticed out the window today that ye was speaking tae the old mon, Mr. Adams. Did he happen tae mention me name?"

Emily caught the woman's soft blush and bit back her smile. "As a matter of fact, he did. He referred to you as Fan and said that he'd like to be courting you."

"Indeed!" Her expression grew indignant. "Why, he's much tae old fer the likes o' me. I've already buried one husband. I dinna intend tae bury another.

"And Frosty Adams had better watch his mouth, or I'll be washing it out wie lye soap and be happy tae do it. I willna have the mon speaking so familiarly of me. I'm a respectable woman, I am."

"I don't think Mr. Adams meant any disrespect. He's sweet on you. And he seemed very upset that Stinky Wallace bore you some affection."

At the mention of the Bar JM cowhand, Frances chuckled softly. "Stinky needs a mother, nae a wife. He's a good-hearted soul, but he would make a terrible husband."

"And Mr. Adams? What kind of husband would he make?" Emily noted how quickly color rose to Mrs. Ferguson's cheeks, and she suspected that the housekeeper felt more than just disdain for the Bar JM's foreman. The insight could prove quite useful, she thought.

"He would benefit from having a good woman fer a wife, that's fer certain. I'm nae sure what kind o' husband he'd be, though, wie his sassy ways and fresh tongue. The mon's daft, he is, if he thinks I'll be sweet-talked by the likes o' him."

"And Jess Murdock? What kind of husband would he make?" It was writer's curiosity, Emily told herself. Strictly research.

"The best. Jess is a good lad. A bit stubborn and head-strong at times, but he's got a good heart. And he's a wonderful father tae Zach. I think any woman would be lucky tae have him fer a husband. But 'tis the getting that be the hard part. Jess says he'll never marry again. Nae after what happened tae him the last time."

"Do you know what happened?"

"I do. But that's nae fer me tae be speakin' of. Ye'll have tae be asking Jess that question, if ye want tae know. And I've said tae much already. Now I've got tae be gettin' back tae the kitchen."

It was obvious that the woman had said all she was going to on the subject of Jess Murdock, and Emily didn't see the point in pressing her right now.

"Tell Zach I'll be down directly to begin his lesson. We'll begin yours after supper."

The older woman nodded, then departed, leaving Emily more curious than ever to find out what had happened between Jess and his former wife and to discover all the other intimate details of his life.

The Bar JM cowboy pulled his horse to a halt in front of the line shack and dismounted, looking about to make sure he hadn't been followed to the rendezvous point. The shack was empty when he entered, and he frowned, thinking that his contact should have been here by now. They'd planned to meet at three o'clock, just like always.

The temptation to make money off Murdock by rustling his cows had been too strong to resist. Murdock was well off, at any rate, while he was still living hand to mouth.

Thirty dollars a month wasn't much for a man to live on. Women, liquor, and cards were expensive pastimes, and he liked to indulge in all three as frequently as he could. He figured Murdock owed him. He knew things about the man that had never been made public.

The sound of horse's hooves had him drawing his gun and moving to the window. Carefully he brushed aside the curtain and looked out, breathing a sigh of relief when he spotted his contact and not Jess Murdock's men.

The Bar JM's hands were loyal. And no man would have hesitated to shoot a cattle rustler or a horse thief, even if he was one of their own and had been for a right good while.

"Goddamn it, Juan! You're late!" He moved outside and holstered his weapon. The dark-haired man's cocksure grin had him clenching his fists in anger.

"Do not wet yourself, *mi amigo*. I have your money, just as I promised. I was late getting back from town, that's why I wasn't here on time. Pleasure often comes before business, no? A man must take his ease."

The Bar JM ranch hand thumbed back his black felt hat, his light eyes as cold as the metal barrel of his gun. "We've got to lay low for a while. Murdock's getting antsy about so many head being taken, and he's tightened up the perimeter. I was lucky to get out today to meet you."

The man rubbed his chin thoughtfully. "The buyers I supply need cows. And you, *mi amigo*, promised me cows." The man's hand eased toward his pearl-handled gun, but he didn't draw it. "I don't like being lied to."

The cowboy swallowed, realizing he'd be no match for the man, if he decided to draw against him. El Lobo didn't come by his ruthless reputation lightly. He was a mean son of a bitch, who tended to shoot first and ask questions later. He had no intention of upsetting him. "I ain't lying. I just need more time to work things out. Murdock's mean when he's crossed, and I ain't looking to get my neck stretched. The man can shoot the eye out of a jackrabbit at two hundred yards, and I ain't anxious to become his target practice."

"It would be interesting, would it not, to meet this Murdock and see who is the better man with a gun?" When the rustler's eyes widened and he didn't answer, Juan said, "I understand that you have some company out at the ranch."

The cowboy shrugged. "A woman. She writes books. I wouldn't mind taking a roll in the hay with her, I can tell you that. She's a real looker, with her black curly hair and big blue eyes. Not much on top, but still a looker."

The outlaw's eyes widened at the description, but he didn't let his interest show. It was never wise to reveal your position, he had learned early on. "Señor Murdock might not like that."

Grinning, the cowboy said, "Jess don't cotton much to women anyhow. And it just might be challenging to rustle his woman, in addition to his cows."

El Lobo was unimpressed by the cowhand's bragging, and his extreme foolishness in going after another man's woman, especially when that man was obviously a much better shot. "When can I expect the next shipment? I can't put my buyers off indefinitely."

"A few weeks. Just let things cool off a bit. I'll send word in the usual way."

"And if I don't hear from you, *amigo*, should I assume that Murdock shot off your balls for messing with the woman?" He laughed at the sudden anger on the cowboy's handsome face.

"You'll hear from me. And if you're real lucky, I'll even let you know in detail how good she was."

El Lobo smiled, for he intended to find that out for himself.

Chapter Six

THE LOUD, DETERMINED BANGING ON THE DOOR
roused Emily from a sound sleep. Fire! was her first thought
as she bounded out of bed, stubbing her toe on the nightstand
in the process. "Dang it all!" She bounced up and down on
her right foot, trying to ease the pain from the left.

"Get up, Emily," came Jess's voice through the door.
"It's time to muck out the barns."

Emily stared daggers at the door, then gazed out the
window. It was still pitch black outside. She couldn't keep
her temper from showing as she glared back at the door.
"It's the middle of the night. Even the rooster's not up yet.
Go away."

She heard a chuckle. "'Fraid I can't do that. The
horses can't wait to be fed, and neither can the chores that
need doing.

"You did say you wanted to learn all about living on
a ranch, didn't you? If you've changed your mind . . ."

The gauntlet had been thrown. Again. "I'll be right
there," she shouted back at the hateful man, wondering

why she'd ever offered such a stupid challenge. It was as obvious as her throbbing toe that she wasn't cut out for ranch life. And it was just as obvious that Jess Murdock was determined to make her sorry that she had ever entertained the idea of writing his life story.

She donned the pair of Levi's and flannel shirt that Mrs. Ferguson had appropriated from somewhere, then yanked on a pair of tooled leather boots that the housekeeper had confessed had been bought for her one Christmas but never worn. The pants and shirt were snug, the boots too large, but Emily was dressed and determined to see this fiasco through if it killed her.

"I hope you're appreciating this, Max," she said under her breath as she wobbled to the door in the too large boots.

Downstairs she found Jess in the kitchen. He had just swallowed a mouthful of coffee when he spotted her, and the dark liquid came spewing forth all over his shirtfront.

"What the hell are you wearing, woman!" His eyes widened as he perused the way the flannel clung to her breasts, revealing a very lush form, the way the jeans cupped her bottom, leaving no doubt that the wearer of the men's clothing was a woman.

Emily smiled, pleased that she'd been able to ruin his morning as effectively as he'd ruined hers. "Mrs. Ferguson thoughtfully procured these garments for me. She didn't want me ruining my clothing. Wasn't that kind of her?" Not waiting for his answer, she moved to the stove and the enamel coffeepot simmering there, and poured herself a cup.

"You can't wear that around the ranch."

She took a sip of her coffee and sighed contentedly, grateful that coffee always had the power to make things right again. "Why ever not? These clothes are perfectly decent and acceptable for ranch life. You wear them. And no one is going to see me anyway, except for the people who work here." The pants and shirt were ten times more comfortable and unfettering to wear than the dresses she'd brought with her, and far more practical. And Emily always prided herself on being a practical person.

Jess wondered if any work would get done once the men took a gander at Emily. He thought not. He glanced down at her feet and the boots that were a size too big for her. "How are you going to get around in those? You'll fall and break your neck."

"I stuffed the ends with socks. They're a bit big, but I'll manage. You'll find that I'm a very resourceful woman when I put my mind to it." She smiled sweetly and continued sipping her coffee.

"Suit yourself. But if any of the men get out of hand, you're to tell me immediately. Do you understand?"

Spotting the plate of freshly made doughnuts, Emily moved to grab one, then shook her head in confusion while taking a bite. "Why should they get out of hand?" she asked, her mouth half-full. "I'm not going to interfere in their work."

Jess rolled his eyes, wishing that were true. "I know you're unfamiliar with life out west, Emily, but surely you must realize that these men don't get into town all that often. Women are still a scarcity out here. Especially pretty ones."

The corners of her mouth tipped up. "Is that a compliment?"

"No!" he thundered, moving to the door, wondering how the woman could be so oblivious of the temptation she presented. Not only to the men, but to himself. He'd felt the stirrings of awareness, the dull throbbing in his groin, at the sight of her in those revealing clothes, and he wasn't the least bit happy about it.

"Hurry up and eat your doughnut," he said more harshly than he intended. "It's time to get to work."

"You are obviously not a morning person, Mr. Murdock. I'm not, either, but I try not to bite other people's heads off just because I'm tired and cranky."

He looked at her as if she'd lost her mind. "I am not tired and cranky. What I am is sorry that I ever consented to let you stay on my ranch."

Deciding not to let his comment upset her, Emily followed him out the door and into the darkness and cold morning air. Clutching her arms about herself to ward off the chill, she wished Mrs. Ferguson's largesse had included a warm jacket.

"Now that you've brought that up, I've been meaning to ask you when you think we can sit down and talk about your adventures. I'm just dying to hear all—"

"Never! I told you that you could stay here, but that I wasn't going to let you write any books about me. I haven't changed my mind."

"You're just being stubborn. Mrs. Ferguson said you were stubborn and headstrong."

He cracked his head so swiftly, his hat nearly fell off. "She said what?"

Emily bit her lip, unwilling to get the housekeeper in trouble. "Nothing. But it's obvious that you're used to having your own way about things. I guess someone with your background is naturally bent on being first, best, and right. At least that's what I've heard."

He paused by the barn door and lit the kerosene lantern hanging just inside on a nail. The large area was immediately bathed in a golden glow. The horses whinnied in greeting, and the odor of stale hay and manure assaulted her senses. Wrinkling her nose in disgust, she lamented that it was a bit early for inhaling animal droppings.

"Just what have you heard, Emily? I'm curious to know."

Without so much as batting an eyelash, she replied, "That you killed fifty-seven men while you were marshal of Abilene."

"Fifty-seven men! Where the hell did you hear that?"

He seemed astounded by the revelation, and that gave Emily pause. "It's common knowledge. Are you trying to say that you didn't?"

He shrugged, unwilling to defend himself against rumors. "Would it make any difference? Folks are apt to believe what they want, whether or not it's true. Writers tend to write lies, especially when they don't have their facts straight," he added, thrusting a pitchfork in her direction.

Emily grew instantly wary. Manual labor was not in her job description. "It's true that we take some license with the truth, but that's what writing fiction is all about.

It's the fantasy of the Wild West that is so appealing to readers back east.

"Most men, like Cody, and before him, Hickock, didn't seem to mind the exaggerations written about them. If anything, they enjoyed the mystique. Dime novels made them into larger-than-life heroes. And the reading public is always clamoring for heroes."

"Men should be judged on their own merits, for what they do, not for what folks *think* they do. Trust me, there's a world of difference.

"Cody and Hickock did many heroic things in their lifetimes, but there were also events in their past that I'm sure they weren't too proud of."

His face grew pained when he said it, and Emily's curiosity was piqued again. There might be something in Jess's background that he didn't want anyone to know about. Perhaps the reason for his wife's desertion, she mused. "I heard you were an Indian scout for a time. Is that true?"

He heaved a sigh, nodded, but said nothing.

"I heard you were a hero."

His eyes grew cold and flat, as did his voice. "I'm not a hero, Emily Jean. So get that ridiculous notion right out of your head. I did what had to be done because that was my job, and I'm not proud of the way the Indians were dealt with, in any case." The memory of the massacres he'd participated in, the senseless killing of women and children, still had the power to sicken his stomach.

The white man had lied to the Indians, mistreated

them, and stolen their heritage, so they could flourish on land that wasn't rightfully theirs. Jess bore the guilt for that as well. His ranch had once been part of the hunting grounds of the northern Cheyenne.

Leaning on her pitchfork, Emily heaved an exasperated sigh. "You're not giving me much to go on."

"I think you're starting to get the picture. Now get to work. These stalls aren't going to clean themselves."

Emily was tempted to take the pitchfork and shove it right into Jess Murdock's rear end. The man was as irritating as all get-out.

"You're making my job much harder than it needs to be."

"Good."

"You said you'd meet me halfway."

He turned his head to look at her. "I did? I don't recall saying any such thing."

"Well, it was understood."

"By who?" He arched an eyebrow. "You?"

"You leave me little choice, then." Emily intended to interview as many of the people on the ranch as she could, in order to find out what she needed to know. She would start with Frosty Adams, who seemed to think that a book about Jess was a great idea.

"No one at the Bar JM who wants to keep their job is going to talk to you about me," he replied, as if he could read her mind. The fact that he could was getting to be damn irritating.

Her blue eyes widened in disbelief. "You threatened people with their jobs?"

"It's my ranch, my life that you're trying to invade and exploit, Emily. I have to protect myself, my son, and my privacy, the best way I know how."

"You should know that I'm not going to give up. There's too much at stake for me and for my publisher, Maxwell Wise."

He shrugged. "I guess we're at an impasse, then."

However true Jess's statement may have been, it only served to fuel Emily's determination to succeed. Maxwell Wise could have told Jess that Emily Jean Bartlett was a formidable opponent. But unfortunately for Jess, Max was in New York, and the cowboy would have to find out that truth the hard way.

"Jess told me to come and help you with your riding lesson, Miss Emily."

Looking over her shoulder, Emily brushed the hair out of her face with the back of her hand to find Frosty Adams standing behind her. She straightened, easing the pain in her lower back with the palm of one hand while holding the pitchfork with the other. "I'm almost done. This is the last stall to clean, Mr. Adams."

He observed her handiwork and nodded, inhaling the scent of fresh hay. "Looks to me like you've done a right good job. Horses are like people. Always appreciate a clean bed to sleep on."

"I'm filthy."

He nodded. "'Fore a stable can get clean, someone has to get dirty. Them horses are mighty grateful, though."

She gave a halfhearted smile. "I'm so pleased for

them." If she never saw another horse or the inside of a barn again, it would be too soon. No matter how many times she bathed or washed her clothes, she was sure she would never get the stench of horse off her.

She thought of what her mother would say if she could see her at this very moment, with straw in her hair and manure covering her work gloves and clothing, and a smile suddenly crossed her face. Marian Bartlett would be horrified and would mostly likely faint dead away. Emily's mother always fainted at the most propitious moments, like when Emily had refused to marry Tom Neeley.

"I can see why Jess wanted me to give the riding lessons this morning." He perused her unusual attire from top to bottom, then chuckled, spitting a wad of chewing tobacco into the clean hay. "Couldn't understand what my age had to do with it. But I can now. The younger men might get a bit distracted seeing you in that getup."

"How thoughtful of your boss to see to my welfare." Emily did her best not to grimace. Jess wasn't nearly so considerate when he'd demanded that she muck out all of the stalls in the entire horse barn. The chore had taken her nearly three hours.

"Jess takes his responsibilities to heart, Miss Emily, and I guess he deems you his responsibility while you're living here at the ranch."

Setting aside the pitchfork, she wondered if Jess would have been so magnanimous if he had known that he had played right into her hands. She intended to use his foreman as a source of information. "I'm happy you'll be acting as my new riding instructor, Mr. Adams. I'm sure you'll have far more patience than your predecessor."

The old man scratched his head. "Don't know about that, ma'am, but I'm willing to give it a try, iff'n you are. And you just call me Frosty. Most folks here are pretty informal, except for Fanny, that is."

"I welcome the chance to get to know you better. I'm sure we'll have plenty to talk about."

He stiffened and grew immediately apprehensive. "I guess you know that Jess don't want any of us talking to you about him."

"I do indeed. And I wouldn't dream of asking you to put your job in jeopardy." He seemed relieved by that. "I was merely going to ask you for your help, in exchange for my own."

His forehead wrinkled in confusion. "I don't rightly understand what you're getting at, ma'am. Even though I disagree with Jess about you writing them books, that don't mean that I can go agin his wishes. We go back a long ways, Jess and me do."

Emily turned over a feed bucket and seated herself. Frosty squatted beside her. "I think you know that Jess deserves the recognition that a series of books would bring to him, Frosty. Just as I know that you and Mrs. Ferguson would make a very nice couple."

His jaw dropped again. "Me and Fan?"

"I'd be willing to help you in your amorous pursuit of Mrs. Ferguson, if you'd help me convince Jess that my writing the series is a good idea. It's obvious he trusts your judgment, or you wouldn't be his ranch foreman."

"Just how would you be able to help me with Fan, if you don't mind me askin'? She's a hard woman. And she's made it clear as rainwater that she ain't interested in me courting her."

Emily's smile was full of confidence. "But she's a woman, same as me. I can put in a good word for you now and again. Point out your finer qualities. And perhaps give you some suggestions that might soften her heart."

He thought for a moment, rubbing his whiskered chin as if contemplating the idea. Then he said, "And all I'd have to do is try to convince Jess that he should let you write his books? That don't seem too hard."

"You said that you and Jess go back a long way. Did you know him when he rode with the Wild West show?"

"I surely did. But I knew him way before that. Met him when he was riding scout for the cavalry." His chest puffed up with pride. "I like to think I taught him most everything he knows about reading sign and scouting."

Emily smiled at that.

"He was a mite cocky and arrogant in his younger days, too sure of himself for his own good. I took him under my wing and gave him the benefit of my knowledge and experience. If I hadn't, he might have ended up like that stubborn fool Custer. A more conceited man I've yet to meet."

It was obvious that Frosty bore a great deal of affection for Jess and that he was more than willing to take credit for Jess's abilities and accomplishments. "Guess it must have been quite dangerous back when the Indians were on the warpath and settlers were getting killed."

He nodded matter-of-factly. "Damn near lost my scalp a few times. Woulda been killed if Jess hadn't come along and saved my hide. Guess I taught him right." He grinned.

Before the older man could reveal any more information, the barn door slammed open and one of the cowboys entered.

"Hey, Rusty!" Frosty called out when he saw who it was. "Why ain't you out rounding up strays?"

The man paused, holding out his bridle. "Bit's come loose. I need to get another before I can ride out. Howdy, ma'am," he said, smiling at Emily, his light eyes roaming covertly over every inch of her. "I didn't see you sitting down there." He removed his hat to reveal a mop of rust-colored hair.

"Miss Emily, this here's Rusty Doyle. He rides for the brand, same as me. Been with Jess a right good while now."

"Speaking of Jess," Rusty said to Frosty, tearing his gaze away from the fetching woman, "he's wondering why you ain't out in the corral giving Miss Emily her riding lessons."

"'Cause we've been finishing up here." Frosty gave Emily a conspiratorial wink. "Guess we'd better get to our lesson, Miss Emily. The boss don't like any lollygagging, ain't that right, Rusty?"

The cowboy nodded. "I'd best be on my way, too. Pleasure to finally meet you, ma'am." He strolled out, leaving Emily with the impression that Jess Murdock's men didn't pose much of a threat to her safety.

Most of the cowhands she'd met had been polite, like Rusty Doyle. He was a nice-looking man with impeccable manners who didn't seem at all intimidating, unlike his boss, who could make a mountain lion cower in fear.

Emily had always heard that cowboys held women in very high regard and took umbrage with anyone who was wont to insult them. It was part of the code they lived by, just like not taking another man's horse, not complaining when the work got too hard, and not breaking their word—the latter being by far the most important.

Emily wondered if Jess Murdock was aware of the cowboy code. She thought not.

Emily grunted and groaned as she attempted for the fourth time to get the heavy saddle hoisted up and over the stall partition. Taking care of the tack was as important as taking care of the horse, Frosty had explained.

Her first riding lesson with the foreman had gone well. Frosty had far more patience for teaching than Jess—Mrs. Ferguson had been right about that—and had even complimented her on the fact that she'd managed to stay on the horse for an entire turn around the corral. She'd felt a real sense of accomplishment when Caesar had actually given up trying to buck her off and had consented to let her ride him.

Now, if I can just get this darn saddle up, I can go into the house and—"Dang it all!" she cursed when the weight of the saddle had her falling backward onto the hay. "Hellfire and spit!" She pounded the ground next to her in frustration.

The sound of laughter had her looking up into a pair of brilliant blue eyes. She fought the urge to shout out more obscenities. Jess Murdock was by far the most irritating man on the face of the earth, probably in the entire solar system.

"*Tsk. Tsk.* Ladies shouldn't swear."

Emily knew that. And normally she didn't. But when she got really mad or frustrated, the western vernacular that she used in her writing seemed to creep into her speech.

"Having a bit of trouble, are we?"

She wouldn't give him the satisfaction of admitting any such thing. "I slipped. The hay was wet."

"You're not a very good liar, Emily. I noticed that right off. Need some help with the saddle?"

She shook her head. "I'll manage. Was there something you wanted, or did you just come here to gloat over my ineptitude?" She rose to her feet, brushing the debris off her backside.

Jess's eyes followed the movement with more than a passing interest, then he grinned. "We like to keep the hay in the stall."

Her fists knotted. "You—!"

She was about to retort something quite unflattering when Jess added, "Eggs need to be collected. Thought I'd show you how to go about it."

Emily tried to hide her disappointment. She'd been envisioning a soak in a hot tub. Her taut muscles were screaming for release. "You mean I've got more chores to do once I'm done here?"

"Living on a ranch is hard work, Emily. If you're going to be accurate in your books, convey authenticity in your writing, then you need—"

Heaving a sigh, she held up her hand to forestall the lecture. "Never mind."

Jess entered the stall, bent over, and hoisted up the saddle with one hand, placing it atop the partition. "Once you get some muscles in those skinny arms of yours, you'll be able to do that yourself."

She looked down at her arms. "What do you mean, skinny arms? My arms are perfectly well developed."

As was the rest of her body, but he wasn't about to admit that. He squeezed her biceps. "A few more weeks of hard work and this puny little thing will be bulging." A few more minutes of Emily Jean's company and something else would be bulging, too, he thought, mindful of the tightening in his loins and doing his best to ignore it as they headed outside to the chicken coop located at the rear of the house.

The hens were carrying on and making an awful racket when Emily approached the coop door cautiously and peered in. "I don't see any eggs. And those chickens don't look too happy to see me." They looked downright hostile, in her opinion.

Hiding his smile, Jess pushed her farther into the coop, reaching under one of the hens to pull out a fresh brown egg. "They're sitting on the eggs, Emily. You've got to reach under the chickens to pull them out."

Horrified at the prospect, she drew in a sharp breath and her mouth fell open. "You want me to steal their offspring while they're still sitting on them? That's barbaric. I can't do that. I'd feel like a kidnapper."

His look was disbelieving. "How the hell do you think we get our eggs?"

She shrugged. "I hadn't really thought about it. In the city I just wait for the grocer to deliver them."

He handed her a wicker basket that had seen better days. "We're not in the city, and here we gather our own. It's necessary to raise enough chickens to feed everyone on the ranch. Same with the milk cow, and—"

"You've got a milk cow, too?" Her expression turned sickly.

"We'll save that lesson for another day."

It wasn't a comforting thought. "I thought you were a rancher, not a farmer."

"Ranchers have to eat, same as everyone else. We don't get our groceries delivered. We grow them." He pointed to the vegetable garden adjacent to the coop. "We've got squash, pole beans, pumpkins, and other vegetables growing out there. We use the chicken and cow droppings to fertilize the plants."

Emily pulled a face. "You put cow manure on the food you eat?" She shuddered at the very idea. "How disgusting!"

"We wash them off before we eat them, Emily. We're self-sufficient here. Winters in Montana are long and sometimes quite harsh. We've got to put away enough foodstuffs to get us by. You'll be helping Mrs. Ferguson with the canning and storing when the time's right, so you can learn how it's done."

"I can hardly wait," she replied, moving closer to the broody hen and reaching under her. She felt the egg and clasped it in her palm, but when the bird started squawking and flapping her wings in protest, Emily jumped back. "I can see this is going to take a bit of practice."

Jess stood by the door, arms folded, and watched with admiration shining in his eyes. Emily, for all her city ways and naiveté, had grit. She hadn't backed down from her goal of writing her series, hadn't ducked the challenge of learning the ways of the ranch.

And she hadn't run away, like Nora Murdock.

Jess's wife hadn't adjusted to married life after having a child. She'd complained constantly about feeling confined, missing her friends, losing her figure, and having to care for a bawling brat. They'd had many arguments over her indifference to the child, to shirking her duties as a wife and mother. But instead of her trying to work things out, his wife had opted to desert him and their three-month-old child and run away. To this day he had no idea where she was. It was as if she had disappeared off the face of the earth, and it made ending their marriage extremely difficult.

Nora had taken the coward's way out of a situation she hadn't been willing to accept. Unlike Emily Jean Bartlett, whom Jess was certain didn't possess a cowardly bone in her body.

Chapter Seven

Aᴄᴛᴇʀ ꜱᴜᴘᴘᴇʀ ᴛʜᴀᴛ ᴇᴠᴇɴɪɴɢ, Eᴍɪʟʏ ꜱᴇᴛᴛʟᴇᴅ ʜᴇʀ-self at the old maple kitchen table with Frances Ferguson to begin the housekeeper's instruction in the reading and writing of the English language.

Emily hoped Mrs. Ferguson was better at learning her letters than she, Emily, had been at mastering the art of equestrianism and performing ranch chores. She hadn't had much to show for her first effort at gathering eggs.

Returning to the house with four cracked ones in her basket had earned her a tongue-lashing from the older woman, then a comforting hug when Emily, tired and upset, had burst into tears. It had been a singularly embarrassing moment in her life and one she'd been grateful Jess hadn't witnessed.

Watching as the housekeeper penned the letter "A" several times, Emily nodded her approval. "That's excellent, Mrs. Ferguson. I think you'll be writing correspondence in no time." The woman had confided that one of the reasons for wanting to learn to read and write was so that she could correspond with her only surviving relative, a sister now living in Philadelphia.

"Ye make me feel small, Emily, after the way I behaved over the eggs."

Emily brushed away the apology. "It's hard not to feel frustrated and inept when learning things for the first time, but we'll both get the hang of our lessons eventually."

Three raps sounded at the back door, and Emily looked up to see Frosty through the window. She guessed the old man had decided to take her suggestions for wooing Frances Ferguson. "You've got company, it seems, Mrs. Ferguson."

When the housekeeper saw who it was, she harrumped loudly, then hurried to answer the summons, patting her hair in place as she went. "Since when do ye stand outside, old mon?" she asked. "Ye've nae knocked on me kitchen door before. Ye usually just waltz in, brazen as all get-out."

From behind his back, Frosty brought forth a bedraggled-looking bouquet of what were supposed to be flowers but looked more like weeds. Mrs. Ferguson looked astounded by the gesture and somewhat pleased, though she did her best to hide it. "What's this?" she asked, her cheeks pinkening.

Removing his hat, Jess's foreman declared, "I'm officially paying court to you, Fan. Please accept these here flowers as a token—"

"I'll do no such thing, ye daft mon. And don't be calling me Fan." She took the flowers anyway. "Now get ye gone, Frosty Adams. I'm doing me lessons wie Emily Jean."

Frances turned to put her bouquet into a pitcher of water, and Frosty took that moment to give Emily a conspiratorial wink and a smile. "How do, Miss Emily."

"Hello, Frosty. You're looking awfully resplendent this evening." His white hair was still wet from having been freshly washed, and he smelled as if he'd borrowed some of Stinky Wallace's sandalwood cologne.

"Perhaps we should continue our lesson tomorrow, Mrs. Ferguson," Emily offered, and received a grateful look from the foreman. "I'm sure you'd much rather spend your time with Mr. Adams." She attempted to rise, but Mrs. Ferguson pushed her back down with a firm hand to her shoulder.

"I do nae!" the woman declared emphatically. "Thank ye fer the flowers, Mr. Adams, but I am otherwise engaged."

Frosty looked crushed. "But I took a bath, Fan, and it ain't even Saturday."

Emily swallowed her smile.

"And I'm sure ye needed it, old mon. Now be gone wie ye. I'm much tae busy tae be bothering wie the likes of ye right now."

Discouraged but not defeated, Frosty bowed gallantly before the woman he adored. "I'll be saying good night, then, Fanny. But I'll be back. You can count on that, ol' gal." He exited through the doorway and headed toward the rear of the house, where Jess's office was located.

"Old gal, am I?" Indignation rode Frances hard. "The nerve of the mon, thinking he can come calling on me anytime he pleases."

"It's obvious that he's smitten, Mrs. Ferguson. I think Frosty Adams is just a darling man. I like him very much."

"Ye do?" Frances seemed surprised by that and seated herself back at the table. "And what do ye find so appealing about him, I'd like tae know?"

"Well, Mr. Adams has a lot more patience than Jess when it comes to giving riding lessons. And he's a very kind individual, always quick to compliment and give encouragement. He's just the opposite of my father, who was always very stern and critical of everything I did or wanted to do." It had been difficult trying to earn Louis Bartlett's approval. In the end, Emily had ceased trying.

"Frosty has a good sense of humor, too. That's not always easy to find in a man." Jess had a good sense of humor, too, but it was usually directed at her.

Mrs. Ferguson seemed to consider Emily's words. "What ye say may be true. I havena paid much attention to the mon's good points, only his bad."

"A woman could do worse, I imagine," Emily said as nonchalantly as possible, but the woman was wise to her motives.

"I see that ye fancy yerself tae be a matchmaker as well as a tutor, Emily Jean. We had professional matchmakers in Scotland. Men and women who were paid tae make a suitable match between two parties. Arranged marriages are very acceptable in my country."

"I assure you, Mrs. Ferguson, that I am not getting paid for speaking the truth about Mr. Adams." Not in money, anyway, Emily thought, hoping that Frosty intended to keep his end of the bargain.

*   *   *

Seated in the leather wing chair fronting the desk in Jess's office, the foreman of the Bar JM attempted to do just that as he extolled Emily Jean's virtues to Jess while the rancher continued working on his books.

"Miss Emily is a quick learner, Jess. She managed to stay on Caesar a right good while today. I don't think it'll take long at all for her to become a good rider."

"That's nice," Jess said absently.

Sipping his whiskey, Frosty settled back in the comfortable leather chair. "I like her."

Jess sighed and finally looked up from his accounts, wondering when the old man was going to get around to making his point. He'd been hemming and hawing for fifteen minutes, and that wasn't like him. Of all the men he knew, Frosty Adams spoke his mind and gave no apologies for doing so.

"Did you come here tonight for any particular reason? Maybe to tell me that you've caught the bastard who's been stealing my cows?" Figuring he wasn't going to get any more work done tonight, Jess closed the ledger and poured himself a drink from the bottle he always kept in the right-hand drawer of his desk.

"Nope. Don't have any news on that. But that don't mean squat. You know eventually that whoever's doing the stealing is going to mess up. Then we'll grab him."

Jess shook his head. "Don't have that many cows to spare, old man. I was hoping to sell this herd and make a profit." Jess had been hit hard by the drought and the disastrous winter of 1887 and was only now making a financial recovery. He couldn't afford to lose any more head of cattle, and if he caught the bastard who was stealing from him, he was going to string him up.

"I ain't never led you astray before, boy. Guess you know that."

"Guess that's so. But that don't mean there won't be a first time."

"If I was to give you some good advice, do you suppose you'd take it?"

Jess leaned back, intrigued. "Depends on what it is. If you've found a way to make the ranch more productive, then of course I—"

Frosty shook his head. "It don't have nothing to do with the Bar JM, not directly, anyway. It's about Miss Emily. I think you're selling her short."

Arching a disbelieving brow, Jess said, "What's this? Frosty Adams smitten with a woman half his age?" Then he chuckled, knowing how easy it was to get a rise out of his old friend.

"Don't be a horse's ass, Jess. I ain't smitten with Emily Jean. You know my heart's with Fan. But I sure as heck do like that little gal. She's smart, and spunky, too. And I think you should let her do them books she wants to write. What could it hurt?"

Jess swallowed his liquor in one gulp, his eyes hardening into bits of blue ice. "She put you up to this, didn't she?"

"No." Frosty shifted nervously in his seat. "Well, not directly, anyway."

"I knew it. I'm going to kick her pretty butt off this ranch first thing tomorrow morning."

The old man's face whitened to match his beard. "You can't do that! She ain't got nowhere to go."

"I'll give her the money myself to get back to New York. I figure it'll be a wise investment."

"What are you afraid of? I think maybe you're becoming sweet on the gal yourself and just don't want to admit it. You think every woman's going to be like Nora. And they ain't. Miss Emily's as sweet as apple pie and a whole lot prettier than that snooty woman you married."

"This has nothing to do with my wife. We're talking about Emily Jean Bartlett and her conniving ways. All women are the same, far as I can tell. They get what they want, then cut out, giving no thought to whom they hurt and the consequences of their actions."

"Sounds like you're still festering, boy."

"I'm over the selfish bitch, Frosty. But I don't want to borrow trouble from anyone else. Me and Zach have made our own lives here. We don't need anyone interfering in them, and we sure as hell don't need some woman writer invading our privacy and telling our secrets to the world."

Frosty sipped thoughtfully on his drink. He'd been with Jess a long time, knew there wasn't a smack of cowardice within him, but the man still had demons about his past mistakes. "You're worried that everyone will find out about what happened, aren't you? It was an accident, for chrissake, Jess. Give it up."

"I don't want any ugliness touching my boy. I don't want him thinking less of me because of what happened."

"Even a small child like Zach would understand that what happened was an accident, that you didn't mean to shoot that kid. Why are you being so damn hard on yourself? It was nearly a year ago."

Jess's eyes clouded with pain. "Rory Connors's face still haunts me to this day, Frosty. The boy was only four when he died, and I killed him. No matter that it was an accident. I was to blame." He'd never get over the possibility that it could have been Zach lying dead in that small coffin. His son had played with Rory on numerous occasions. He could very well have been in the tent that night— Jess shuddered at the thought.

"Law didn't see it like that. And neither did the boy's parents. They understood it was an accident, one you had no control over."

"I'm sure Bill Cody paid to keep them quiet. It wouldn't have done for the 'star' of his Wild West extravaganza to be accused of murder."

The foreman let loose with a string of curses. "You are one stubborn son of a bitch, Murdock. Always have been. It's probably what's kept you alive all these years. But you're wrong about the boy. And you're wrong about Emily Jean.

"Maybe if you did get all your secrets out in the open, you'd be able to live with yourself. Hiding from the world, from your mistake, ain't gonna make it go away. You know it. And I know it. Think about it, Jess." Frosty stalked out, slamming the door behind him.

Jess watched him go, then leaned back in his chair and poured himself another glass of whiskey, heaving a sigh. The old man was probably right. He usually was. But that didn't make accepting his responsibility for killing that child any easier. He had only to close his eyes to bring back every sickening, heart-wrenching moment.

It had been a cold, clear January night, the kind where you could see your breath every time you exhaled. A thousand stars had shimmered in the sky against a backdrop of black velvet. The huge arena had been packed to capacity, the crowd cheering enthusiastically as he entered the ring dressed in his fringed buckskins atop his white stallion, Brutus.

He'd done the performance a hundred times before, holding his two six-shooters out at his sides and firing into the air. But that night Brutus had stumbled, throwing off his aim, and the bullets had gone astray, one entering the tent of Tim Connors, one of the show's employees. Rory Connors, Tim's youngest, a sweet, towheaded boy of four, had been killed instantly.

After a brief investigation, in which Jess had been judged innocent of any wrongdoing by the local authorities, he had quit the show and retired to his ranch in Montana, hoping desperately to put the ugly memory behind him.

But though almost ten months had passed since the incident, it would forever be etched into Jess's memory, a painful reminder of what fame had cost him and Rory Connors.

Frosty had urged him to allow Emily to write his life story, to reveal to the world all the horrible details of the accidental killing of the child. But how could he?

Jess Murdock had been labeled a hero, a legend in his own lifetime. What would folks—his own son—think if they found out what had happened on that winter's night? What would they do when they discovered that Jess Murdock was only a man, not an icon? A man with a past and an upbringing that held its own share of horrific secrets.

By the time the soft knock sounded on the door, Jess was well on his way to becoming drunk. He'd imbibed half a bottle of sourmash whiskey, and he was feeling no pain.

"Who is it?" he called out, his tongue thick with the alcohol he'd consumed. "I'm busy."

"It's Emily. I was wondering if you had a moment."

He frowned at the voice that was beginning to haunt his dreams at night, at the woman who was turning his normally staid life topsy-turvy with her never-ending questions and engaging grin. Emily Jean Bartlett, with her pert nose and equally pert breasts, was a temptation he was finding hard to resist.

He called for her to enter. When she did, his eyes widened at the sight of her dressed in her nightclothes. Emily looked like a damn virgin with her high-necked, white cotton nightgown and wool robe, her tiny pink toes peeking out from beneath the hem. But she also looked damned desirable.

"You wanted to ask me something?"

Emily stepped toward the desk, noting the half-empty bottle of whiskey, and nodded, an unsure smile flashing across her face like summer lightning. "I was getting ready for bed, as you can see"—her cheeks pinkened to match her robe—"and my kerosene lantern went out. I can't get it to work. I need to work on my book this evening, and I was wondering if you could fix it."

The woman was asking him to go up to her bedroom and fix her lamp? Was this a joke? Or did she have some other, more serious intention? Like seduction, perhaps?

He rose to his feet and came toward her, his gait steady despite the large amount of alcohol he'd consumed.

Suddenly the room seemed awfully small to Emily, and she swallowed nervously, wondering how wise it had been to put herself in such a compromising position with a man she felt attracted to but hardly knew.

She backed toward the door, but he kept coming toward her, his gaze intent. "Uh, maybe I should come back another time," she suggested. "You're probably busy." He was standing so close now, she could smell the alcohol on his warm breath and the musky scent of his cologne. His overwhelming masculinity scared the heck out of her, even as it flowed into all the sensual areas of her body.

When he reached out to finger the satin lapel of her robe, Emily stopped breathing for a moment. "You smell nice," he said.

She'd just bathed in lavender-scented water—the scent he was so fond of—and now was sorry she had. "Tha . . . thank you. I'd better go. It's getting late."

"Why not have a drink with me? Then we can go up and see what's wrong with the lamp."

"A drink?" She shook her head. "I'm afraid I don't drink spirits, but thank you anyway."

"Not drink? How in hell do you expect your male characters to behave authentically if you've never had a drink, experienced what it feels like to be intoxicated? Surely some of those rough, tough heroes of yours must imbibe 'spirits,'" he said mockingly.

Her face heated. "I'm a writer. I don't have to experience every detail in order to write about it." She'd had plenty of murders in her books and had yet to kill anyone herself.

"Your books would be a whole lot better if you did."

The man had the audacity to act as if he knew what the heck he was talking about, but it was obvious to Emily that he didn't. Annoyed, she took a calming breath. "My books are thoroughly researched and well written."

He cocked a brow. "Really? Is that why you chose to write dime novels instead of romantic novels? Maybe you've got more experience with outlaws and gunfights than you do with kissing and making love."

Frightened by the intensity she saw in his eyes, by the seductive grin on his face, Emily bolted for the door. But he was quicker and grabbed on to the back of her robe, spinning her back toward him. "I told you I was going to teach you all you needed to know about writing your novels, Emily Jean." He pulled her closer. "I thought we'd start by—"

She pushed at his chest. "Let me go, Mr. Murdock! You're obviously drunk. And I am not the least bit interested in your amorous advances."

He dismissed her protests with a laugh. "I told you that you weren't a very good liar, Emily. Shall I prove it?" Without waiting for a response, he pressed his lips to hers.

The kiss was punishing at first, and Emily sensed that he was acting on pure animal instinct and unable to control his behavior. But then it gentled, his lips moving over hers with masterful persuasion, his tongue seeking entry into her mouth, and Emily was caught up in the sheer wonder of it. And him.

His caressing lips and searching tongue sent shivers of awareness darting through her. Her stomach fluttered, her heart pounded, and she felt herself growing weak-kneed and light-headed. Just when she thought she might pass out, he kissed the pulsing area at the base of her throat, her cheeks, then his lips landed light as a butterfly's wing on her eyelids. Finally he took her mouth again, and Emily knew she was lost.

No one had ever kissed her like this before. No one had ever made her feel the way Jess Murdock made her feel. She was damned for all eternity. A fallen woman. A—

Suddenly his mouth was no longer upon hers, and Emily felt confused and devastated. She opened her eyes to find him gazing intently at her. The mocking smile she expected wasn't there, and in his eyes she thought she detected a small measure of regret.

"You've never been kissed before, have you? I mean—really kissed. Not just some chaste peck on the cheek by some silk-suited New York City dandy."

She shook her head, unable to voice a response. Her

heart lodged in her throat, and it was pounding so hard that she was sure he could hear it.

"You'd better go now, Emily. Run to your room and lock the door. Because if you don't, I won't be responsible for what happens next."

She searched his eyes for a moment. Then without a word, she scampered around him, pulled open the study door, and took flight up the stairs and into the safety of her darkened bedroom.

Breathing hard, she closed the door, then felt for the lock. There was none. She dragged over the chair standing near the door and propped it up under the doorknob, wondering all the while if she was seeking protection from Jess Murdock or from herself.

Chapter Eight

THE FOLLOWING MORNING JESS HAD COME TO A DECIsion: Emily Jean Bartlett had to go. She had not only tried to turn his foreman against him, she had attempted to seduce him with her innocent ways and had nearly succeeded.

Last night his resistance to her had weakened owing to the excessive amount of alcohol he'd consumed. He couldn't take the chance that the same thing would happen again if she remained at the ranch.

He was attracted to her. Emily was obviously attracted to him. She hadn't resisted his kisses; rather, she had welcomed them. Their mutual awareness of each other was sure to become explosive at some point. Sooner or later he would lose control and take what she was offering. It was as simple as that, and he wasn't about to let that happen. He liked his life just the way it was, with no entanglements.

Entering the kitchen, Jess saw Emily and his son together, and his heart twisted. She was very good with the child, very patient, and he knew that Zach relished the attention that she lavished on him. Heads bent, the two were intent on studying something in Zach's primer, and he almost hated having to interrupt the cozy scene.

"Miss Bartlett, I'd like to speak to you."

"Papa!" Zach flashed him an engaging grin. "Emily's teaching me my numbers. Want to hear me recite them from one to a hundred?"

His son's face glowed with pride and happiness, making Jess feel even worse for what he was about to say. "Not right now, Zach. Emily and I need to talk."

Judging from the tenseness in Jess's voice, Emily was fairly certain that he wanted to discuss what had happened between them last night, a topic she wanted to avoid like a case of the measles. She had spent over half the night trying to force the memory of his delectable kisses from her mind. "Can't it wait? Zach is making such wonderful progress, and—"

"Zach's progress is no longer your concern, Emily. I've decided to terminate our arrangement. I will give you the money to return to New York. You can leave first thing in the morning."

Emily's face paled. Mrs. Ferguson, who had just stepped into the room and overheard Jess's comment, gasped audibly. Zach burst into tears and rushed toward his father.

"Please don't send Emily away, Papa," the child pleaded, grabbing on to Jess's pant leg. "I want her to stay. She likes it here. And she plays with me. You can't send her away."

Jess sighed, squatting down to reason with the small boy. "Zach"—his tone softened—"Emily needs to return to her own home. We've kept her here far longer than she wanted to stay. I'm sure she misses her family and wants to see them."

Zach sniffed, then turned to face Emily. "Is that true, Emily? Do you want to leave me and Papa?"

Emily Jean refused to lie to the innocent child, of whom she'd grown inordinately fond. "No, Zach, I don't wish to leave. But if your father wants me to, then I have no choice but to do as he asks." Her honesty earned her a scathing look from Jess.

Mrs. Ferguson stepped forward, her expression combative. "Emily is teaching Zach and me tae read and write, Jess. Ye know she's been doing a good job. So why are ye being so unreasonable all of a sudden? She's hardly been here a week, and she's nae bothering anyone on the ranch." The housekeeper went to stand next to Emily's chair, an indication of whose side she was taking.

She's bothering me, Jess wanted to shout, but he couldn't. Instead he said, "I—I didn't want to impose on Emily any more than we already had."

Emily smiled sweetly. "It's no imposition at all, Mr. Murdock, if that's what you're worried about. I'm enjoying my stay at the ranch. And I'm quite loath to leave here at the moment." Her eyes widened, and she was the picture of complete innocence. "Why, I'm learning so many interesting things—things I've never experienced before. Shall I tell you what they are?"

Jess's face reddened at the veiled threat, and he shook his head, unwilling to allow his housekeeper or son to learn what had transpired last evening. "That won't be necessary."

Zach let out a yell. "Hear that, Papa? Emily doesn't want to leave yet." The child rushed forward to hug his tutor, and Emily responded in kind, bussing the boy on the top of his head and ruffling his hair.

Jess knew when to retreat in the face of formidable odds—he'd done it dozens of times before—but he didn't have to like Emily Jean getting the best of him, and his expression turned as sour as his disposition.

Jess had no intention of accepting defeat graciously. Emily may have won the first skirmish, but the battle between them was far from over.

Jess's desire to teach her a lesson was clearly evident an hour later when she was summoned to the barn by the imperious rancher.

One look at the cow's big pink udders, and Emily's blue eyes widened in disbelief. She'd never realized that cow's breasts were so . . . so gigantic. She stared down at her own slight form and sighed wistfully.

"We're not here to engage in a beauty competition, Miss Bartlett," Jess pointed out, and Emily's face reddened in mortification. "I believe Cora would win hands down, if that were the case."

Cranking her head, she gave the chuckling rancher a contemptuous look. "You're just doing this to punish me, Jess, because Zach and Mrs. Ferguson want me to stay. You're afraid to have me around. Admit it. You're afraid because of what happened between us last night. But what happened last night wasn't my fault, it was yours. You're the one who was drunk on your—"

His eyes narrowed at the veracity of her deduction. "Yes?"

"Whiskey." She swallowed her outrage. "And just because you forced yourself on me—"

"Forced?" He threw back his head and laughed, and the sound rippled down Emily's spine like a tickling feather.

"Listen here, lady, I was the one whose virtue was in jeopardy last night. You imposed yourself on me, remember?"

She gasped at his contention. "I came to your office to ask you to fix my lantern! Or were you too drunk to recall the reason for my visit?"

He shook his head in disbelief. "I've heard some pretty implausible seduction excuses in my time, but fixing a lamp has got to be—"

She bolted from the stool so quickly, the cow mooed in protest, turning her head and giving Emily an annoyed look. "Seduction! You think I came to seduce you?" She could see by his smug expression that he had. "Hellfire and spit! Of all the conceited, stupid, ridiculous—I told you once before that I'm not interested in you personally, Mr. Murdock, only professionally.

"And I think it's time that we got down to some serious interviewing. If you want to get rid of me, the fastest way to do that is to cooperate and let me write your damn book."

Jess found himself becoming aroused by her anger. His eyes were drawn to her heaving breasts, which were outlined quite clearly by her taut flannel shirt. "Maybe I was a bit too hasty. Maybe you could give Cora some serious competition," he teased.

Blue eyes flashed like summer lightning. "Are you mocking me, Mr. Murdock? I may not be as well endowed as some, but I hardly think that gives you the right to—"

He stepped toward her as if pulled by a magnet. "You felt well endowed to me last night. In fact, I got the impression when you were pressed up against me, Emily, that you didn't have a stitch on beneath that robe and nightdress of yours, am I right?"

Turning several shades of crimson, she stiffened in outrage. "I will not stand here a moment longer and be insulted."

Crossing his arms over his chest, he shook his head in mock confusion. "I just paid you a compliment. Most women like to hear that they've got big—"

Emily started to walk away, but he clasped her arm. "I thought you were interested in asking me some questions."

Gazing up into his face, she saw that he was serious. "Have you changed your mind, then?"

He shrugged. "Not entirely. But I might allow you to ask a few general questions, see where they lead." He couldn't believe what he was saying. But, damn it, he enjoyed being around her, matching wits, and sparring with her. Kissing her.

So what if she presented a threat to his sanity, to his very existence? He really didn't want her to leave, despite what he'd said earlier. Not just yet. Too much was unsettled between them. She filled the void he so keenly felt in his loneliness.

And to be fair, Emily had kept up her half of the challenge quite admirably, and Jess Murdock wasn't one to welsh on a bet.

"Do I still have to milk the cow?" She looked at Cora, who blinked her big brown eyes at her and looked horrified at the prospect.

Jess shook his head. "No. Cora was milked hours ago. I was just teasing you."

Emily bit the inside of her cheek and counted silently to twenty. Ten wouldn't have been nearly long enough. She couldn't afford to lose her temper right now. Jess Murdock had actually agreed to cooperate. Somewhat. It was a start. And at least she didn't have to milk the damn cow.

"Where would you like to conduct our interview? It would be nice if we could go someplace where we won't be disturbed. And no," she said when his eyes widened, "I'm not trying to seduce you."

"Pity. I was just starting to get used to the idea." When she heaved an impatient sigh, he added, "Tell you what—I've got to go into town to pick up supplies, so you may as well ride along with me. You can interrogate—I mean interview—me on the way."

She brightened at the prospect. "I'll need fifteen minutes to freshen up and change my clothes."

He cocked a disbelieving brow. "I've never known a woman who could change clothes in just fifteen minutes."

"But then, you don't know me all that well, do you, Jess?" Her confident smile disappeared when he replied:

"I guess not as well as I'm going to, Emily Jean."

While Jess fetched the buckboard and Mrs. Ferguson's grocery list, Emily dashed upstairs and quickly discarded her men's clothing, garbing herself instead in a navy wool skirt and white cotton shirtwaist that looked tidy and professional in appearance.

When she returned downstairs not ten minutes later it was to find Jess pacing the hallway. She smiled to herself, for he reminded her of Max, who was always impatient to get where he was going, even if they had all the time in the world.

Impatience was definitely a perverse male thing, Emily concluded as she made her way out the door.

The sun had disappeared behind a cover of dark clouds, turning the sky a gunmetal gray as they began the trek into True Love. Blue grama grass covered the surrounding countryside like thick, plush carpeting, and a meadowlark dipped its wing as if in greeting before soaring into the heavens.

The trip to town was the first since Emily's arrival, and she was a bit nervous at the prospect of facing Reverend Higgbotham again, should they happen to run into him. He didn't yet know that she'd lied, and she couldn't bear to see the disappointment on the man's face when he found out what her real motive had been in visiting Jess Murdock. No doubt he'd be just as "delighted" as Jess had been to discover her true intentions.

Chewing her lower lip indecisively, she finally asked, "Do you usually visit with the reverend and his wife on your trips to town?"

Jess shrugged. "Depends. Sometimes I stop at the rectory and pay my respects. Why?"

"Oh, nothing. I was just thinking how nice the Higg-bothams were."

"And how you lied to them?"

She sighed, wishing he couldn't read her mind so ef-fectively. The man was positively clairvoyant. "I'm not proud of lying to them, but I did what I thought was nec-essary at the time. And I was in dire straits. Surely a man with your considerable reputation must have told some whoppers in his day."

Jess grinned like a naughty schoolboy. "When I was a kid of nine I used to sneak out behind the barn and smoke. My ma would have tanned my hide had she known, but I told her that I was cutting firewood. Don't think she be-lieved me—I never did bring in any wood—but she never called me on it."

"Are your parents still alive?" For some strange rea-son she'd never thought of a man like Jess Murdock, a man so commanding and dynamic, as having parents. Of course, upon reflection, she realized that the notion of him springing into form as a full-grown man was totally ab-surd.

"No." His voice grew as cold as the stones littering the ground. "They're both dead."

"I'm sorry."

"Don't be. I've learned to live with it."

Emily thought his comment odd but passed it off to self-consciousness. Most men made light of their true feel-ings; apparently Jess was no different in that regard.

"My parents are still alive, for all the good it does me. They've never forgiven me for going against their wishes and becoming a novelist, so they don't want anything more to do with me." The thought had the power to hurt. More than she'd ever admit.

As he turned to look at her, the horse whinnied loudly. "That's the most ridiculous thing I've ever heard. You're a grown woman, for chrissake! You should be able to do what you want with your life."

Spoken like a man, she thought, wishing that women were afforded the same choices and opportunities as men, but she knew from firsthand experience that it just wasn't so.

She'd struggled hard against her parents' biases, against male prejudice, against pubic opinion in general, to pursue her dream of a writing career. It had been an uphill battle all the way, and there had been casualties along the way.

"Though writing is a respectable profession, it wasn't one my parents would have chosen for their eldest daughter. They're rather affluent and wanted me to marry a man of their choosing and social standing, so that I could give them grandchildren."

"Instead you gave them novels. I think it's a fair trade-off."

She smiled ruefully. "I gave them grief, above all else. But I had to follow my heart. I'd always wanted to write. Even as a small child I would make up stories and jot them down on paper. I guess it's just part of who I am, like you being a hell-raising cowboy."

He ignored the prevailing, inaccurate opinion of him. "Seems like you turned out all right. Don't know what they've got to complain about."

Emily warmed to Jess's compliment, particularly since he rarely offered one. Then, realizing that most of their conversation had been about her, she changed the subject. "Were you born here in Montana?"

"Nope. Born and bred in Kansas on a dirt poor farm to a father who was a drunken bastard and a mother he used as a punching bag."

Her face paled, and she clutched his arm. "I'm so sorry, Jess."

"Like I said before, don't be. They're both better off dead. Ma's at peace now, and Pa's exactly where he belongs—in hell."

"How did they die, if you don't mind my asking?"

Knowing Emily's persistent nature, Jess decided that she would ask, and continue asking, whether he minded or not. "After being nearly beaten to death, my mother decided that she couldn't take it anymore. She was worried that Pa would eventually turn his drunken anger on me, so she shot the bastard, then turned the gun on herself."

Finding his mother dead had been the hardest thing he'd ever had to face, until the death of Rory Connors. Both experiences had been turning points in his life and haunted him to this day.

"She took her own life?" Emily's voice lowered to a whisper.

"Yeah. Even though some might view it as a mortal sin, Ma probably thought she was already in hell, so it didn't matter much anyway."

"How awful it must have been for you growing up

without a family." At least she'd had hers until she was well past her majority.

He shrugged. "Frosty has a theory that it was because of my childhood that I became the man I am today." He smiled ruefully. "Such as that is."

"I'm anxious to get to know that man."

He gazed at her out of the corner of his eye and saw the sincerity there. "Are you? Well, I don't think I'm up for any more talk about my past right now. I've told you more than I ever intended." Why that was, he had no idea. He'd never told a soul about his parents, except for Frosty, whom he trusted, and who had been more like a father to him than his old man. But there was something about Emily that inspired trust.

Unwilling to open any more raw wounds at the moment, Emily said, "So we'll change the subject. Tell me about True Love. That's a very unusual name for a town. Is there a story behind it?"

"As a matter of fact, there is. A man by the name of Mortimer Peet founded the town many years ago. He hailed from somewhere back east—Maine, I think—and decided to come west to make his fortune by selling tools and implements to the miners.

"Mortimer did well for himself. In a few years he had saved enough money to build a house, so he sent for his fiancée. Unfortunately the woman contracted cholera while crossing the plains in a wagon train and died en route."

"How awful!"

Jess nodded. "When Mortimer found out that his true love was dead, he scrapped the idea of building a house and built a mercantile instead. It was the first building in the town he named True Love, after his departed fiancée—his one true love. Or so the story goes."

She sighed wistfully. "It's a wonderful story. But so sad. Whatever happened to Mortimer?"

"He died ten years later of heart failure."

Her voice filled with sadness. "A broken heart, you mean. It's so tragic when one loses the person he loves."

Jess's voice hardened. "I wouldn't know. I don't believe there's such a thing as true love and all that romantic drivel that women are so fond of believing." If he'd told Emily the truth—that Mortimer Peet had actually died while making love to a whore—he wondered if she'd believe him. It was doubtful. The woman dealt in fantasy, whereas he was a realist from the ground up.

"Of course there is," she countered. "There's a special someone for everyone. It's just finding that someone that's the hard part. But I have every confidence that when you do, you'll know it immediately. I know I will."

"I hope your illusions are never shattered, Emily Jean," he said, maneuvering the buckboard down the bustling main street of the town they'd just entered. Jess knew only too well how disillusioned one could become by believing in something as all-consuming and heart-breaking as love.

Jess and Emily entered the mercantile a short time later and were greeted by the proprietress, Flossie Camden. She was a tall, rawboned, no-nonsense kind of woman who epitomized the West and the females in it. The writer in Emily was immediately intrigued.

"Well, howdy, folks." Flossie pumped Jess's hand like a well handle. "I had no idea that you up and married, Jess. Why didn't you say something to somebody?" She turned to Emily. "Howdy do, ma'am. Ain't you a pretty little thing!"

Emily's cheeks flushed red at the woman's outspoken and effusive greeting. "I . . . you've made a mistake," she said, grateful when Jess came to her rescue, looking somewhat florid himself.

"This is Emily Jean Bartlett of New York City, Flossie. Emily's not my wife, but a writer come to pen my memoirs."

The woman's eyes practically bugged out of her flaccid face as she looked Emily over from top to bottom. "Well, ain't that just the most exciting thing I've ever heard.

"Frank! Frank!" she shouted toward the back of the store. "Come out here and meet a real live author. We got us a celebrity here in our store."

Jess grinned at his startled and mortified companion. "Now you'll know what it's like to be famous, Emily. I can assure you that it's not what it's cracked up to be."

"Ssh!" she cautioned, unwilling to hurt the woman's feelings. It was obvious that these people thought she was somebody important.

As large as Flossie Camden was, her husband, Frank, was just the opposite. Wiry of frame, the bespectacled man came around the counter to greet them. "Don't rightly know what to say to a real writer, ma'am, having never met one before."

Smiling warmly, Emily held out her hand in greeting,

saying, "Hello will do quite nicely," then turned to survey the shelves loaded with all kinds of colorful fabrics and various articles of ready-made clothing. Beaver hats lined the top shelf, while the glass counter case held an assortment of mens' and ladies' gloves in both leather and cotton, an array of hair combs, and a large amount of various and other sundry items.

Farm implements hung on the walls and from the ceiling, and glass jars filled with pickles, black licorice, and colorful gumdrops rode the countertop like enticing sirens.

"Is this the same mercantile that Mortimer Peet started?" she asked, and Flossie laughed so hard that her cheeks turned red.

"I see you've told Miss Bartlett about Mortimer, Jess. It's a touching tale, ain't it, ma'am? Bet you write some touching tales as well. Think you might write Mortimer Peet's story someday?"

"Why, I hadn't really thought about it, but I suppose it's possible," Emily replied, and the woman leaned closer in conspiratorial fashion.

"I wouldn't mention the part about the whorehouse," she advised. "Mortimer's relatives still live in the area, and they wouldn't like it if old Mortimer Peet's reputation was tarnished."

Emily's eyes widened. "Whorehouse?" She looked at Jess, who smiled sheepishly.

"Mortimer died a happy man. I heard his grin was permanently plastered on his face when they planted him six feet under." With a wink at Emily, he turned his attention to Frank. "How about getting me a keg of nails. And I can use—" The two men floated to the other side of the store to conduct their business, leaving Emily and Flossie alone.

Emily's face was still florid when Flossie asked, "Will you be doing any shopping today, ma'am? We're having a sale on drawers and corsets this week." She indicated the piles of garments at the far end of the store. "All good quality merchandise. And we've got plenty of long underwear, of course, for the coming winter months. You'll be needin' some, if you're fixing to stay."

If there was one thing Emily did not want to purchase while in Jess's company, it was underwear. The remark he had made about her alleged nudity beneath her nightwear had been humiliating, totally improper, and all too accurate.

Observing the neatly stacked piles of denim pants on the shelf, she said, "I'm learning to ride and could use another pair of dunagree trousers. Do you have some that would fit me? And I need a flannel shirt to go with them." She had finally received a small amount of money from Max and decided that the clothing would be a worthwhile expenditure.

"I do." Flossie Camden grinned, rubbing her hands together, and Emily thought she could see dollar signs reflecting in her eyes. "And you're right sensible to be buying such practical garments. Most women ain't that smart, and their bottoms get chafed all to hell from trying to ride in them bustles.

"Ain't that so, Jess?"

The rancher had just stepped up behind Emily and

was grinning like a hyena. Emily, whose face was nearly purple with embarrassment and felt as if it were on fire, was horrified that he'd been privy to the woman's indelicate conversation. She prayed that the floor would just open up and swallow her whole.

Western women were definitely a different breed of female, she decided, shaking her head in dismay.

"Having never worn a bustle, Flossie, I can't comment on the chafing, but if Miss Bartlett has any problems with it, I know a good liniment and just how to apply it." He grinned at her mortification, stepping back just in time to avoid being hit when the door was swung open and Emily made a mad dash out of the store.

Chapter Nine

IN LIGHT OF HER HUMILIATING ENCOUNTER AT THE mercantile, Emily decided it was safer to wait in the buckboard while Jess visited the grocer to fill Mrs. Ferguson's order. He'd been gone about ten minutes, and while she waited she took the time to observe the hustle and bustle of True Love's main thoroughfare.

Though it was far different from New York City's Broadway, the town's Main Street had a lively pulse of its own. Farmers hauling wagons laden with vegetables and foodstuffs were bartering and selling right in the street; a young boy from the local paper hawked his publisher's wares, the same way newsboys did in the city.

People here seemed friendlier, far more talkative, than they did where she lived. They stopped to chat and catch up on family news and gossip, and mothers carted their children around on their hips without the benefit of nannies or perambulators.

Emily decided that she liked the differences and meant to ask Jess his opinion of small-town life, as compared with the larger cities he'd lived in.

As if conjured up by her thoughts, the rancher stepped onto the wooden sidewalk a moment later. He was hailed immediately by a tall, lanky man in a black-and-white-checked suit, who was waving frantically at Jess as he approached. Jess's groan was audible, and Emily surmised that he wasn't thrilled to have been detained.

"Jess Murdock, just the man I've been wanting to talk to," the man declared, hurrying to catch up.

Pausing outside the grocery store, Jess nodded politely in greeting, Emily thought, despite the pained look on his face. "Howdy, Mayor. What can I do for you?"

Fred Dandy adjusted his spotless white shirt collar, though there was absolutely nothing wrong with it. Nervous at having to bring up a subject that he knew was likely to annoy Jess Murdock, he cleared his throat several times. "I'm sure you know why we need to talk, Jess. The sheriff's job is still open, and we want you to take it."

Sucking in his angry response, Jess did his best to hold his temper and remain reasonable, as he'd done many times before when this subject had come up. "I told you and the other members of the town council, Fred, that I'm not interested in renewing a law career. Those days are over for me."

"But, Jess—"

"Why can't you just take no for an answer? We've had this discussion many times over, and my answer is still the same: I'm not interested. That's not going to change."

Ignoring Emily's wide-eyed, curious gaze, he began loading the sacks of flour and sugar he'd just purchased onto the back of the buckboard, hoping the mayor would get the hint and disappear. Unfortunately the man was more tenacious than Jess had given him credit for.

"You, as sheriff, would bring a lot of notoriety to this town, Jess. We're talking about increased revenue to hire a schoolteacher. Why, your boy would be one of the children to benefit."

"My boy's got a good teacher." He winked at Emily, who grinned in response.

It was then the mayor noticed the pretty dark-haired woman seated in the wagon. He gave her a curt nod before continuing. "You've got the experience. Not just anyone can handle such an important position."

"This town's got little trouble to police, Mayor Dandy. Be glad of it. If I took the job, it would likely attract the wrong element—gunslingers with something to prove and reputations to enhance. No thanks. I've done my part for keeping the peace. Now I only want to keep my own." And he wished everyone would leave him alone to do just that, instead of treating him like some prized commodity on the New York Stock Exchange.

The mayor looked clearly frustrated and disappointed, and Emily knew exactly how he felt, having come up against Jess's intractable position on things. But now she understood a little bit better his rationale and reluctance to seek the limelight, though she didn't agree with him one hundred percent.

"If that's your last word . . ."

"It is. Now I'll be saying good-bye. Me and Miss Bartlett need to start back for the ranch, if we're going to get there before dark. Give my regards to your wife, Mayor."

At the mention of Emily's name, the mayor's eyes widened in recognition. "So you're the writer Flossie and Frank mentioned?" His attention focused solely on the young woman. "Welcome to True Love, Miss Bartlett. We're honored to have such a famous person in our midst.

"I'm Mayor Fred Dandy." He held out a hand clammy with perspiration. "I'm sure my wife, Cecilia, would love to make your acquaintance next time you're in town."

Emily smiled graciously, made the suitable response, then breathed a sigh of relief when the man strolled off down the street to accost another citizen and Jess climbed back onto the wagon.

She was beginning to see just how bothersome fame could be. The fawning attitude of the Camdens at the mercantile, and now the mayor, had embarrassed her. If Jess experienced that kind of response every time he went out in public, she could understand why he disliked it.

Another episode happened a few minutes later to further cement her unfavorable opinion of notoriety when Jess stopped at the post office to check on his mail. She had accompanied him into the small brick building to see if Max had sent any news, but no letter had been waiting for her.

Emily wasn't sure if that was good news or bad. Max's financial situation was uppermost on her mind, and not a day went by that she didn't worry about him.

Jess encountered four members of the school board at

the post office who insisted that he hold a shooting exhibition to raise money for the new school they were trying to erect. The exhibition, he'd been told, was to be held the following month to coincide with the admittance of Montana as the forty-first state to enter the Union. A big celebration was planned, and they needed Jess's assistance and notoriety to entice more people to attend.

Posting her letter, Emily did her best to stay in the background, while the men continued to badger Jess and remind him in no uncertain terms of his civic duty to the community.

Emily could see that Jess had a tight rein on his temper. The vein in his temple was throbbing; his teeth were clenched as if his jaw would break in two at any moment. Having encountered that temper in the past, she had no wish to experience it again and was therefore grateful when the men finished their heated discussion and departed without incident.

"Whatever did you say to those men?" she asked when they were alone, though it was really none of her business. A moot point, she decided, considering everything she'd gone through to discover details about Jess Murdock's life.

His voice was silken steel when he spoke. "I told them to leave me the hell alone, or I was going to give them a personal and private exhibition of just how accurate and deadly I can shoot."

Her eyes widened. "Really? You told them that?" She shook her head, her lips curving into a smile. "You're a wicked man, Jess Murdock."

He arched an eyebrow. "Are you just finding that out, Emily? I thought that's why you wanted to write my series."

"Looks like we've got company." Jess pulled the buckboard into the yard and stepped on the brake. "That looks like Reverend Higgbotham's buggy to me."

Emily recognized the conveyance at once and swallowed at the truth of his words. "Would you like me to help you unload the items you bought?" she offered, eager to postpone her meeting with the clergyman.

Jess grinned and shook his head. "I've got plenty of men to do that. See?" He waved at the two men crossing the yard from the corral area, and Emily recognized Stinky Wallace, but not the other man. "Webb Parker and Stinky are coming to unload, which will leave us plenty of time to visit with the reverend. I'm sure he's anxious to talk to you. Word travels fast in a small town."

Her voice filled with dismay. "But we just left True Love a few hours ago." She hadn't had time to prepare what she was going to say, what excuse she could give for her falsehoods. It was extremely doubtful that Jess would offer any help.

"Obviously Higgbotham wasted no time in beating us home. He must have gotten a head start when we stopped at Wilkinson's Bootery to check on Frosty's new boots. Guess the reverend's mighty anxious to talk to you."

A sickly smile crossed her face, and Emily entered the house, bracing herself for the encounter. Though the reverend was a kind gentleman, she had lied through her teeth to get him to help her and was pretty darn sure he was going to be angry with her.

But when she entered the front room it was to find Reverend and Mrs. Higgbotham dining on Mrs. Ferguson's lemon tarts, looking giddy as all get-out and not the least bit upset.

"Emily Jean!" Clara rose to her feet when she spotted Emily. Eyes wide, her smile that of an eager schoolgirl, the woman fairly gushed her enthusiasm. "The reverend and I have just discovered who you really are. We came to tell you how very excited and honored we are that you chose us to assist you in your time of need."

"Indeed, young woman. I'm happy I could be of help." The reverend stuffed another tart into his mouth, then licked his lips in satisfaction.

More confused than ever, Emily cast a sidelong glance at Jess, who was doing his best to hide his knowing smile.

Why aren't they furious with me? Why are they treating me with reverence instead of disdain?

"Th . . . thank you," she replied. "It's so nice to see you both again. What brings you out to the ranch?" As if she didn't already know. Apparently her fame was spreading faster than an unwanted case of poison sumac.

Emily and Jess took a seat on the sofa opposite the Higgbothams. "I'm sure Reverend and Mrs. Higgbotham were quite anxious to renew their acquaintance with such a notable person," Jess said with an innocent smile, hoping to give Emily Jean a small taste of her own medicine.

"You'll be getting all kinds of social calls now that word's out on your true profession as a famous novelist."

"Would you consider speaking to our local women's club?" Clara asked. "We're always looking for ways to raise money for charitable causes. And since you're so active in charity work back home, I thought you wouldn't mind lending us a hand.

"I know folks around here would pay good money to hear you speak. Your life must be so glamorous and very exciting." Mrs. Higgbotham sighed enviously.

Emily gasped, nearly choking on the tea that Mrs. Ferguson had just handed her. She absolutely abhorred public speaking. It was definitely not her forte. The few times she'd attempted to give a speech her voice had cracked, sounding like a bullfrog in heat, and she'd forgotten every word she'd planned to say. The experience had been totally mortifying.

"I'm not really sure I'll have the time, Mrs. Higgbotham," she said finally. "I'm very flattered to be asked. But you see, I'm under a rather tight deadline to complete Mr. Murdock's series, and, well . . ."

Clara waved away the apology, though she looked clearly disappointed. "Don't give it another thought, dear. You artist types must do what you think best. Isn't that right, Mr. Murdock?" the older woman asked, lumping Jess into that category as well.

The cowboy chose his words carefully. "Emily's been working extremely hard to achieve her goals, ma'am. I don't think I've ever met anyone quite as tenacious as this young woman."

His smile was decidedly smug, and Emily had the greatest urge to dump her hot tea over the top of his head. Instead she said, "I'm sure you both realize what a famous celebrity you have in your midst, in the form of Mr. Murdock. My publisher is quite eager to tell his story to the world."

Jess shot Emily a scathing look, but if Phinneas Higgbotham noticed, he gave no indication of it. "Yes indeed. We're quite aware of Jess's fame," the reverend said, then addressed the rancher. "I was wondering, Jess, if you'd consent to attend church service a little more often than you do. My services are usually full when folks know you're going to be there."

Emily saw Jess open his mouth, no doubt to say something rude, and she quickly butted in. What the reverend had suggested was totally unfair, and she intended to let him know it, but in a manner that wouldn't offend. "I'm sure you must realize, Reverend Higgbotham, that having notoriety in any form can be a burden. I don't think it would be right to infringe on Mr. Murdock's time of worship so that others in the congregation can gawk at him. He and his son have every right to praise God in their own way, and their privacy should be respected."

Jess's eyes widened in surprise, then filled with gratitude and admiration. Emily's sensitivity was welcome and quite astounding, given her present preoccupation with his memoirs. "I couldn't have said it better myself."

Phinneas cloaked himself in self-chastisement, and the hair shirt he wore looked to be very uncomfortable. "You're quite right. God's house is not a place of exploitation. I don't know what possessed me to say such a thing. In fact, if you like, I can erect a special partition that will shield you from—"

"That won't be necessary, Reverend," Jess interrupted. "I want Zach to grow up as normally as possible. To him, I'm just Papa; he isn't aware of all the other callings I've dealt with in my life."

Clara flashed her husband a glowering look that promised retribution and quickly changed the subject. "How long are you planning to remain in True Love, Emily? I hope you'll be able to attend our statehood celebration next month."

The young woman smiled. "That depends solely on Mr. Murdock, and how quickly we can come to an agreement about how the story should be written. I have some new ideas that I intend to approach him about later."

Jess cranked his head, noting the mischievous smile curving Emily's lips, and wondered what she was up to now. He'd learned early on that Emily Jean Bartlett had more tricks up her sleeve than a cardsharp at a high-stakes poker game. It was not a comforting thought.

"Later" came after dinner that evening. Emily had offered to wash the dishes after Mrs. Ferguson had complained of an upset stomach. Jess had taken over the duty of bathing his son and putting him to bed and had just returned to the kitchen after settling Zach down for the night.

Eyeing the stack of wet dishes growing tall on the counter, he picked up a linen dishtowel and began to dry.

"Guess you inherited kitchen detail tonight. Hope you don't mind."

Wiping beads of perspiration off her forehead with her forearm, she smiled at the sight of the hell-raising cowboy wiping the dinner dishes. It was as unexpected as it was incongruous. "I don't mind at all. I wouldn't have offered if I had. Mrs. Ferguson looked quite peaked to me. I hope she'll be all right."

"I'm sure she'll be fine by morning. Chili tends to affect her like that."

The chili had been hot enough to burn the roof off her mouth, and Emily could well imagine what it was doing to the lining of Mrs. Ferguson's stomach. "I suppose you're right."

"Frances likes you. She doesn't warm to that many people, but she really took a shine to you in a short time."

His comment made Emily smile. "I like her, too. She's very motherly, and I miss that. Although my mother was never one to cuddle and joke the way Mrs. Ferguson does. You're lucky to have such a kind, caring woman looking after Zach."

"Frances is a jewel. I'd hate to lose her if your plan to marry her off to Frosty succeeds."

Emily's face crimsoned, and it had nothing to do with the steam rising off the water. "It's obvious they like each other. I was just trying to give them a shove in the right direction."

"Heard you've been interviewing some of the boys about me. Guess that's all right, as long as you don't interfere in their work. But I'd much prefer that you spoke to me directly if you want to know something, so you'll get the truth and not the exaggerated version."

She handed him a dish. "You needn't worry. I didn't find out anything, except that they all hold you in very high regard. It seems you're a saint to work for, a paragon among men. Hardly fodder for a dime novelist to use." She needed sordid revelations to spice up her books, and so far she'd come up empty-handed.

The disappointment he heard in her voice made him laugh. "I'm sorry you weren't able to dig up more dirt, Emily. My life is probably not as interesting as you thought it would be."

After placing the last dish on the counter, she wiped her hands on the blue gingham apron she'd borrowed from Mrs. Ferguson and turned to face him. "I think after today I have a much better insight into why you are so reluctant to cooperate with me in the writing of the series."

Jess tensed, wondering if she had somehow learned of the killing of Rory Connors. He breathed easier when she said:

"It can't be easy being the object of everyone's adoration, being the major asset in a growing community, with everyone wanting a piece of you. That insight became more evident by the way Reverend Higgbotham behaved today."

"I never thanked you for coming to my defense."

"There's no need. What he suggested was wrong. And it led me to believe that perhaps what I've been suggesting is wrong, too."

He arched his eyebrows so high that they nearly reached the dark curl drooping down on his forehead. "You don't want to write your series now? I'm surprised, to say the least." And relieved, he added silently.

After what she'd witnessed today, Emily had given the situation a great deal of thought. Jess's friends and neighbors viewed him as a means to an end—a savior of sorts. It was the same way she had perceived him, she was embarrassed to admit. She hadn't considered him as a man, a father, an employer, but as someone, a celebrity, who could save Max's publishing business.

She realized now that the dime novel series would cheapen what Jess Murdock had accomplished during his lifetime, would make him out to be a dime novel idol instead of the real man, the real hero, that he was.

Jess was no fictitious character, but a flesh-and-blood man who had loved and lost and somehow survived, faced his childhood demons and overcome them, carved a career for himself, sometimes facing great odds, and lived to talk about it.

He was the stuff of a real biography. And that's what she intended to write. Convincing him of that, however, would be an entirely different matter. Convincing Max would likely take an act of Congress.

"Emily?" Jess shook her shoulder when she didn't respond right away.

Smiling apologetically, she grabbed the coffeepot off the stove and seated herself at the table. "Why not sit down and listen to what I have to say?"

"Uh-oh." He pulled out a chair, scraping it across the pine floorboards. "If coffee is necessary to make it more palatable, I'm probably not going to like it much."

"Before you go getting all pigheaded on me, just hear me out. I think you'll agree that I've come up with a wonderful solution to our mutual difference of opinion where your series is concerned."

He studied her intently, noting the enthusiasm that effused her face, the way her brilliant blue eyes glowed like sparkling sapphires, the way her lips looked so tempting. He heaved a sigh at the memory of how those soft lips felt beneath his. The pleasurable recollection brought discomfort, and he shifted his weight. "Go on."

"I finally realized that what you're probably objecting to about the series of dime novels I planned are the inaccuracies and glorified exaggerations that are so much a part of the genre. What I propose instead is to write a true biography, a factual account of your life, your accomplishments, a recounting of all the major events that would let people know who Jess Murdock really is." Hoping Jess would be impressed by the idea, she was disappointed when he frowned and continued to sip his coffee.

Jess's voice was gentle when he spoke. "Emily, I'm flattered that you think folks would want to read a story about my life. And I'd like to help you and your publisher out, really I would. But I don't want to expose my life story to strangers. I have my reasons."

"What reasons?" she pressed.

"There are things . . ." He paused, his eyes filling with sadness. "Things in my past that I'm not proud of. I don't want to reveal them to the world. Think how it would affect my son if he were to ever find out."

Her eyes lit with compassion, and she covered his hand with her own, offering strength. "Your childhood isn't something to be ashamed of, Jess. The shame must be shouldered by your father, not you."

"You don't understand." How could he tell her about Rory Connors, an innocent child who'd been killed through no fault of his own? About the incident back in Texas many years ago where he'd been forced to defend a woman's honor by strangling a man with his bare hands?

The woman had been a prostitute in a border town whose name he couldn't even recall. Her customer had been beating her up when Jess had come upon them in a darkened alley. The sight had triggered memories of his childhood, and he'd flown into a murderous rage, choking the man to death and wishing all the time that it had been his father he had in his clutches.

There was nothing heroic about his exploits, nothing to be proud of. He'd let people think what they would because the lies were easier to live with than the truth. And while he had told Emily to seek the truth in her writing, he couldn't allow her to expose his.

"I would like to understand, Jess. I'm here to listen, if you want to tell me. I'm offering you the chance to set the record straight about your life, about all the fictitious stories, like those fifty-seven men you supposedly killed." She knew now with certainty that Jess Murdock could never have murdered those men. There was too much goodness in him.

Emily had seen the many kindnesses he'd bestowed upon Mrs. Ferguson, the tender way he gazed at his son.

And she hadn't been exaggerating about how his cowhands held him in such high esteem. Jess never asked anyone to do a job he wasn't willing to do himself. Except, perhaps, for mucking out the barn, she amended.

"I would like to provide a true depiction of life as a cowboy in the real West. It would be something your son could read in later years and be proud of. It would be a legacy every bit as meaningful as the ranch Zach will one day inherit.

"You've lived the kind of life, witnessed things, that most men only dream about. The Wild West will soon be gone. Modernization is already encroaching on the western states. You yourself have indoor plumbing."

His lips twitched. "A necessity when the temperature drops down below freezing and your butt sticks to the—"

Her cheeks warmed. "I get the picture."

"Emily, I'd—"

She clasped his hand and shook her head, sensing that he was going to refuse again. "Don't make up your mind right now. Take some time to think about it. I'm not going anywhere, unless Max drags me back to New York or you decide to kick me out." Both were strong possibilities.

He squeezed the small soft hand beneath his own and wondered how he would feel if Emily Jean Bartlett suddenly disappeared from his life.

It was a prospect he hoped he wouldn't have to face for a very long time.

Chapter Ten

UPON AWAKENING THE NEXT MORNING, EMILY DIS-covered that Mrs. Ferguson was still abed. Alarmed to think that the older woman might be far more ill than either she or Jess had realized, she knocked softly on the housekeeper's door and waited a few moments.

She entered to find Mrs. Ferguson with her head in an emesis basin, giving up what was left of last night's dinner.

"Mrs. Ferguson!" Emily rushed forward and grabbed a wet cloth from the nightstand. Wiping the woman's forehead and face with it, she said, "You truly are ill. Is there anything I can do?"

Despite her pale complexion, the housekeeper's cheeks turned rosy with embarrassment. Shaking her head, she settled back against the down pillows, pulling the colorful starburst quilt up to her chin. "It's me own fault, hinny. I shouldna hae eaten that chili. I made it extra spicy, the way Jess and the wee lad like it, and now I'm paying the price fer me generosity and stupidity."

"Are you sure that's all it is? I can send someone for the doctor."

"I'm sure. 'Tis happened afore, but not fer a long while now."

"Is there anything I can do to help out while you're sick?"

"Ye'll be needin' tae prepare breakfast fer the men, Emily. 'Tis Saturday, and on the weekend I always invite the boys in fer a good hearty meal." She glanced at the clock on the mantel. "They'll be doing chores first, so ye'll hae a while tae prepare. Ye'll have tae build a fire under Zach. He likes tae dawdle in the morning. And Jess'll be lookin' fer his clean shirts. I always hae them ready on Saturday."

Emily had always considered herself a proficient woman when it came to business, but domestic matters were a different matter. At least cooking breakfast wouldn't be a problem, though she'd never cooked for large groups of men before. "Don't worry," she told Frances confidently. "I'll take care of everything. You rest, and a bit later I'll bring you up some tea and plain toast. That might settle your stomach somewhat."

"Ye're a true blessin', Emily Jean, and I thank ye fer taking such good care o' me and mine. Now, if ye don't mind, I'll be taking a wee nap." She closed her eyes and soon fell into a restful slumber.

After shutting the door behind her quietly, Emily hurried down the hall to wake Zach, trying to remember which bedroom was his. Certain it was the second door on the right, she barged in without knocking, intending to surprise the child. "Wake up, sleepy he—"

She pulled up short at the sight of Jess half-naked and standing at the shaving mirror. Her mouth fell open, her eyes widened, and when he turned and she caught sight of his muscular chest, lightly furred with hair that disappeared into the waistband of his pants, she nearly fainted.

"I . . . I'm so sorry!" she stammered, her cheeks glowing. "I thought this was Zach's room."

Swallowing his amusement, Jess grabbed a towel and began to wipe soap from his face and behind his ears. "He's next door getting dressed." he indicated with a jerk of his head that she'd missed the correct room by only one door.

"I checked on Frances earlier to find that she was still under the weather," he added, "so I took the boy under my wing. He'll be down directly."

Feeling as if she'd just been kicked in the stomach by a mule, Emily nodded, waiting for the breathless feeling to subside. She'd never seen a bare-chested man before. Certainly not one whose muscles rippled every time he moved. Swallowing with difficulty, she said, "Well, then, I—I'll just go and fix breakfast."

His brow cocked. "If you're sure you won't be needing anything else."

His meaning was quite clear, making Emily's cheeks glow even brighter. "I'm quite sure."

"In that case, make the breakfast hearty, ma'am. I'm starving this morning." He rubbed his belly, and Emily's gaze drifted down again, lower this time.

"You did say you were sure?"

His voice was seductive, suggestive, and it sent shivers of awareness tripping down her spine. Indecent thoughts cluttered her brain, and for a moment she couldn't think, let alone speak.

Finally she looked up and saw the grin on his face. Her mortification returned in full force. "No! Yes!" Dashing out of the room as if Satan himself were on her heels, Emily could hear the devil's laughter all the way down the stairs.

Two hours later the men filed into the kitchen and took a seat at the long maple table, their faces filled with eager anticipation of what was to come. Mrs. Ferguson's weekend meals were a treat after eating the plain fare served up by Herb Lassister—or Grubby, as he was better known—all week.

Emily introduced herself to those cowhands she didn't know, did her best to avoid Jess's knowing looks, and hurried to fetch the cheese soufflé and croissants she had slaved over. Then she took a seat at the opposite end of the table from Jess and bowed her head.

"Shall we say grace?" she asked, and was greeted with some very strange looks by the men.

"Grace!" Zach shouted, and everyone laughed, including Jess.

He explained, "When the hands are present we usually dispense with the religious formalities, Emily. It makes some of them uncomfortable."

Her blue eyes widened. Emily didn't consider herself an overly religious woman, but she always said a blessing before beginning her meals, and she knew that Mrs. Ferguson did, too. "Does Mrs. Ferguson approve of your skipping the blessing on the weekend?" She could hardly believe so.

Looking somewhat sheepish, Frosty shook his head. "No, ma'am. Fan's a devout Christian woman, but she's done given up on us. Says her prayers to herself now when we're around."

"Well, Zach"—Emily turned to the small boy seated next to her, hoping he, at least, would join her—"I guess you and I can say the blessing together, if no one else wants to participate."

The child blurted, "Hellfire and spit! Let's eat," making Emily gasp.

"Zachary Murdock!"

"I'm afraid the boy's picked up some of your bad habits, Emily," Jess pointed out before admonishing his son.

"Food's getting cold," Stinky pointed out, and a chorus of murmurs followed.

"Such as it is," Webb Parker added, eyeing the cheese concoction with distaste and screwing up his face to let everyone know what he thought of it.

Before anyone else could express an opinion, Emily blurted out in a rush, "Dear Lord, bless this food and bless us all. Amen."

"Amen," Zach responded, looking contrite.

Jess looked down the length of the table at the rusty-haired cowboy. "Pass the bacon and sausage, Doyle. I'm starving."

"There ain't none," the man replied. "Just some kinda biscuits and gooey stuff."

Emily's face warmed. "That 'gooey stuff,' as you call it, Mr. Doyle, is a cheese soufflé. It's a very famous French recipe that my mother's chef taught me. I think you're going to enjoy it very much."

"Fan usually makes us hotcakes and eggs with plenty of sausage and bacon," Frosty informed her, trying to keep his disappointment from showing. "A man needs food that's going to stick to his ribs while he's out working all day, Miss Emily."

Noting that Emily's face had fallen somewhere in the vicinity of her feet, Jess took pity on her. "I'll try some of that soufflé. Guess it wouldn't hurt to sample something new every once in a while, eh, Frosty?"

Taking the hint, the older man nodded. "Sure, boss. No man's gonna say that Frosty Adams ain't up for a little adventurous eating. French, you say? Well don't that beat all."

"What kinda biscuits are these, ma'am, if you don't mind me askin'? They don't look regular-like." Webb took a bite of the flaky pastry, and his eyes widened in surprise and approval. "Not bad. Not bad, at all."

"Those happen to be croissants," Emily replied. "They're also French."

"I knew me a French whore once," Stinky said, and the other men snickered loudly.

Webb poked his sidekick in the arm. "That whore weren't French, Stinky. She just used some of that French parfume, like the kind you're always dousing yourself with."

Jess laughed at that, then everyone joined in, and Emily's cheeks blossomed with color.

"These croissants are mighty tasty, ma'am," Rusty pronounced, eager to make a favorable impression.

Grateful that the courteous man had thought to change the subject, Emily smiled warmly in response. "Thank you, Mr. Doyle," she replied, purposely ignoring Jess's blatant amusement.

After five of the men had filled their plates with the soufflé, it soon became painfully obvious that Emily hadn't made enough. Gazing in dismay at the now empty bowl, she said, "I guess I miscalculated."

Jess pushed back his chair and stood. "I'll whip up some scrambled eggs. Frosty, you fetch the bacon and sausage from the icebox. It won't hurt any of us to lend Miss Emily a hand, seeing as how she's new here and not used to our ways or how much we eat."

Tears burned behind Emily's eyes at the thoughtful gesture, and she could have kissed Jess for his kindness. "Shall I make some biscuits? Some regular biscuits, I mean?" Her offer was greeted with much enthusiasm.

After everyone had eaten their fill, Zach and the men went out to finish their chores, leaving Jess and Frosty to linger over their coffee and discuss the day's events.

At the sink, Emily began to wonder how someone of Mrs. Ferguson's age could keep up with all the work involved on a ranch. It was barely eight o'clock, and she was already tired from cooking and washing dishes. She hadn't yet cleaned the house, washed and ironed any clothes, baked bread for tomorrow's meals, or done any of the dozens of chores Mrs. Ferguson was so proficient at handling. The woman was truly a marvel.

"You'll be getting your riding lesson from Rusty today, Miss Emily," Frosty said. "Me'n Jess need to check the fences, make sure none have been cut again."

"That'll be just fine. Mr. Doyle seems very nice."

It was obvious from Emily's smile that she was pleased by the idea, and that didn't sit well with Jess. "Didn't think you knew Doyle all that well to have formed an opinion."

"Mr. Doyle and I have been introduced," she replied, surprised by the animosity in his voice. "I found him to be a very courteous and kind individual, and not the least bit coarse or crass." *As you would have had me believe about all the men working at the Bar JM,* she added silently.

Jess's frown deepened. He'd known Rusty Doyle from his Wild West show days, when the cowboy had been a wrangler for Bill Cody. About six months ago Rusty had shown up at the Bar JM looking for work, and Jess had reluctantly hired him.

The cowboy had always been somewhat of a gambler and a ladies' man. His good looks and pleasing personality just naturally lent themselves to successful seductions of naive women and to getting him into trouble. Though he'd kept his nose clean since he'd been working at the ranch, Jess didn't know if he could trust Rusty around Emily. Hell, he thought, he couldn't trust himself.

The thought of Rusty and Emily together had the vein in his neck throbbing wildly. "You watch yourself, young woman. Men are men, no matter how courteous they may appear on the surface."

At his overbearing tone, Emily swung around to face him, fire flashing in her eyes. "Are you lumping yourself in that category?"

The tension in the air had grown so thick, it could have been cut with a buck knife. Frosty cleared his throat and stood. "I'd best be gettin' back to work now." Then he beat a hasty retreat out the door.

Jess crossed the room in three strides, took the dishtowel from Emily's hands, then pulled her up against him. "I am." He kissed her passionately, thoroughly, until Emily could feel the wild rhythm of it soaring through her head like a thousand violins, pounding in her heart like the roll of a kettledrum.

The music played through Emily's veins finer than any symphony, but when Jess spoke to break the spell the notes suddenly went out of tune.

"Heed my warning, Emily Jean. Little girls who play with fire usually get burned."

She watched him stomp out the door, her chest heaving with indignation and a large dose of frustration. "Damn you, Jess Murdock!" she shouted, raising her fist in the air. "Damn you for making me want you," she whispered.

"Hey, *mi amigo*. What took you so long? I have been waiting in this cold barn for a very long time." The outlaw smiled at the startled man who had just entered the darkened building.

Hearing the familiar voice, the cowboy pulled up short, then squinted as he tried to focus. He spotted El Lobo, arms folded nonchalantly, leaning against one of the horse stalls and became furious. "Are you crazy? What the hell are you doing here, Juan? I told you I'd contact you when I was ready to deliver the cows."

"So you did, my friend. But it is taking too long, and my buyers are getting anxious. I have come to hurry things up a bit. Maybe even steal them myself." He grinned at the possibility, and his teeth flashed white against his tanned skin.

"You'll get your fool head shot off, if you try that. Murdock's been watching the herd like a hawk. Even now he's about to ride out to check the fences to make sure they've not been cut."

Juan lit a thin cigar, and the sulfur match flared brightly to illuminate his displeasure. "I cannot wait much longer. I have expensive tastes like you. We are two of a kind, no?"

The ranch hand had never killed anyone, had never robbed anyone, except for Jess Murdock, and he wasn't about to lump himself in the same category as El Lobo, an outlaw with a price on his head. "There's going to be a big shindig in a couple of weeks to celebrate Montana's statehood," he explained. "I'm sure everyone, including Jess, will be going. That's when I intend to break out some of the cows and make the delivery."

Shaking his head, Juan puffed his cigar, and the smoke rings circled his head like a halo. "Is this my reward for working with amateurs? I should have known you were not reliable."

"Mr. Doyle? Are you in there?"

Cracking open the barn door, Rusty Doyle glanced

out to see Emily Bartlett crossing the yard in his direction.
"Shit!" He'd nearly forgotten that he was to give the riding
lesson this morning. "You've got to go. Miss Bartlett's on
her way here for her riding lesson."

"And what kind of ride are you going to give the
pretty *señorita, mi amigo?* Maybe a long, hard one, eh?
Aren't you going to share with Juan?" The outlaw laughed.

Disgusted with the cocky Mexican, Rusty grew more
impatient. "You've got to leave now, or you're going to
spoil everything we've worked hard to bring about."

Juan straightened, no longer amused or amicable. "I'll
go, Doyle. But before I do, know this: If you double-cross
me in any way, I'll come for you. And I will make you very
sorry that you were ever born. *Comprende, mi amigo?"*

"Don't worry. You'll have your cows. Just be patient
a while longer. Now get the hell outta here. And don't
come back till I send for you."

Emily came through the barn door just as the outlaw
was making his exit out the back. She caught a glimpse of
a tall, lanky man dressed all in black. The pearl handle of
his gun flashed in the sunlight as he made his escape, and
Emily knew a moment of real fear.

"Who was that man? I didn't recognize him from the
ranch."

Rusty smiled smoothly. "It's doubtful you would
know everyone who works here, Miss Emily, seeing as
how you're new here and all. But to put your mind at ease,
that man was Tim Little from one of the neighboring
ranches. He's thinking about buying one of our horses. We

do a lot of trading with the other ranchers. Jess is known throughout the territory for his excellent breeding stock."

Though she breathed a sigh of relief, Emily couldn't shake the uneasy feeling flowing through her. "Guess my overactive writer's imagination is playing tricks on me. I thought I knew that man."

"Lotsa men look alike." Rusty quickly changed the subject. "You ready for your lesson? I hear from Frosty that you're doing real good for a city gal."

Her fear forgotten for the moment, Emily smiled. "High praise indeed coming from Frosty."

While Emily saddled the bay gelding that she would be riding, she took the opportunity to ask the cowboy a few questions. "Have you worked here long, Mr. Doyle?"

Tipping his hat back, Rusty stared appreciatively at the woman's enticing form, which was clearly outlined by her snug denim pants. He'd like nothing better than to find his way into those pants and have a taste of all that sweetness. He figured her for a virgin, and Rusty had a real fondness for virgins and sweet young things. He'd worn enough hand-me-downs in his lifetime to appreciate something pretty and brand new.

" 'Bout six months, I reckon. Me and Jess used to work for Buffalo Bill Cody. That's where I met him." Her interest was immediately piqued, as Rusty knew it would be.

"What was it like working with the Wild West show?"

"You'll probably need to ask Jess that question, ma'am. He was the star. I was only wrangling the ponies."

"But it must have been exciting just the same."

The cowboy grabbed hold of the horse's bridle, and

Emily followed him out of the barn and into the corral. "I reckon. Got to travel to a lot of places I might not otherwise have seen. And I met a lot of nice people." Women, mostly. But he didn't mention that.

"Sounds like you've led an interesting life."

He grinned, and she was taken aback by how handsome he was. His eyes were an unusual shade of gray, almost silver in appearance. "Want to write my life story instead, Miss Emily? I could tell you all kinds of interesting stuff."

"I appreciate the offer, but I'm already committed to writing Mr. Murdock's."

"Thought you were interested in writing adventure stories, not sorrowful tales."

Emily's eyes widened, and her writer's instincts homed in. "What do you mean by that?"

He shrugged. "Nothing. Forget I said anything. Now, are you ready to begin your lesson?"

She nodded, but he could see that he'd hooked her. And that knowledge would likely prove useful in the near future, Rusty decided, cupping his hands and giving her a boost up before mounting behind her.

"Mr. Doyle! What on earth are you doing?"

Wrapping his arms around her to grab on to the reins, he replied, "I go about my lessons a bit differently from Frosty, ma'am. I think it'll be more helpful if I guide you through the paces, so you can get a feel of what it's like having all that power between your legs."

Heat rose to her cheeks, and Emily tried to scoot forward, but there was little room. "I'm not sure this is a good idea."

"Just relax and lean back against me." He clutched the reins tighter, purposely brushing the sides of her breasts with his arms as he did, then sniffed the lavender scent of her hair. "You sure do smell nice, Miss Emily."

His blatant touch could have been an accident, but for some reason Emily didn't think it was and grew alarmed. "I think I've had enough riding for one day, Mr. Doyle. I think I need to get down."

"Don't be afraid, Miss Emily. This horse needs to be shown who's boss. Just press your knees into his sides, let him know which way you want him to go." He attempted to place his hands on her thighs to illustrate, but Emily reared back with enough force to unseat the bold cowboy and knock him to the ground.

"Holy shit!" someone yelled. "Rusty's just been knocked off the horse and onto his ass. Don't that beat all."

Jess came around the barn at that instant to find Doyle sprawled on the ground and Emily attempting to get control of her horse. When the horse reared suddenly and Emily screamed, he took off at a run, jumping the corral fence to approach the frightened steed.

"Whoa, Caesar," he crooned, grabbing the bridle and murmuring reassuring words until the horse settled down. Reaching up, he helped Emily dismount. "What the hell happened?" He gazed at Doyle with murder in his eyes.

Noting Jess's fierce reaction, Emily shook her head. "It was my fault. Mr. Doyle was trying to show me how to steer the horse while mounted behind me, and—"

"Doyle was mounted on the horse with you?" Satisfied that she had not been harmed, Jess approached the cowboy. "What the hell were you thinking of, Doyle? As if I didn't know."

Several of the cowboys who had now gathered around the corral fence snickered at that. Doyle's reputation as a ladies' man was well-known around the Bar JM.

Rusty paled slightly. He couldn't afford to lose his job. Not yet. Juan would kill him for sure if that happened. "I was just showing Miss Emily how to control the horse, Jess. That's all."

The cowboy's expression turned immediately contrite as he faced Emily. "I'm real sorry, ma'am. I didn't mean to frighten you. Guess I'm not much of a riding instructor."

His apology seemed so genuine, his look so innocent, Emily wondered if she had imagined his seductive manner. She was sure she hadn't. "No harm's been done, Mr. Doyle. I'm fine now."

Inclining his head, the cowboy picked up his hat off the ground, slapped it against his leg, throwing up a billow of dust, and walked away. The other men dispersed as well, leaving Emily alone with Jess.

"Are you sure you're all right?" he asked, looking her over so thoroughly from top to bottom that she blushed.

"Yes. I'm sure."

"And are you equally sure that Doyle didn't act improperly? If he did, I'll have no qualms about firing the bastard. He's got a history of that sort of thing."

She was not altogether surprised to hear that, but she was still unwilling to be the cause of the man losing his job. "Nothing untoward happened. The horse reared, I couldn't bring him under control, and then Rusty fell off the back."

Jess wondered if she meant the horse or the man was out of control, but he didn't press her on it. "From here on out you're to ride only with Frosty or myself. I'm not putting temptation in front of any more of my men."

Her cheeks crimsoned, and she stiffened in righteous indignation. "I can assure you that I'm not some femme fatale who goes around trying to lure men."

"Dressed as you are, you don't have to be any damn female siren. You could be wearing a burlap sack and you'd still look damn desirable. We're only men, Emily Jean. I wish you'd try to remember that."

"Is that why you stormed out of the kitchen earlier? Because you were afraid of me?" The thought seemed utterly preposterous and totally provocative.

He tipped back his hat, stared into her innocent blue eyes, and heaved a sigh. "That's right. I shouldn't have kissed you. It would have led to something neither one of us wants. And it's not going to happen again. I've already made up my mind about that."

"Oh, really?" The gall of the man, to decide that he wasn't going to kiss her again. "And what if I want it to happen again? What if I want you to kiss me?" Her boldness surprised even her.

"Jesus, Emily! You don't know what you're saying. You're naive. And I'm not going to take advantage of your innocence. I'm considerably older than you, and a whole lot more experienced."

Her eyes lit with confusion. "But you just said that you found me desirable."

"I do. That's why I'm not going to kiss you again. Kissing only leads to trouble. And I've got enough trouble as it is."

His high-handed, unreasonable decision infuriated her. She wanted Jess Murdock's kisses and caresses. She wanted to feel giddy and breathless and sick to her stomach with longing. And she wasn't about to let him dictate to her or deprive her of that. "So I guess if you don't want to kiss me, you won't mind if I find someone else to do it. I'm sure there are several cowboys here at the ranch who—"

He grasped her arms tightly, and his eyes grew wild with something that looked suspiciously like jealousy. "Don't even think about it. You'll not conduct your sexual experimentation on any of my men. Is that understood?"

She tapped her chin, as if to contemplate his dictate. "Gee. I don't know. I mean—I've got a lot of time on my hands to experiment."

"Emily!"

The warning tone in his voice would have frightened lesser women, but Emily had a definite agenda. "I guess if I could keep busy writing your biography, I might not think about getting myself into trouble."

He was neatly cornered, and she knew it. "You, Miss Bartlett, are nothing but one compact package of trouble." He sighed in defeat. "All right, you win. We'll begin work on the book as soon as I return from checking the fence-line. But you have to promise not to press me about subjects I don't want to talk about."

Trying not to gloat, Emily crossed her fingers behind her back and smiled sweetly. "I promise."

Jess snorted, shook his head, and walked away, wondering how such a small bit of a woman could wreak so much havoc on his life.

Emily wondered how she was going to get Jess to kiss her again.

Chapter Eleven

"EMILY! EMILY!" ZACH BURST INTO THE KITCHEN, HIS face flushed, his eyes sparkling with excitement. "Papa said to come fetch you. He's waiting outside in the buckboard. We're going to the pumpkin patch to pick us out some jack-o'-lanterns for Halloween."

Emily ruffled the small boy's hair, then turned to see if Mrs. Ferguson approved of the idea. The housekeeper had indicated that she was fully recovered from her ordeal, but Emily didn't want to leave if she still needed help with the chores.

Sensing Emily's indecision, Frances Ferguson took matters into her own capable hands. "Go on wie ye, Emily. I can take care of everything that needs tae be done today. You did more than yer share yesterday, and I truly appreciate it." When Emily hesitated, she added, "You wouldn't want tae disappoint the wee lad, now would ye?"

"Please say you'll come, Emily," Zach pleaded, tugging her arm impatiently. "Papa says we're going to have a picnic."

"A picnic?" Eyes wide, Emily glanced out the window at the sunless sky and shivered at the thought of picnicking out in the chilly autumn weather on the damp ground.

"Pretty *pleeeese*, Emily."

Unable to disappoint the eager child, Emily finally nodded. "All right. I'll just go and fetch my new jacket. I'll be down before you can count to one hundred."

With a "Yippee!" and a "Hooray!" Zach ran outside to wait, slamming the door loudly behind him before Emily or Mrs. Ferguson could admonish him not to.

A few minutes later, cloaked, hatted, and gloved for her trek to the pumpkin patch, Emily approached the wagon. Seated atop the buckboard, Jess took one look at the bundled woman and burst out laughing. "I was planning to build a fire, Emily, but I guess now I won't have to." He gave her a hand up.

"Emily looks like a snowman, doesn't she, Papa?" Zach asked from his perch in the back of the wagon, then began to giggle.

Emily refused to apologize for her sensible apparel. "I despise being cold." The warm fleece-lined jacket had been a recent gift from Jess. "And I have no care to get sick. I've got a deadline to meet, in case you've forgotten, *Mr. Murdock.*"

Her comment made Jess frown. "Hard to forget when you remind me every moment of the day, *Miss Bartlett.*" He hitched the reins and clicked to the horses, ignoring her loud harrumph.

Emily had begun her interview of Jess yesterday, shortly after he had returned from checking the herd. They had sequestered themselves inside his office, and the whole while she sat listening to him relate the details of his unhappy childhood, she couldn't help but recall what had recently taken place in that very room: the passionate embrace, heated caresses, tantalizing kisses.

Twice he'd had to raise his voice to gain her attention, and twice her cheeks had flushed hot as the memories of their mutual passion came flooding to the forefront.

"Did you get any writing done last night? You were holed up in your room most of the night." Jess had missed having her around, but he wasn't about to admit it.

"Yes, as a matter of fact I was able to finish the first chapter of the book. And as you can well imagine, I'm quite anxious to resume our interviews so I can continue on." Emily believed the biography of Jess was going to be some of her best work. She only hoped Max agreed. As yet, she'd had no reply to the telegram she'd sent informing him of the change in plans. Max hated surprises, so she wasn't feeling any too confident that he was going to approve.

"We'll continue, Emily, but not today. Today I've got reserved for the boy. Every year before Halloween we go out to the pumpkin patch to select the perfect jack-o'-lantern. You're welcome to pick one out yourself if you like."

Her eyes lit. "I've never carved a pumpkin before," she admitted, and was suddenly filled with childish glee at the prospect.

"Really, Emily? How come?" Zach wanted to know. "Didn't your mama and papa like them?"

She shook her head. "My parents considered Halloween to be a pagan holiday and never allowed any of us to participate or attend our friends' parties. Of course, when I was older I attended several costume events on my own, but had my parents known, they would not have approved."

"They sound like stick-in-the-muds to me," Jess said, not bothering to hide his disdain.

Emily's smile was rueful. "That description fits my parents to a tee, I'm afraid. Their conservative values and opinions didn't lend themselves to childhood escapades."

The wistfulness in Emily's voice touched Jess deeply. He could now understand why she had chosen to live out her fantasies and childish dreams within the pages of a book; she'd never been allowed to experience them firsthand.

As a product of an unhappy home, he could empathize with her. But at least he'd been fortunate in the fact that his mother had done her best to provide him with as many of the normal trappings of childhood as she could while she'd been alive.

The fond memories of carving pumpkins with her, baking cookies at Christmas, were what prompted him to share those similar experiences with his son. It had been difficult these past five years to be both mother and father to Zach. But he was determined that Zach would never feel deprived or rejected because of his mother's callous ways.

"Your parents not only deprived you of some wonderful childhood memories, Emily, they deprived themselves as well. I enjoy doing these activities with my son. Someday it's likely they'll be sorry that they never did them with you."

She shrugged. "I suspect my siblings and I were raised in the same vein my parents were. I guess it's the only way they knew, so it's hard to blame them."

Jess pulled the buckboard to a halt beneath a large cottonwood tree whose leaves snapped loudly in the steady wind. The temperature was bone numbing, and he wondered how Emily would fare. Not many folks were prepared for their first Montana autumn or winter. "The pumpkin patch is yonder," he said, pointing to the field filled with row upon row of orange melons. "You and Zach go ahead and see if you can find anything that suits your fancy, while I fix us a fire to warm up. I'll be there directly."

Zach and Emily went skipping off, oohing and aahing their delight as they scouted the colorful fruit. Emily looked every bit as childlike as Zach, and Jess grinned at her antics.

The woman was full of contradictions: one moment childish, the next a sultry siren demanding to be kissed. But she was also honest to a fault. He suspected that with Emily Jean you got exactly what you saw: a woman with a passion for life and the strength and determination to live it to the fullest.

She was a pint-sized package of dynamite ready to explode. And as much as he denied it, Jess wanted to be the one, the only one, to set off Emily's fuse.

While Jess was pondering explosive techniques, his foreman was spending his Sunday trying to set off sparks with the woman he adored.

"These cookies are mighty tasty, Fanny." Frosty took another bite and savored the sweet, subtle lemony flavor, watching as the woman removed another batch of sugar cookies from the oven. "You surely are a fine cook. Yes indeed!"

Frances looked back over her shoulder and frowned. "Don't ye have someone else tae pester, Mr. Adams? I'm busy, as ye can see." Though she was secretly delighted that he'd come to call, Frances Ferguson was not a woman of easy virtue and would not be trifled with. There wasn't much a woman could claim besides her good reputation. "And don't ye be calling me by that impertinent nickname. My name is Frances, or Mrs. Ferguson, tae ye."

Frosty ignored the woman's chastisement and plunged ahead. "Heard there was fixin' to be a shindig over at the Town Hall next month. And I was wondering"—he cleared his throat—"if you was planning on going?"

She took the blue enamel coffeepot from the stove and refilled his cup, then hers. Sitting down at the table across from him, she looked him square in the eye. "I might be. And what business is it o' yers if I do, Mr. Adams?" Though Frances was loath to admit it, it was awfully nice having a man to share coffee and conversation with. That was one of the things she'd missed most after Ennis had died. He'd been a man with a rare sense of humor and a gift for gab, not unlike Frosty Adams. The unwelcome comparison made Frances reach for her coffee cup once again.

Heat rose up Frosty's neck, and he pulled his bandanna from his pants pocket and wiped his sweating forehead with it. Frances Ferguson was a direct woman, and her come-right-to-the-point attitude always took him by surprise.

A confirmed bachelor, he'd never thought to meet a woman who would fill his thoughts with marriage and settling down. But he was pushing sixty, and Frosty didn't relish spending his twilight years alone. And Frances was a very attractive woman. The kind of woman who could make even an old man like him sit up and take notice.

"I was kinda . . . kinda hoping that you'd consider going with me." He swallowed nervously, and his Adam's apple bobbed.

She arched a brow. "Are ye asking me out fer the evening, Mr. Adams? Is that what ye're about?"

"Yes, ma'am, I am." He cleared his throat before continuing. "I—I know you don't cotton to me much. But if you'd just give me a chance, I'd like to keep company with you and show you what an excellent catch I am."

His look was so earnest that Frances almost felt sorry for the dear old man. He'd spruced up for the visit, that was clear. His hair was combed neatly, and the wool plaid shirt he wore was fairly new. And he'd been considerate enough to bring her a rope of red licorice, which just happened to be her favorite candy. But none of that meant that she was going to let him off the hook too easily. That wasn't Frances's way.

"I'll have tae give yer offer some thought, Mr. Adams. As a respectable widow I canna afford tae hae tongues waggin' about me doings."

Frosty reached out across the table to cover her hand with his own. Her eyes widened at the bold gesture, but she didn't pull away. "You're a fine woman, Fan—I mean, Frances." Her face warmed, and he grinned. "And you sure do bake a mean cookie, too. I'd be honored if you'd think about going with me."

"We'll see, Mr. Adams. We'll see." But Frances was already thinking about what dress she was going to wear.

* * *

Later that same evening, Zach and Emily sat at the kitchen table, admiring the jack-o'-lanterns they had just spent the last hour carving. Emily couldn't remember when she'd had more fun, and she had Jess to thank for it.

He had made the outing truly memorable, first by helping her and Zach pick out their pumpkins, then by bringing forth a sack of marshmallows, which they'd roasted over the campfire while singing silly songs they'd composed.

After smiling warmly at him, she turned her attention to his son, who had lost a front tooth in his exuberance to find the best pumpkin. "I think your pumpkin looks the scariest, Zach. Mine's too funny looking."

Pleased by the compliment, the boy grinned, and the gap where his tooth had once been showed prominently. "They're thuppothed to be funny, Emily. Ithn't that right, Papa?"

Jess wore an amused grin as he watched the pair. It was obvious that Emily bore Zach a great deal of affection, and that affection was reciprocated in spades. The boy was definitely smitten. "That's right, son. Jack-o'-lanterns can look any way you wish. There are no rules when it comes to making them."

Mrs. Ferguson entered the kitchen just then, and Zach showed off his pumpkin proudly. "Me and Emily made up a thong today about our pumpkin, Gran. Do you want to hear it?"

The older woman smiled. "Yes, lad. And then 'tis off tae bed we ye. Ye've had a busy day. And I'm sure Emily and yer father can use a bit o' rest as well."

Not the least bit embarrassed by his impaired speech,

Zach stood and began to sing. "I'm a little pumpkin thort and fat. I hath two eyes and a nothe that's flat. I have a candle that makes me glow. I light up the night so the kids can go . . . beg or borrow goodies to eat. They have lots of fun and thcare me till I die, then they cut me up and make pumpkin pie. Oh . . . I'm a little pumpkin thort and fat. I hath two eyes and a nose that's flat."

Everyone laughed and clapped loudly, then Frances shook her head. "I'm thinking ye'll be appearing on the stage someday, lad." Winking at Emily, she clasped the child's hand. "Give yer papa and Miss Emily a kiss now. And we'll be off tae bed."

The small boy did as instructed, then skipped out of the room, singing the new song at the top of his lungs.

His father could only shake his head in bemusement. "I'm not sure whether or not to thank you for making up that little ditty, Emily. I have a feeling we'll be hearing a lot more of it from here on out."

She smiled, happy she'd been able to give something back for all the wonderful amusement she'd been given today. "I think Zach had a lot of fun today. I know I did. Thank you." She placed her hand over his and squeezed.

But Jess, who wanted nothing more than to take her in his arms and kiss her, pulled back, suddenly afraid of his feelings—feelings he'd been harboring throughout the day. "Guess I'd better go settle the horses down for the night. I've got a mare that's about to foal." He stood so quickly, he nearly upended the chair he'd been sitting on.

Hiding her frustration behind a smile, Emily nodded. "Well, good night, then. Thanks again for a wonderful day." And a disappointing evening, she added silently, trying not to feel rejected.

In her room, Emily disrobed and donned her nightgown, wondering the whole time if Jess was still outside in the barn. Though he'd made it clear that he didn't want any involvement between them—his hasty departure had made that even more obvious—she still wouldn't give up hope that some type of a relationship between them was possible.

Emily wasn't experienced when it came to men or matters of the heart, but she was fairly positive that she was falling in love with Jess Murdock. He occupied her every waking thought, and when she wasn't with him, she felt miserable, incomplete, as if a piece of her were missing.

She couldn't foresee the future, but she knew that she wanted Jess to be part of her life, wanted him like no decent woman should want a man who wasn't her husband. Her body cried out for his touch. Her aching heart yearned for the balm that only his words of love could supply. Her soul wanted to be joined to his forever and ever.

Emily didn't want to think about the career she had worked so long and hard to establish, or Jess's remote existence on a Montana ranch that was totally foreign to her upbringing, or the fact that she had no idea how to be a mother. She wanted only to think about now, this very moment, and what it would be like to make love with Jess, give him her most precious gift: her heart.

At the window, Emily looked out toward the building to see the light of the lantern still glowing, and her mind was made up. She grabbed her jacket and boots and left the security of her room to face the unknown entity of sexual desire.

Jess knelt beside the laboring mare and crooned words of comfort to her. Fairly certain that the horse wouldn't foal this night, he was almost relieved.

It was difficult concentrating on anything but his need for Emily Jean. A need that was growing with every day she remained on the ranch and becoming increasingly difficult to ignore. But he didn't want to act upon that desire, couldn't act upon it, in all good conscience.

Jess was still a married man. And as much as he wanted to be otherwise, it was still a fact he had to face. Nora had left without resolving their relationship. There was no way to institute divorce proceedings even if he wanted to, for he had no idea where his errant wife had run off to. The Pinkerton Agency had yet to come up with any worthwhile leads. He'd been left in limbo, a man who couldn't get on with his life— a man legally bound to a woman he despised.

There'd been a time when he'd actually thought he loved Nora. They'd met at a party of a mutual acquaintance, and he'd been dazzled by her beauty. She'd been taken with his dashing image of a Wild West performer, he with her brilliant smile and lighthearted ways. It hadn't taken long for them to consummate that attraction, and a few weeks later they had learned that Nora was with child—his child.

Jess had been overjoyed at the news of impending fatherhood. He wanted a chance to offer his child the love, affection, and interest that his own father had withheld from him. But Nora had viewed her pregnancy as a major inconvenience, a life sentence of drudgery, and an end to her good times. She'd talked about taking the easy way out and ending the child's life, but Jess wanted no part of that unthinkable act and had convinced her to marry him.

It became painfully obvious in just a few short months that Nora wasn't cut out to be a wife or a mother and that what had seemed like shared interests between them was nothing more than superficial attraction with no substance on which to base a marriage.

The shaky foundation had crumbled shortly after Zach's birth, and Nora had fled, he assumed to resume her normal carefree life without the hindrance of a baby or husband.

Absorbed in his disquieting thoughts, Jess didn't hear Emily's approach until she was standing right next to him.

"How's the horse doing? Is she going to be all right?" She knelt beside him in the hay, and the fragrance of lavender overpowered him, as did his hunger for her.

His voice was harsh when he spoke. "What are you doing out here? It's freezing, and you're not exactly fond of cold weather, as I recall."

"I noticed the light from my bedroom window and decided to come and see if everything was all right." It wasn't quite the truth, but it would have to do, she decided.

"I think you should leave. It's not a good idea for you to be out here." Alone, with me, in your nightclothes, he wanted to add.

She reached out to pat the horse's velvety muzzle. "I thought maybe you wouldn't mind some company."

Turning to face her, he caught the yearning in her eyes that mirrored his own. "God, Emily! You're torturing me. What am I supposed to think when you come out here half-undressed and smelling like a field of wildflowers? I told you before that men are weak creatures when it comes to things of a sexual nature."

"Sometimes women are weak, too," she admitted.

He turned away from her. "Go away and leave me be. I'm not interested." It was a lie, of course, but it would have to suffice. He cared about Emily and didn't want to hurt her.

Most women would have taken offense at such blatant rejection, but not Emily Jean, who had made up her mind to seduce Jess, no matter what insults she had to endure. Problem was, she didn't exactly know how to go about doing that. Obviously she was going about this seduction thing all wrong. She needed to take a more subtle approach, play hard to get, like the vapid heroines in her dime novels.

Fluttering her lashes, she presented him with what she considered to be an enticing smile. "I'm . . . I'm very surprised to hear that." Her voice was purposely breathless and, she hoped, alluring.

"Why should you be? I told you before—" Suddenly he stopped and stared at her strangely. "Is there something wrong with your eyes? You keep blinking them like you've got some dirt in them or something."

Blushing, she shook her head and in her best imitation of a femme fatale replied, "How you do go on, Jess." She forced a giggle. "Why, I just feel so small and helpless next to a big strong man like you." Her hand covered her heart, and her eyes widened in wonder.

Confusion at Emily's unorthodox behavior flashed across Jess's features, and it took him another minute to figure out just what she was doing; or hoping to do. He came to the frightening conclusion that the exasperating woman was indeed trying her damnedest to seduce him, though it was painfully obvious that she had no idea how to go about it.

The realization that she wanted him as much as he wanted her was humbling. Exciting. Damn frustrating!

"Emily, I—"

She licked her lips, though he doubted it was an artifice. She was too naive for that. "Yes?"

Clasping her shoulders, he pulled her to him. "God, woman! You don't know what you're asking." He lowered his mouth to hers and plundered her lips like a thief intent to rob all.

The feel of Jess's lips upon hers made Emily feel triumphant. He wanted her, and she certainly wanted him. When he moved his hands to remove her jacket, she didn't object. Jess's kisses had the power to ignite her body into a blazing inferno.

"Oh, Jess," she murmured as his tongue entered to duel with her own. Soon his hands found her breasts through the flannel material of her nightgown, and Emily knew there was no turning back.

Lowering her to the hay, Jess covered Emily's body with his own and lost himself in the joy of having her soft and willing beneath him. He was still fully clothed, but as good as she felt, as much as he wanted her, he might as well have been buck naked.

Emily arched up against him, trying to assuage the tension building within her and making him even harder than before. Jess reached down to pull up her nightdress, caressing every inch of her and feeling how wet and ready she'd become in just a few short minutes.

Pressing his hardened member to her, he rotated his hips, allowing her to feel that his need was every bit as strong and powerful as her own. She moaned in response.

"Make love to me, Jess. I want us to be together."

Pulling the nightgown up and over her head, he feasted his eyes upon her silken perfection, illuminated by the lantern light. He brought her small breasts to his mouth, drawing the hardened nipples into his mouth and suckling to slake his hunger.

"Jess! Jess!" Emily cried out, her head rocking back and forth at the exquisite torture.

"You're beautiful, Emily. More beautiful than any woman I've ever known."

Emily did feel beautiful at that moment, and cherished, and when Jess's hands parted her thighs and his mouth descended to that place where no man had ever touched, she didn't object.

As thoroughly as he'd savored her breasts, he now pleasured her with his tongue, and it was unlike any pleasure she had ever experienced. With his mouth and his hands he explored, tasted, touched, playing her body like a finely tuned instrument until the need to cry out for release became unbearable.

But the tortured sound that resulted was not her own, but the distraught mare's cries for attention.

"Goddamn!" Jess stopped what he was doing and sighed deeply. "I'm sorry, Emily, but the mare sounds like she's in distress. The foal could die if I don't help her."

It was obvious by the pained look on his face that Jess was in as much distress as his horse. Emily reached for her nightgown and put it on, knowing he had no choice but hating the interruption just the same. "I understand."

With an apologetic smile, he kissed her on the cheek. "I'm sorry, babe."

He left her to see to the horse, and Emily felt bereft. Throbbing with a need she couldn't control or fully comprehend, she wanted to call him back, beg him to finish what he had started. But she couldn't.

She didn't mean anything to Jess Murdock, certainly not as much as his horse. And she couldn't bring herself to ask for what he would most likely refuse: his undying love and devotion.

But what had started this night would one day be finished. Emily knew that with a certainty. And she would have it no other way.

Chapter Twelve

Rusty Doyle spotted Emily just as she disappeared into the chicken coop, and he made his way in her direction, intent on talking to her. He'd been outside having a smoke the previous night and had seen her leave the barn, then had watched Jess depart shortly after her. They'd obviously been sequestered in there together, and it didn't take a genius to figure out what they'd been doing. It was the very same thing he himself wanted to be doing with pretty Miss Emily.

The coop door banged shut, and Emily's heart lurched to her throat. She turned, expecting to find Jess. She hadn't wanted to face him this morning, so she'd hurried out to the chicken coop to gather the eggs at Mrs. Ferguson's request. Not only did she feel embarrassed about what had happened between them last night, but she'd learned from Mrs. Ferguson that the foal had died, and she felt somewhat responsible.

Rusty stood on the threshold, arms folded across his chest, a cocky grin splitting his face. "Howdy, Miss Emily.

Looks like you're mighty busy this morning. Did you sleep well last night?"

Heat rose up Emily's neck as memories of last night came to mind, but she willed it back down, determined to keep her composure at all costs or else be branded a loose woman. There was something about the way he'd asked the question that bordered on impertinent, as if he actually knew what she and Jess had been doing in the barn last evening.

"I slept quite well, thank you. What brings you out here so early in the day? I thought you'd be at the cook-house eating breakfast with the other hands."

"I only eat when tempted, Miss Emily. And there was nothing tempting 'bout Grubby's cooking this morning." He looked her over from top to bottom, licking his lips suggestively, and her cheeks turned bright pink.

Turning away from him, Emily wondered how she could have ever thought him polite. Probing beneath the disgruntled hen, she extracted an egg on her first try, feeling triumphant at the small accomplishment. The hens usually protested loudly whenever they saw her coming, her ineptness at ranching apparently obvious even to them.

"Was there something you needed? I'm afraid I'm a bit short on time. Mrs. Ferguson is waiting for these eggs, and she doesn't like to be kept waiting."

"Thought you might want to continue our conversation about the Wild West show. I know some things you may find interesting. Things you could put in your book."

Interest flared brightly in her eyes, and she turned to look at him. "If you have information, then certainly I'd like to hear it. I'm always looking for ways to make my books more accurate."

"I've got to be getting back to work right now, Miss Emily, but perhaps you can meet me later and we can discuss what I know."

Warning signals went off in Emily's brain. She didn't trust Rusty Doyle, and she certainly didn't want to be alone with him. "I'm not sure—"

"What I have to tell is something you aren't likely to hear from Jess. He's got secrets that he doesn't want anyone to know. I doubt he's been telling you what I know. And you did say you wanted your book to be accurate. It won't be without the information I've got." The hook had been baited, now Rusty waited to reel in the catch.

"Where and when do you propose to meet? I'm busy with Zach this afternoon, and I'm obligated to teach Mrs. Ferguson her letters after dinner."

"How about you meet me out in the barn tonight after everyone goes to bed?" What he had to tell her wouldn't take long, then they'd have the rest of the night to themselves. Rusty had no doubt that Emily wanted him as badly as he wanted her. He'd seen her shy smiles and interested looks. Women always played hard to get, but in the end he usually had his way.

"The barn?" Her eyes widened, her heart thudding in her ears.

Rusty nodded. "We'll be private there. No one can disturb us."

She knew that only too well, and that was what worried her. "I—I'm not sure that's a good idea, Rusty. It wouldn't be proper for me to meet you alone at night like that."

He shrugged, feigning indifference. "Have it your own way. I was only trying to help," he said, turning to leave.

"Wait!" she called out, halting him in his tracks. "All right. I'll meet you. But only for a few minutes."

Flashing a grin, he winked. "See you later, Miss Emily. And wear some of that perfume I like so much."

Before she could tell him that she'd changed her mind, Rusty departed, and Emily worried that she had made a huge mistake. She didn't trust Rusty. He was too forward, too sure of himself. On the other hand, if he knew something about Jess's past that could help her with the book, she had to find out what it was.

A good writer lets nothing stop him from seeking the truth.

Max's words came to mind, and Emily realized just how silly she was being. Rusty was just living up to his reputation as a ladies' man. He probably teased every woman he came into contact with. And he'd never really done or said anything to make her fear him.

It was true that he'd acted a bit brazen while giving her the riding lesson, but most likely he'd only been joking with her. Cowboys were notorious for playing practical jokes on one another.

Emily decided to set her mind at ease about the cowboy by asking Mrs. Ferguson a few pointed questions. The woman knew everything that went on at the ranch. If there was anything suspicious about any of the hands, Frances Ferguson would know.

Fifteen minutes later Emily found the housekeeper in the kitchen, rolling out pie dough for the apple pie she was preparing for dinner.

"I managed to find six eggs this morning, Mrs. Ferguson," she announced with pride. "I think I'm getting better at this ranching stuff." She placed the basket of eggs on the table, returning the woman's indulgent smile.

"That ye are, lass. Ye'll make a Montana woman yet. I knew ye were of strong stock the moment I laid eyes on ye, I did."

Emily pulled out a chair and sat. "You wouldn't be saying that if you'd met my mother. She faints at the most inconvenient times."

"*Tsk. Tsk.* Women and the vapors. Seems a useless reaction tae me. I canna see what purpose it serves tae be doing that."

"Mrs. Ferguson," Emily began, searching for the right words so as not to arouse suspicion. The older woman had a mind like a steel trap, and there wasn't much that got by her. "Do you know a neighbor by the name of Tim Little?"

"Aye. He comes around every once in a while, buying horses from Jess. Why?"

Relief shot through Emily. At least Rusty had been telling her the truth about that. "I heard the name the other day and wondered who he was, that's all."

The housekeeper lifted the thin dough onto the pie tin and began to crimp the edges. "The Littles live a few miles east of here. They're very nice people. Gertrude Little is quite active in the church, and her two girls sing in the choir."

"Are you familiar with all of the hands who work at the ranch?"

The housekeeper glanced up, surprised by the question. "Well, sure I am, lass. Most have been wie Jess a right good while now. All good lads, they are. I canna think o' one who's caused me any grief."

Satisfied with the answers, Emily decided to keep her appointment with Rusty after all, and she deftly changed the subject. "I heard Mr. Adams came calling yesterday. Weren't you going to tell me?"

Frances's face turned as red as her hair. "Nothing much tae tell. And 'tis doubtful that ye'll be wantin' tae tell me what it was ye was doing outside in yer nightclothes last night, I'm thinking, lass."

It was now Emily's turn to blush. "I—I was helping Jess with his mare. She was about to foal and—"

"Aye. And I'm Mary, Queen of Scots." The woman's throaty laughter forced Emily out of the chair, and she made a hasty departure, mumbling an excuse about editing her book.

Intent on hurrying up the stairs to the safety of her room, away from any more knowing looks and laughter, Emily wasn't watching where she was going. She ran headlong into Jess's midsection, the feeling not unlike running into a brick wall.

Jess grunted, then clasped her shoulders to steady her. "Whoa there, woman! Why are you in such an all-fired hurry? Anxious to see me, are you?"

Emily's cheeks flamed red. "Ssh! Someone might hear you." She looked about to make sure they were alone, then added, "And it's ungentlemanly of you to speak of such things."

"It's not me who has 'such things' on the mind, babe." His grin was incredibly sexy, setting Emily's pulse to pounding. "But now that you mention it, when are we going to finish what we started last night? I'm sorry I had to leave like I did." The loss of the foal had been a bitter pill to swallow in light of what had almost happened between them last night.

Jess had thought long and hard about that and had decided to put himself out of his misery and take what Emily was offering. It was obvious that she wanted him as desperately as he wanted her. And until he satisfied the longing eating away at him, he wasn't going to be able to concentrate on anything else.

He'd damn near broke his neck this morning while breaking a green horse. Because his mind had been occupied with thoughts of making love to Emily, he hadn't been paying attention to the horse's subtle movements, and the frightened stallion had tossed him up and over his head.

Jess had almost paid the ultimate price for his inattention, and he'd finally come to the conclusion that making love to Emily would be a hell of a lot safer than losing his concentration again.

He'd given his marital status a great deal of thought as well. In his mind, he and Nora weren't really married any longer, even if he didn't have the legal paper to prove it. He considered himself a single man with singular needs, one of which was Emily Jean Bartlett.

"I—" Emily wanted desperately to meet Jess tonight, to consummate what they had begun the night before, but she had already made a commitment for the evening. *Damn, Rusty Doyle!* She felt conflicted about choosing between her desire and her duty to Max, agonizing over the promise she had made to herself. In the end, she chose duty.

"I'm eager to be with you, too, Jess, but not tonight."

"Why not? You haven't replaced me with someone else already, have you?" His eyes twinkled when Emily's face flamed again.

"Certainly not! What type of a woman do you take me for? Just because I allowed you to take certain"—her voice lowered to a whisper—"liberties, is no reason—"

"Don't go getting your corset strings all tied up in knots. I was only teasing." He pulled her into his chest. "Now that I've had a taste of you, Emily, I want more."

Emily's heart was pounding, and she thought surely it would explode. "I've got to get some work done tonight. Max is expecting a progress report. And I'm sure you can understand that I must honor my commitment to him. He's counting on me."

He rubbed her back, making small, sensual circles that sent tingles down to her toes. "I'm getting hard just thinking about being with you." He took her hand and placed it on his crotch, which was swollen and bulging. "Feel what you do to me." Pushing her back against the wall, he kissed her until she was breathless, then said, "Remember that, babe, when you're writing your next scene."

Jess left her standing in the darkened hallway with her mouth hanging open and a dull ache centered between her thighs. Emily doubted very much that she was going to get any writing done today.

*   *   *

The barn was wrapped in darkness when Emily pulled open the heavy door and entered. Wrapping her warm coat about her, she shivered violently against the cold night air, vowing that this would be the last clandestine meeting she would have in the barn or anywhere else, for that matter. She was definitely not cut out for cloak-and-dagger melodramas.

She looked about to find that Rusty Doyle was nowhere in sight. Deciding that was probably for the best, that her plan to meet the cowboy was a foolhardy one, she had just turned around to return to the house when a deep voice came out of the darkness to frighten her.

"I see you came."

Clutching her throat, she spun around to see the glowing tip of Rusty's cigarette. "It's not nice to sneak up on people like that. You nearly scared me to death, Rusty Doyle!"

He lit the kerosene lantern hanging on the wall, and the barn was immediately consumed by a golden luminescence. Emily could see clearly that he was amused by her reaction.

"Sorry. I didn't mean to scare you, Miss Emily," he said smoothly, stepping toward her. "I just thought it'd be best if we didn't draw too much attention to ourselves."

She took a deep breath to calm down. "I suppose that was wise. Now, if you don't mind, I'd like to get this discussion over with as quickly as possible and return to my room. I'm freezing."

The cowboy grinned and took another drag on his smoke. He knew lots of ways to warm up cold women. But he'd bide his time until after Emily Jean was sufficiently grateful for what he was about to tell her. "I can see you're anxious, so I won't keep you waiting."

"Thank you."

"Like I told you before, me and Jess used to work with the Wild West show. One night there was a shooting and a child was killed."

Emily gasped. "How awful!"

Rusty nodded. "Yeah, it was. The kid's parents were beside themselves with grief. Especially when they found out who had murdered their only child."

"Murdered? Someone murdered a child? What kind of person would do such a horrible thing?"

"Some say it was an accident, but the kid was killed just the same, and the man responsible was never brought to justice because of who he was."

A sick feeling of dread formed in the pit of her stomach. "Who was he?" Emily asked, her voice barely above a whisper, though she was sure she already knew.

"I think you can guess. Jess Murdock didn't want it to come out that he had shot the kid. Cody covered it up for him, threatened the parents with their jobs if they was to put up a stink, then he paid them off to keep it all quiet.

"It never got into the newspapers. I suspect Cody or Murdock also paid off the police who investigated." He went on to explain about what had happened that fateful night when Rory Connors was shot by Jess Murdock, the star of the show.

Emily was stunned by the revelation. She could certainly understand why Jess wouldn't want anyone to know about what had happened. He no doubt blamed himself.

She didn't believe for a minute that he had intentionally killed the child, and she wondered what Rusty Doyle's motive was in trying to make her think so.

"It sounds as if the incident was nothing more than a tragic accident. Why do you believe otherwise? And why did you want to tell me about it?"

Rusty stepped closer, and she could smell the tobacco on his breath. "I figured if you was going to write a book about Murdock, then you should have all the facts, not just the whitewashed ones he told you. And I also figured that you'd be mighty grateful to me for helping you out."

"If you're looking for money, Mr. Doyle, then I'm afraid I can't help you. I arrived in True Love virtually penniless."

He threw down his cigarette and stomped it out, then reached out to clasp her arms in a viselike grip. "It ain't your money I'm interested in, sugar. You got something worth a whole lot more. And seeing as how you've already given it to Jess, I figured you wouldn't mind sharing with me."

Fear clutched her heart. "I don't know what you're talking about," she brazened out. But she did, realizing that she had made a terrible mistake—a mistake that could cost her everything.

He snorted in disbelief. "I think you do. You city girls are smart, and fast." He pulled her to his chest.

Emily swallowed the scream rising to her throat and struggled to free herself, but the cowboy's hold was too strong. "Let go of me! I should have known better than to believe you. Jess tried to warn me, but I was too stupid to listen."

His eyes darkened. "Don't be playing hard to get, Emily. I saw you leave the barn last night. I figured you and Jess was out here humping in the hay like a couple of love-starved rabbits. I just want me some of the same." He tried to kiss her, but she turned her head and let out a bloodcurdling scream.

Filled with sexual frustration and desire, Jess hadn't been able to sleep. Still fully dressed, he was pacing his room like a caged lion, wondering how he was going to get through the night. He'd already poured cold water over his head to cool off. He supposed he should have poured it a bit lower, where it would have done more good.

Cursing under his breath, he decided to ignore Emily's request for solitude and go to her room to see if he could change her mind about taking up where they'd left off the night before. No doubt she just needed a littler persuading. And he could be awfully persuasive when he put his mind to it.

As quietly as he could, he tiptoed down the hall and entered her room without knocking. Pausing, he looked about. The kerosene lamp was still burning on the desk, papers were strewn every which way, but Emily was nowhere to be found.

Thinking that she'd probably gone down to the kitchen for a late night snack, he followed his hunch to find that she wasn't there, either, and he wondered where she could have gone at this hour of the night.

Gazing about the large room, he discovered that the back door had been left ajar. His forehead wrinkled in confusion. It wasn't like Frances to forget such a thing. He then noticed that Emily's coat was missing from the peg by the door and grew alarmed. It wasn't safe for her to be wandering outside by herself in the dark. There were animals out there, both the four-legged and two-legged kind.

After lighting a lantern, he hurried outside to investigate.

"Let go of me, you animal!" Emily shouted, but the cowboy was stronger, and he covered her mouth with his, thrusting his tongue between her tightly clenched lips. Revolted by his touch, by the taste of him, she bit down as hard as she could.

He screamed in agony, pushing her from him. "Goddamn!" He wiped the blood from his mouth with the back of his hand. "You little bitch. I'll get you for that."

Not waiting for him to make good on his threat, Emily made a break for the door, but Doyle lunged for her and grabbed her.

It was at that moment that Jess entered the building.

He ground to a halt, his eyes widening in disbelief at the sight of Emily wrapped in Rusty Doyle's arms. "What the hell is going on here?"

Rusty let go of Emily immediately, and she ran to Jess's side, relieved that he had come looking for her. "He attacked me."

The cowboy shook his head and smirked. "Ain't it just like a woman to be crying rape when she was asking for a little loving? She came to me, Jess, not the other way around."

"That's not true!"

Jess wore a mask of outrage. "Then what the hell are you doing out here in the barn in the middle of the night, Emily?"

"I—"

What could she say? That she'd been investigating him behind his back after he'd asked her not to?

She said nothing.

Jess noted the guilt on her face, and his eyes turned lethal and condemning. His gaze finally settled on Doyle. "Get the hell outta here, Doyle, before I beat the living crap outta you. I told you before to leave Emily alone."

"I'm only a man, Jess. She was wanting a little loving. Said she was disappointed about what happened last night."

The rancher's face paled slightly, and he turned an accusing look on Emily, his voice filled with disbelief. "You told him about last night?"

She shook her head. "No! He's lying. He saw me leave the barn, that's all. I didn't—"

"Shut up, Emily. I'll deal with you in a minute. Doyle . . ." He turned to face his cowhand again. "Get back to the bunkhouse. If I wasn't so shorthanded at the moment, I'd fire your ass in a heartbeat. I don't ever want to see you around Emily again, do I make myself clear?"

The cowboy nodded. "Yes, sir! I didn't know you had put your brand on her, Jess. She played us both for fools."

Rusty beat a hasty retreat, and Jess turned all of his attention and venom on Emily.

"I should have known."

She held out her hands beseechingly, trying to make him understand. "I can explain—"

"Oh, I'm sure you can. If I recall correctly, you're quite good at making up lies and half-truths. It's what you do for a living, after all."

"Surely you can't believe that there's something between Rusty Doyle and myself." He couldn't be that insensitive after what they'd shared last night.

"Weren't you the one who wanted to have some sexual experimentation? Weren't you the one who was left unfulfilled last night and sought to remedy that with some other man?"

Rocking back on her heels as if slapped, she gasped, her eyes filling with unshed tears. "No! You're wrong, Jess. I don't want any man but you. Please believe me." She reached out to him, but he stepped back as if she were contaminated and the mere thought of touching her proved revolting.

"Get back to the house, Emily. I'll let you know in the morning what I decide to do."

She swallowed. "Do?"

His eyes were like chips of blue ice when he said, "I'll let you know in the morning whether or not I'm going to kick your pretty, unfaithful ass off this ranch."

Chapter Thirteen

THE MORNING AIR WAS BITING, AND THE WIND LASHED across Jess's face like a whip, stinging relentlessly. But he didn't care. It served as a reminder of the pain he experienced whenever he allowed himself to get too close to a woman.

Damn Emily's faithless hide! She had played him for a fool and won. When was he going to learn his lesson where treacherous women were concerned?

"Looks like the fence is still intact, boss." Frosty's breath came out in white puffs against the freezing temperature as he inspected the barbed wire for cuts. "Don't know why we had to check before sunup. We ain't lost any head in a while."

"Because I said so, that's why." Jess dismounted, wishing he had a cigarette. But he'd given up the damn things when Zach was born, figuring it wouldn't be too healthy for a baby to be breathing in all that smoke.

"You're as touchy as a sore-titted bitch this morning. What the hell's gotten into you? And don't be telling me

'Nothing." Cause I know better. I've known you too damn long to be buying that horseshit."

Jess rubbed the back of his neck, trying to ease the knots out of it that a restless night had caused. He'd gotten little sleep after witnessing Emily in Doyle's arms.

"It's nothing—nothing I'm not going to get over in a couple of days."

"I hope you're not talking about a woman," Frosty said, shooting his companion a disbelieving look, "because you sure as hell ain't gonna get over any woman that quickly. Look how long it took to get over that woman you're hitched to." Jess's foreman noted the pain reflected in the man's eyes and dismissed the feral look he wore.

"I made a mistake in thinking Emily was different. It won't happen again."

"That little gal is different, son. You're just too damn stubborn to notice."

"I'll tell you what I noticed, old man. I noticed her in the arms of that bastard Doyle last night when I went out to the barn to look for her because I was worried. That's what I noticed."

"And did you notice if she was enjoying herself?" Frosty shook his head at the man's obtuseness. "'Cause Rusty ain't the kind of man to care. If he wants something, he takes it, whether or not the woman's willing. You know the kind of man he is, Jess."

"Emily claims he attacked her, but it didn't look that way from where I was standing. From where I was standing it looked real cozy."

"No doubt you was blinded by your anger. Emily's not the kind of woman to be two-timing a man. She's a nice gal, a decent sort."

Jess's stomach growled as hunger pains tore at his belly. From his saddlebag he retrieved a sack of beef jerky, handed Frosty a piece, and took a chew before mounting his horse again.

"What makes you such an authority on women? Just because you think you're making some headway with Frances doesn't make you a damn expert."

"If I had me a daughter, I'd want her to be just like Emily Jean. That gal is so damned sweet-natured and kind." Jess snorted rudely, and Frosty let loose with a string of curses.

"Look at the way she is with your son. Are you blind? Can't you see how much she cares about Zach? And she's got the patience of Job, teaching Fan her letters and all."

Everything his well-meaning friend said was true, but it didn't excuse Emily's wanton behavior. "She's young, Frosty. A lot younger than me. And she's inexperienced when it comes to men. She's curious about things. And that curiosity led her straight into Rusty Doyle's arms."

"You're plumb crazy, boy. I never figured you for a fool, Jess, but you sure are sounding like one. Miss Emily told me several times during our riding lessons that she didn't trust Rusty, that she found him to be too cocksure of himself. 'A randy rooster,' is what she called him. I remember laughing about it at the time."

"Women are notorious for changing their mind." Nora

had professed to love him, and she'd run out on him and Zach.

As if he could read Jess's mind, Frosty said, "Emily ain't Nora, so quit comparing the two. That gal's as loyal as a three-legged hound. She ain't the kind to cut and run. If she was, she sure as hell wouldn't have stuck it out here at the ranch, while you did everything in your power to make her life miserable." Emily had proven to be every bit as stubborn as Jess, and that wasn't exactly a compliment, in Frosty's opinion.

They reached the rise overlooking the ranch, and Jess reined his horse to a halt, observing the beauty of the lush valley below. The serenity of the landscape was in direct contrast with how he felt at the moment. His stomach was tied up tighter than a buxom whore's corset strings. "Maybe what you say is true, but I'm not taking any chances. I've got Zach to think about. And he's growing awfully attached to Emily. When she leaves, he's going to be heartsick."

"When she leaves?" The old man looked horrified by the prospect. "Who said anything about her leaving?"

Jess had been ready to send her packing after what he'd observed the night before. But in the light of day he just couldn't bring himself to make her go, and he wondered what he would do when he was finally faced with that eventuality. He was starting to care a little too much, and that frightened him.

"Emily will leave when she's done with the book. You know she's only here until then. She's got a life back in New York City."

"She's got a life right here at the Bar JM. Iff'n you wasn't such a dad-blamed fool, Murdock, you'd see that. That gal's in love with you. I see it in her eyes every time she gazes at you like a lovesick puppy. And unless I miss my bet you've got strong feelings for her, too."

Jess opened his mouth to deny it, but Frosty never gave him the chance. "Seems to me you should be doing something about those feelings instead of making false accusations and an ass out of yourself." The disgusted foreman spurred his gelding to a gallop and rode back to the ranch.

Watching him go, Jess shook his head. What the hell did the old man expect him to do? Marry Emily? Hell, he couldn't marry anyone. He was already married, and Frosty knew it.

And he wasn't exactly sure what his feelings were for the woman. Sure he cared about her, enjoyed being with her, and he sure as hell wanted her in his bed. And he couldn't stand the thought of her leaving. But was that love?

"Goddamn!" he cursed. His life was in one hell of a mess. And Emily Jean Bartlett had only complicated matters, not provided a solution.

Emily was at the moment looking for a solution, not for Jess's problems, but for her own. She had made a mess of things. Her eagerness to write an authentic narrative, to delve into Jess's personal history, had impaired her normally sound judgment. And it might have cost her the man she was so desperately in love with.

She cursed her own stupidity, then Jess, who had accused her of improper behavior with Rusty Doyle. She was furious about his unfair condemnation. But that fury was tempered by the fact that she had placed herself in a compromising position with the dishonorable cowboy and had to absorb some of the blame for Jess's misunderstanding.

"You should have listened to your gut instincts, Emily Jean," she chastised herself. But she hadn't. And now she would no doubt pay the price for that foolhardiness.

And if all that wasn't bad enough, she still had to face the consequences of her actions regarding the book and Max. If Jess decided to terminate their professional relationship as well as their personal one, she would have let Max down and jeopardized Wise Publishing in the process.

Pulling aside the curtain, she gazed out the bedroom window to find Jess riding into the yard. *Damn you for being so stubborn, Jess Murdock! And double damn you for making me fall in love with you. My life was much simpler—albeit boring—before you came into it.*

She crossed to the desk and retrieved the letter from Max that had arrived early that morning. Reading her publisher's words, discerning the distress in them, and knowing the obstacles he faced with his creditors made her feel even worse than she already did.

"Please hurry with the book, Emily Jean," he wrote. "Time is running out."

Time was running out for her, too. She needed to figure out a way to make it up to Jess for what happened last night, to mend the damage she'd created. For Max. For her own peace of mind. And to repair the large chasm that had rent her heart in two.

* * *

"One times four is four, Emily." Zach smiled proudly, then went on to recite his multiplication tables to ten.

"You're doing so well, Zach. I'm very proud of you." She bussed him on the cheek at the exact moment his father came into the kitchen, looking not the least bit pleased with the world. Or her.

"I'd like to speak to you in my office, Emily," Jess said.

Emily's heart twisted at the coldness in his voice. He was going to ask her to leave. She bit the inside of her cheek to stem the rising emotion she felt. It wouldn't do to cry in front of the boy. "I'll be there in a moment. I just want to give Zach his homework assignment."

He nodded, then spun on his heel, and Emily reached deep inside herself to draw upon the strength that had always been there in times of adversity.

"How come Papa looks so mad, Emily? Did you do something wrong? When I do something that makes Papa mad I usually get a spanking."

She was saved from answering when Mrs. Ferguson burst through the back door, carrying an armful of clean laundry that she had just taken down from the clothesline.

"'Tis freezing out, that's fer sure." She set down the pile of clothes, took in the worried faces of Emily and Zach, and began to unbutton her coat. "What's this I'm seeing? Such long faces."

"Papa's mad at Emily," Zach announced.

"That's none o' our concern, lad." Frances Ferguson smiled apologetically at Emily. "Now finish up yer work

and be quick about it. I may just be tempted tae bake oatmeal cookies, if ye hurry."

Emily could have kissed the considerate woman for
getting her off the hook. There was no way she wanted to
explain to a small child about the ugly scene that had occurred in the barn the previous night. She hadn't yet confided in the housekeeper, and she gave her credit for not
prying, though Emily knew Frances was dying to ask.

Smiling gratefully, she ruffled the boy's hair, then
said, "I'll be back for some of those cookies. Study hard,
Zach."

Emily's hand was sweaty as she turned the doorknob
to enter Jess's study. He was sitting behind his desk, looking formidable and not the least bit friendly. His gaze
lifted, and he acknowledged her presence.

"Sit down, Emily. I think we need to have another
talk."

She swallowed the grapefruit-size lump in her throat.
"I thought we said everything we had to say last night."
Emily decided that she wouldn't beg for forgiveness, even
though she wanted to.

Jess had replayed the scene in the barn over and over
in his mind. He'd considered Frosty's words, sifted
through the truth of them, and had reached the very disturbing conclusion that he'd been wrong to accuse Emily
of inappropriate behavior. "I may have been a bit harsh in
my judgment last night."

Her eyes widened at what sounded like an apology.
"It was understandable. I was wrong not to have listened to
you." The relief flooding through her proved to be fleeting.

"Why did you meet Doyle out in the barn?"

Her mouth felt dry as cotton. Once she confessed to the true reason for the meeting, Jess would become incensed and ask her to leave. She had to take that chance. She didn't want any further deception to come between them. "Rusty Doyle said he had information he could give me about the Wild West show. I foolishly believed that to be his only motive in asking me to meet him."

"Information about me?" Jess leaned back in his chair and studied the nervous woman, wondering why Emily couldn't see how damn desirable she was to every male on the ranch, especially a womanizer like Doyle.

She nodded. "He told me about the shooting of the child. I'm sorry, Jess. It must have been very difficult for you to deal with such a tragedy."

Jess heaved a sigh and felt almost relieved that she knew. The burden had been a difficult one to bear. "I'm glad you know. I didn't want to tell you, because I was afraid you would put it in the book. I don't want Zach to ever find out what happened."

She crossed to where he was sitting and knelt beside him, placing her hand on his arm. "You mustn't blame yourself any longer, Jess. It was a terrible accident. I know you didn't mean for it to happen."

His voice filled with emotion. "He was only a boy, Emily, younger than Zach is now. And he's dead because of me. God, if I could relive that day over again, do it all different. I would have given my own life to spare Rory Connors's. Every time I look at my son I feel such incredible guilt."

Wrapping her arms about him, she offered comfort. "You've punished yourself enough. And I won't put the incident in the book if you don't want me to."

He was startled by the admission.

"Listen to me, Jess." She clutched his head in her hands and looked deep into eyes filled with pain. "You mustn't hide from what happened or let it destroy you. People are basically decent. They'll understand and admire you even more for admitting your mistake. But that has to be your decision."

He pulled her down on his lap. "Why are you so forgiving, Emily? Why do you make allowances for me? Is it because of the book?"

"Partly. I'm not going to deny that I still want to finish the book. But that's not the main reason. I—" I love you, she wanted to say. But it wasn't the right time. Not when his emotions were so raw. Not when she had no inkling of how he felt about her.

"I admire you greatly, Jess. I always have. You've accomplished a great many things in your lifetime—things you should be very proud of.

"But aside from all of your glory and derring-do, I admire you as a man. You're kind, you're a wonderful father, and you're honest, brutally so at times, but still honest. I—"

"Shut up and kiss me." Jess silenced her accolades with his lips, and Emily sighed into his mouth, then kissed him back with all the pent-up emotion she possessed.

They lost themselves in the sheer pleasure of their joining, lips to lips, breast to chest, heart to heart, and

Emily knew in that moment that she would give everything she possessed to have this man as her own.

Jess broke the contact and took deep breaths to calm himself. "I want you, Emily. But not here. If we continue like this, I won't be able to control myself."

She ran her finger over his lips. "Did I ask you to?"

"God, woman, but you tempt me!"

She smiled and patted his cheek. "Good."

"How would you feel about going for a horseback ride?"

Her eyes widened in surprise. That was one proposition she wasn't expecting, and truth be told, she was disappointed. "Now? You want to ride horses now? I can think of other things I'd rather—"

He silenced her again with another kiss, then said, "There's a line shack a few miles from here. I keep it stocked with provisions, blankets . . . a bed."

Blood heated and rushed to her cheeks. "Wouldn't it be easier to just go upstairs?"

"I know this may sound a bit old-fashioned, but I don't want to make love to you with my boy in the house."

"Oh, Jess." Emily's eyes filled with tears. "That's not being old-fashioned, that's being wonderful. And honorable."

Tell her, Jess. Tell her about Nora, he told himself. But he couldn't. Not now. Not when the one thing he wanted was so close at hand. "I'm not that honorable, Emily. I'm only a man—a man who wants you and will do most anything to have you."

"I want you, too. But . . . won't Mrs. Ferguson and the others wonder where we've gone?"

He considered the question and realized he would have to protect her reputation. "I'll make up some excuse. Borrow a page from your book and make up an elaborate story to explain our absence."

"I don't want any more lies to come between us, Jess. I want us to be truthful with each other from here on out. I think that's important, don't you?"

Though Jess assured her that he did, he knew in his heart that there was something very real that would always stand between them. Perhaps the biggest lie of all.

They rode for what seemed like hours to Emily. She wasn't used to riding for any length of time, and her rear end and back were stiff and sore from the poor way she seated her mount.

While they trotted along toward the line shack, Jess talked of his past, his time with the Wild West show, and the events that had shaped his life, including the accidental shooting of Rory Connors.

Emily didn't think it was possible, but she loved him even more for trusting her with the information. She knew how bad he felt about killing the small child, knew that it tore him up even to discuss it.

There'd been other tragedies in his life as well. Indian raids, and the murder of innocent women and children at the hands of the United States Cavalry, of which he'd been a part. And he had killed a man with his bare hands when he was but twenty-two years old—a man intent on the murder of a prostitute, whom Jess had saved by his actions.

Jess had many skeletons in his closet, many burdens to bear, and it was easy for her to understand why he'd be so reluctant to have her write his life story.

Even now she didn't know what he would allow her to put into print. But she hoped that she'd be able to convince him that his story was worth telling, all of it, and that people would understand that it took more than glamour and daring deeds to make a legend. It took guts and a willingness to put your life on the line over and over again to do what you thought right, and to live with the consequences of those decisions, right or wrong.

"Guess I'm not quite the honorable man you thought me to be, huh, Emily?" Jess's voice was tinged with sadness and apology. "I tried to tell you that there were things in my past that should be left there."

"You've got more to be proud of than not, Jess. Don't ever forget that. My admiration for you hasn't lessened one bit, and it's obvious Frosty Adams's hasn't, either. We both know the whole story, and we're both still one hundred percent behind you."

Not quite the whole story, Jess thought, wondering how he was ever going to confide the fact that he was still married, still legally bound to another woman.

"Frosty's a good friend. I guess you are, too."

She smiled at the admission and was happy he thought so. But she wanted to be so much more than friends. She wanted to be a permanent part of his life. The thought frightened her, for it meant giving up everything she had worked so hard to accomplish.

A man like Jess would want a full-time mother for Zach, a full-time wife for himself. A woman who knew how to do all the wifely things women were supposed to know instinctively. The kinds of attributes she sadly lacked.

"How much farther is it to the line shack? And what's it used for? I mean, besides secret rendezvous?" She was amused by the thought that she was actually having one, at the idea that E. J. Bartlett, whom everyone thought was a man, was about to lose her virginity. She should probably be frightened at the prospect of taking such an important step, but instead she was excited.

"When the ranch was larger than it is now, we ran more head of cattle on free range. There were no barbed-wire fences then, and we needed to patrol the perimeter to make sure the herd didn't stray.

"I keep a few of the shacks stocked and ready for when I feel like getting away by myself, or sometimes I take Zach hunting and we stay overnight a few days. But I've never brought a woman to one before."

Emily was thrilled and relieved by the knowledge. She wanted her first time to be special, for both of them. And she knew that with Jess it would be.

Chapter Fourteen

THE SMALL CABIN WAS DARK AND COLD WHEN THEY entered, and Jess hurried to light the kerosene lantern and build a fire in the potbellied stove.

Now that the moment was at hand, Emily found she was nervous. While Jess busied himself with putting the cabin to rights, she stared out the window, wiping away the grime with the heel of her hand to see how the sky had darkened.

It would likely rain before they headed back, and she was not looking forward to riding her horse in inclement weather. She had enough trouble controlling him on dry ground.

"Are you warming up?" Jess came to stand behind her, placing his hands on her shoulders. His gaze drifted to the bunk, his eyes narrowing slightly. "It looks as if someone's been here. The bed's been disturbed."

She followed his stare but was more concerned about who was going to be disturbing that bed in a few short moments than who'd been it in previously. "Maybe a

drifter borrowed your hospitality during a thunderstorm."
Cowboys riding the trail often used whatever shelter they
could find during bad weather. It was considered inhos-
pitable not to offer a stranded stranger lodging.

"Maybe," he said, not sounding at all convinced. Or
maybe the bastard who'd been rustling his cows had been
using the line shack as a refuge. The thought was unset-
tling.

Interrupting his disquieting thoughts, she said, "You
never told me what excuse you gave Mrs. Ferguson."

"I told her that we were going to hunt for pinecones.
That you wanted to make a centerpiece for the Thanksgiving table and needed them to complete your creation."

Emily burst into laughter. She could just imagine
what the astute housekeeper thought of Jess's bald-faced
lie, especially knowing of Emily's lack of artistic ability.
Writing was about as creative as she got.

"With Thanksgiving still weeks away, I'd be very interested to know just what Mrs. Ferguson had to say."

In his best imitation of a Scottish brogue, Jess replied,
"Laddie, ye're an out-and-out liar, ye are. Ye're going tae
take the lass and hae yer way wie her, now, aren't ye?
Shame on ye, laddie." Jess wrapped his arms about
Emily's midsection and drew her close. "Now how do you
suppose she knew that?"

Emily grinned, nuzzling her lips against his neck. "I
suppose she's seen me lusting after you."

He kissed her then, long and hard, then helped her to
remove her coat. "I think it's time we got down to some se-

rious lusting, then, woman." With a rakish wink, he led Emily to the narrow bed.

"I'm not really afraid, just a bit nervous. I've—I've never done this before."

His eyes widened at the revelation, and he felt pleased that he would be Emily's first. He'd always suspected that she was a virgin, but to have her confirm it was more than he'd ever hoped for.

Taking her hands in his own, he said, "You have to trust me and know that I would never hurt you. You do, don't you?"

"Yes, of course." She began to unbutton her shirt-waist, grateful that she hadn't had time to change into her men's clothing before they'd left. She doubted Jess would have enjoyed making love to a woman dressed like a man.

"Let me," he said, brushing her hands away impatiently. Within moments he had made short work of the buttons and fastenings on her underclothing, pushing them off her shoulders until the upper half of her body was naked to his view. His eyes glowed with appreciation and longing. "You're truly lovely."

Emily fought the urge to cover herself. Though Jess had seen her naked, it felt decadent to be undressed in front of someone who was still fully clothed. "Aren't you going to undress?" she asked.

"In a moment. But first I want to see you completely naked in the light of day. I want to look my fill with no interruptions."

Her cheeks flushed, and she began to unfasten her skirt, slipping out of it, then her drawers, until she was standing before the bed and him in nothing but an uncertain smile. "I'm afraid I'm not very big on top."

He reached out to fondle her breasts, and her nipples hardened instantly. "You've got more than enough to satisfy my needs, babe." To prove his point he drew her down on the bed beside him and began to suckle her breasts. Emily's blood heated to a fever pitch.

"Now it's your turn to undress." Her voice sounded breathless when she brazenly admitted, "I want to see you naked, too."

In a moment he was as naked as she, and Emily's eyes widened at the large, stiff member jutting forth like a spear ready to impale her. It was doubtful something so large was going to fit inside her. She spoke her thoughts aloud. "There's no way that's going to fit."

Jess threw back his head and laughed, then lay down beside her, covering her body with his own. "You flatter me, woman. But don't worry, it'll fit. God in his wisdom just happened to make it so it would."

It seemed blasphemous to be speaking of the Lord at such a time, so Emily didn't respond. "Is it . . . is it normal for people to be chatting this way when they're about to make love?" Her parents hardly ever conversed during normal times. She couldn't imagine them having such a casual conversation while in bed.

Jess stroked her thighs, then his hand moved up her side and gooseflesh erupted everywhere. "What folks do in their beds is up to them. There aren't any rules about how to make love. You just do what comes natural. If it makes it easier to talk first, then we talk."

"I've never talked with a naked man before."

He grinned. "I'm happy to hear that."

She looked down the length of him to discover that his member was now flaccid. "Oh dear! I hope I'm not the cause of that."

"Put your hand there and see what happens. I've got a feeling that it'll perk right up and be ready for action."

Heat infused Emily's cheeks, but she went ahead and did what he suggested. Her curiosity wouldn't be satisfied until she had touched him as intimately as he had touched her. Within moments his member hardened and grew long in her palm. "Oh my!" She wrapped her hand around him, and Jess moaned, beads of sweat forming on his upper lip at the exquisite torture.

"I wouldn't do that, babe, unless you've changed your mind about making love. I'm not going to be able to hold on much longer."

She stared at his maleness in fascination. "I'd never imagined—"

"I think the anatomy lesson's over for today. It's time to get down to business." Before she could reply, he rolled over on top of her and pressed his mouth to hers.

While his lips and tongue did a thorough probing of her mouth, Jess's hands investigated every inch of Emily's body. Like an explorer in uncharted territory, he mapped the hills and contours, slowly, maddeningly, until Emily wanted to scream out her frustration. She writhed beneath him, bucked against him, but still the torture did not abate.

"We're going to take it nice and slow," he said, trailing his finger down her thigh until he found her womanhood. He palmed her, then made certain she was wet and ready for their coupling until she begged him to stop.

"I can't stop, babe. I want to taste you now."

With her head lolling from side to side, Emily opened herself to the onslaught of Jess's tongue as he teased, tasted, and tormented the very essence of her being. "Oh God!" she cried out, clutching the blanket beneath her. Her body was on fire, a light sheen of perspiration covered her heated flesh, and only sheer willpower kept her from floating to the ceiling.

"You're so damn sweet, Emily."

"Please, Jess! I can't take any more."

Rising up, he placed his hardened member against her, gently guiding her legs apart. "This may hurt a bit, but only for a moment."

She bucked against him, urgently, frantically, trying to quench her longing. Jess thrust deep inside, waiting a moment for her to adjust to the fullness of him before increasing his pace.

Where there once was pain, now there was only pleasure as Emily met Jess stroke for stroke in a frenzied mating ritual. Wrapping her arms about him, she urged him deeper, reveling in the throaty sounds of enjoyment he made—sounds that mirrored her own frantic cries of yearning.

The pace increased, as did the pleasure. Jess clasped her hips, rotating her up and around as he drove them both ever higher toward the pinnacle of pleasure they sought.

Just as he took them over the precipice, Emily cried out, "Jess! Jess! I love you, Jess," then she shattered into a million pieces, heard a thousand violins play in her head, watched as stars glittered like brilliant diamonds before her eyes.

Emily's confession of love touched Jess deeply. He wanted to shout out his own feelings of caring, wanted to tell her how much she meant to him, that he, too, was in love, truly and deeply, for the very first time in his life.

But he knew that to do so would only compound his sin. He wasn't free to declare his feelings. And until he was, he would have to hold them in his heart and hope that his actions spoke much louder than the words he couldn't voice.

They awoke a few hours later to find that a heavy snow was falling and had already blanketed the ground.

Jess frowned as he gazed out the window. Only hours before he had vowed never to hurt Emily. She'd entrusted him with her most precious gift, and in return he had given only deceit. When she'd cried out her love for him, he hadn't been able to respond in kind, and his deafening silence had tortured him.

As soon as they returned, he intended to rectify matters by telegraphing the Pinkerton Agency and insisting that they renew their efforts to locate his wife. No matter the cost, he had to find Nora and put an end to their farce of a marriage. When he was free to marry again, then he would tell Emily that he loved her.

Turning from the window, he gazed at her shivering beneath the thin blanket. "We won't be going anywhere for a while, Emily Jean. Not until this storm abates." Emily wasn't an experienced enough rider to handle the treacherous conditions, and he couldn't risk having her fall off the horse. "It looks like we'll be spending the night here."

Staring at Jess's naked muscular backside, Emily couldn't muster up too much disappointment. Making love with him had been the most wonderfully fulfilling experience of her life.

It had bothered her when she had declared her love for him and he hadn't responded. But she was determined not to dwell on it. In time, she hoped his feelings for her would change. Until then she would be content to wait and enjoy the time they had together.

Pasting on a smile, she finally replied, "Really? Gee, that's too bad. I wonder how we'll occupy our time till then."

He hurried back to bed, and Emily screeched when his cold feet touched hers, sending shivers up her spine. "You've become a wicked woman, Emily Jean Bartlett. What will your legion of fans think when they discover the truth about you?"

"Well, considering that they think I'm a man, I guess they're going to be pretty darn shocked."

Chuckling, he drew her warm body to him. "Even though we've got time to kill, we won't be making love again for a while. You're going to be sore, and I don't want to make it uncomfortable for you."

She stroked his stubbled cheek and felt grateful for his consideration. In truth she was a bit tender, but it had been a small price to pay for the exquisite way he made her feel. "Being naked and in bed with you is already making me pretty darn uncomfortable," Emily admitted. Then she added, "But since we're not going to indulge in any more lovemaking for the time being, what do you say we continue our interview?"

He groaned at the suggestion. "I thought I told you everything you needed to know."

"We've barely scratched the surface, Jess. For instance, you've never really explained what it was like traveling with the Wild West show, about working for Buffalo Bill Cody."

"What's there to tell? Bill Cody's a consummate showman. He loves the limelight, is a bit taken with himself, but his heart's always been in the right place. And he always treated those who worked for him with respect and generosity."

"I saw you perform once. I was awed by the spectacle."

"That was the whole point of the show, Emily. Bill figured that easterners were dying to see real live Indians and cowboys, and that they would pay good money to do so. He recognized the immense popularity of his dime novels, knew that the public hungered for the western experience, and he was right on the money. The show is a huge success."

"Do you know Annie Oakley?" Emily's eyes grew wide with wonder as she waited for him to answer, and Jess fought the urge to smile at her childlike enthusiasm.

"Annie's real name is Phoebe Anne Mozee. She started hunting game to feed her family when she was nine and has developed into the best damn rifle shot I've ever seen, far better than me. She can split a playing card from thirty paces, and she makes it look damn easy. I expect she'll stay with the show a right good while. Annie loves performing."

"Did you love performing?"

He shrugged. "At first when Bill asked me to join the show I said no. But then I got to thinking about the money I could make. I needed the money to buy this ranch, so the idea became more palatable. I'd done a lot of things in my lifetime, jobs that kept me traveling from town to town, with no real roots, and I had a hankering to settle down. But I never had any desire to exploit myself like I did."

"You gave the people who attended those shows real enjoyment, Jess. A chance to view the Wild West without actually going there."

"I guess. But it all seemed so phony. We were giving folks an idealized version of what cowboys and Indians were like. There wasn't much truth in it. The Wild West show was kind of like those dime novels you write—mostly fabrication based on truth with no real substance."

Emily couldn't help but feel insulted, though she knew that wasn't his intention. Jess's view of things was just different from hers. "Popular fiction has been around since Shakespeare's time, probably even before that. If readers get enjoyment out of living vicariously through the pages of a book, or viewers get the same thrill by watching a Wild West show, then what harm's been done?"

Frowning deeply, he said, "I'll tell you what harm's been done. The Indians who perform with the show are depicted as bloodthirsty savages who plunder wagon trains, scalp people, and murder innocent women and children.

It's hardly the truth, and it's made folks scared of them. Cody would have been closer to the truth had he featured the U.S. Cavalry in their place."

Pain etched his face, and Emily sensed that Jess was reliving another unpleasant memory. She placed her hand on his arm. "Neither one of us can be responsible for the wickedness of the human race. But if we can make it better through our words and deeds, then we have a responsibility to do so.

"If you've read my books, then you know that justice always prevails, that good always triumphs over evil. Maybe it's not the truth, the way it really is, but I like to think that it's the way it should and will be one day."

He stroked her cheek, wishing he had her unfailing optimism. "I guess I've seen too much ugliness in my life, been a part of it, and I don't want it glorified."

"The Bible says that 'the truth shall make us free.' Think about it. And when you're done thinking about it, you can kiss me. Because I'm tired of talking and we're wasting a wonderful opportunity to be together."

"Now that's one truth I'm likely to believe," he said before covering her body with his own.

Frosty threw his weight against the kitchen door to shut it, then stomped his feet on the rag rug to rid his boots of the powdery snow. The storm was blowing like a son of a bitch, and there were no signs that it would let up any time soon.

Frances frowned at the wet puddle forming on her newly waxed floor, biting back words of chastisement. She was actually quite relieved to see the old man this night. "Thank God ye've come, Mr. Adams! I've been worried sick about Emily and Jess. 'Tis pitch black out and they're nae home yet."

"And here I thought you was missing me and glad to see me, Fanny girl."

He winked, and a soft blush crossed her cheeks. There was more truth to his words than not. "Ye musna be tae full o' yerself, Frosty Adams. I've got more important matters tae think about at the moment. There's a blizzard brewing out there in case ye havena noticed, and Jess and Emily havena come back from their ride."

Eyeing the apple pie sitting on the table, Frosty smacked his lips. "I surely could use a cup of hot coffee and a piece of that pie, Fan. I'm a mite cold and need some warming up." Though he'd much prefer her arms about him, if he had his druthers.

"How can ye be thinking o' eating at a time like this, Mr. Adams? The people we love and care about could be stranded in this storm, dyin' even." She wrung her hands nervously. "And what are we tae do about the big state-hood celebration? It's tomorrow evening, and Jess has volunteered tae help decorate the Town Hall."

"Jess isn't going to risk his life or that of Miss Emily's by trying to get back here tonight, Fan. I've known the boy long enough to know that he'll stay put until the storm breaks. And if that's tomorrow, then he'll be back. You're frettin' for no reason."

Not the least bit comforted by his words, she never-theless cut two slices of pie, poured coffee into the mugs, and set Frosty's portion in front of him. "'Tis nae just the weather or the party that I'm worried about. I think ye know what else is bothering me. It's nae right fer Emily tae be spending the night alone wie Jess. She's an unmarried woman who'll surely hae her reputation compromised by morning."

"I figure Jess'll do what's right. There ain't no sense in us worrying ourselves to death over what we can't control."

Her lips pinched in disapproval, and she shook her head. "Ye know he canna do right by Emily, Mr. Adams. Jess is already promised tae another, and that's nae changed tae the best of my knowledge."

Frosty thought it was a waste of a perfectly good blizzard to be chewing the fat about Jess and Emily when he and Frances could be setting off a few sparks of their own right here in the kitchen. He sure had a strong hankering to kiss her. Reaching for her hand, he felt encouraged when she didn't pull back.

"Jess's wife hasn't been seen or heard from since Zach was a baby, Fan. It's likely she's dead or long gone by now. I think she would have come back to see the child if that wasn't the case."

The older woman heaved a sigh, her look still filled with uncertainty. "Ye could be right. I never understood how the woman could abandon such a fine mon like Jess. And Zach . . ." She shook her head. "The wee lad's a pure delight, that's fer certain."

Frances Ferguson had never had the displeasure of meeting Nora Murdock, or she would have understood as clearly as Frosty that Jess's wife was a selfish bitch who'd cared more for her own pleasures than her child. He had never liked the snooty woman, had warned Jess about her, but the boy had been smitten by her beauty and sophistication and hadn't heeded his words.

"I know you're worried about Emily, but you mustn't be. She's a grown woman with a mind of her own. Nothing's going to happen between her and Jess that she doesn't want to happen."

"But she loves him, Mr. . . . Frosty. I can see it in her eyes, hear it in her voice every time she speaks o' him. A woman thinks differently about these things than a mon. A woman thinks of marriage and settling down, about making a home and sharing a life, having wee ones tae care fer. A woman in love isna likely tae be thinking o' the consequences o' her actions. She'll be thinking wie her heart and nae her head."

Worry filled the old man's eyes, mirroring Frances's own. Though Frosty loved Jess like a son, he wouldn't be forgiving if he hurt Emily in any way. The kind woman deserved better, and he wasn't entirely certain that Jess would tell her about his marriage to Nora. Men tended to think about the immediate moment, not about all the permanent things Frances was talking about.

He sought to reassure the concerned woman. "Jess Murdock has always been an honorable man. I'd bet money that he'll come clean with Miss Emily and tell her everything."

Frances wasn't convinced, but she decided to let the matter drop for now and see what developed on the morrow. "And do ye think that they're going tae be all right in this storm? 'Tis snowing like there's no tomorrow." She squeezed his hand. "I'm thinking that ye might be having a bit o' trouble yerself getting back out tae the bunkhouse."

Frosty's mouth opened so wide that the piece of apple pie he was chewing nearly fell onto the plate. It would have taken an awfully dense man not to understand what Fan was getting at, and he'd always prided himself on being sharp as an Indian arrowhead. But now that she'd said the words, made the overture, he wasn't ready to take her up on it, not after hearing her views on what a woman wanted, how a woman felt about giving herself to a man.

For once in his life, Frosty had honorable intentions, and he had no desire to consummate a wedding night before the actual ceremony took place. With all the willpower he possessed, he pushed back his chair and stood.

"I'll be sleeping in the bunkhouse this night, Frances. We'll not be having any hanky-panky between us until we are properly married."

Her eyes round as saucers at his presumption, Frances drew her lips into a thin line as rigid as her spine. "Why, ye daft, old mon! How dare ye be thinkin' that I would give meself to ye like some painted harlot! I was merely going tae offer ye the sofa, so ye didn't freeze yer fool head off."

Realizing his mistake, Frosty crimsoned, and he held out his hands beseechingly, trying to rectify matters. "Frances, darlin'—"

She pointed to the door. "Leave me be, you deranged old mon. I'll nae have ye cast aspersions on me good name and character. I'm a respectable woman, I am. And ye'd do well tae remember that."

As if Satan's handmaiden were on his heels, Frosty beat a hasty retreat out the door, yanking it shut behind him. When she was alone once again Frances burst out laughing.

"The dear old mon is going tae make a wonderful husband," she predicted, wiping away tears of joy with the edge of her apron.

"Ah, Ennis. I hope ye're happy fer me. For I truly am in love."

Chapter Fifteen

Emily and Jess returned to the ranch early the following morning. Jess wore the look of a contented man—most of the day his grin was so wide, you could have driven a cattle herd through it—and Emily's eyes sparkled with love, adoration, and happiness.

Neither Frances, Frosty, nor anyone else on the ranch commented openly on their absence. Speculation was rife about what had occurred between the two, and gossip had been bandied about the bunkhouse and cookhouse that would have burned Emily's cheeks and infuriated Jess had they heard it.

Thirty minutes before they were to leave for True Love to attend the statehood celebration, Frances Ferguson knocked on Emily's door. Though she'd told herself a hundred times that what Emily and Jess had done, and were likely to do again, was none of her business, she worried just the same that the young woman had bitten off more than she could chew and would eventually get hurt. If she could prevent that from happening, she would.

" 'Tis me, Emily dear," Frances announced before entering. "I've come tae make certain ye're ready fer the journey. And tae remind ye tae wear yer warmest coat. 'Tis deadly cold outside."

Emily swung about, her smile radiating happiness. "I'm dressed and ready to go." She had donned her nicest gown—a navy-and-red plaid taffeta with white lace-trimmed cuffs and collar—and hoped it would be suitable for the occasion.

The housekeeper's smile was filled with admiration. "You look just lovely, lass. I feel like a dowdy brown wren next tae ye."

As it happened, Mrs. Ferguson was stunning in a russet brown satin skirt and ecru lace shirtwaist, and Emily told her so, making the woman's cheeks blush a becoming peach. "I take it that you're going as Frosty's companion, Frances."

"I am. And the old fool had better watch his step.

"But that's nae what I came here tae talk tae ye about, hinny." After closing the door behind her, she stepped forward, looking a bit ill at ease. "I know 'tis none o' me business what ye and the lad do, Emily, but I worry fer ye. I want ye tae be happy."

"I'm deliriously happy, Frances. Please believe that." She took the woman's hands in her own and squeezed them affectionately. "I'm in love for the first time in my life, and it feels wonderful."

"And does the lad share those same sentiments, lass?"

A frown replaced the smile of moments before. "Jess hasn't declared himself yet, but I'm sure he has feelings for me. I know deep in my heart that he cares." She was positive of it. Though he hadn't actually said the words she longed to hear, he had communicated his feelings with every kiss, every caress.

If Jess hadn't declared his love to Emily, then it was likely he hadn't bothered to mention the obstacle standing between them. Frances felt conflicted between her loyalty to the man she loved like a son and her deep feelings of friendship for Emily. She wondered what action she should take to rectify matters. In the end she opted for discretion.

"I'm sure Jess cares for ye, Emily. But sometimes there are things—things that prevent a mon from speaking from his heart."

Emily nodded. "Jess told me some of his past experiences, the heartaches he's endured."

Frances's brow rose at that, for Jess usually guarded his secrets like a rich man hoarded his gold. "And has he told ye about Nora, Zach's mother?" she asked.

"No. He's never mentioned her. And I didn't think it was my place to ask him about his former wife." Though she'd been dying to know what had caused the problems between them, now she wasn't so sure she wanted to be privy to that information. Thinking of Jess with another woman filled her with insecurity and jealousy, emotions that had been totally alien to her before.

"Perhaps 'tis time ye did, lass. Perhaps 'tis time tae ask Jess about Nora Murdock."

The housekeeper's suggestion was shrouded in such mystery that a feeling of foreboding tripped down Emily's spine; but she quickly dismissed it as foolishness. Jess loved her. She was sure of it. And she loved him. And no one, not even the well-meaning Frances Ferguson, could put a pall on that.

Forcing a bright smile, she linked her arm through the older woman's. "Shall we go and make every other woman at the party drool with envy? I know we're going to have the two handsomest escorts."

Despite the sadness behind her eyes, Frances chuckled, and they headed out the door to make the short journey to True Love.

"Well, well, Miss Emily. Don't you look pretty as a picture this evening?"

Her cheeks flushed from dancing, Emily had just paused at the refreshment table to quench her thirst when she recognized the familiar but unwelcome voice of Rusty Doyle. Caught off-guard, she nearly spilled her glass of punch down the front of her gown.

She spun about, her eyes darting around the large hall to find Jess, but he was nowhere in sight. Music played loudly, revelers laughed and carried on, and it would have done her little good to shout. She'd never be heard above the din.

In a voice filled with anger, she said, "What do you want? I believe you've been told to leave me alone, Mr. Doyle."

His gaze roamed over her in an insulting fashion, leaving no doubt as to his intentions. "Seems a shame when a man can't tell a beautiful woman how lovely she looks. And you do look good enough to eat, Miss Emily."

Incensed, she tried to move past him, but he stepped in front to block her path. "Not so fast, sugar. You and me have some unfinished business to attend to."

Fear clutched her throat at the deadly determination she heard in his voice. "I've got nothing more to say to you. Now leave me be."

"You owe me for that information I gave you on Murdock, Emily. We got interrupted the other night. I aim to collect on our bargain."

Searching frantically once more for Jess, Emily finally spotted him across the room, engaged in conversation with a group of men. Her heart sank when she realized that she would not be able to gain his attention.

Rusty followed her gaze and smiled ferally. "I wouldn't cry out for assistance from Murdock. I've got a knife in my boot, and I won't hesitate to use it." She gasped, and he grabbed her arm. "Come with me. I don't want an audience."

"Let go of me, Mr. Doyle, or I will scream so loud everyone in this room will come running." Several of the townsfolk had begun to stare in their direction, and Emily prayed that one of them would report what they'd overheard to Jess or Mrs. Ferguson.

His silver eyes darkened, narrowing dangerously. "I know you've got a soft spot for Murdock's kid. It'd be a real shame if something were to happen to him."

She drew back her hand to slap him, but he grabbed it. "You filthy bastard! How could you even think of harming an innocent child?"

"Nobody will be hurt if you just shut your mouth and do as I say."

Seething with fury, she nodded her acquiescence and allowed him to lead her toward the back door.

"Murdock's a lucky man, Miss Emily. But you should know that he doesn't deserve your love. There are things about him you still aren't privy to. He ain't worth your loyalty. But I won't waste my breath trying to convince you of that. You wouldn't believe me anyway."

When they reached a dark secluded corner of the hall and were out of sight of the other partygoers, he pulled her into him. "I want a few kisses to remind me of what I missed the other night, sugar. Surely you won't deny me that."

Bile rose in Emily's throat when she thought of kissing him again, especially after the wondrous kisses she'd shared with Jess. "Why would you want to kiss a woman who despises you? Don't you have more pride than that?"

"You're Murdock's woman. I can smell him on you. Everyone's talking about how the two of you spent the night together at the line shack. Was he good, Emily? Did he make you cry out when he took you? Or were you disappointed again?" Without giving her a chance to respond, he crushed his lips to hers, thrusting his thick tongue into her mouth and cutting off her breath.

Emily felt violated and sick to her stomach and tried to think of other things, of Jess, but the feel of the man's hands on her breasts, the feel of his hard member against her leg, wasn't easily dismissed.

She struggled hard to escape his hold, but he only held her tighter, pushing himself into her. As his hand moved to unfasten his pants, she was filled with terror and revulsion and brought up her knee in an attempt to injure him, but he pulled back just in time.

"Be glad you missed, sugar." Just then two young boys Emily had never seen before appeared, and Doyle stepped back. When they disappeared, Doyle decided that his luck wasn't going to hold for much longer. He didn't intend to wait around for Murdock to show up.

"Good-bye, sugar. It's been a real pleasure knowing you. I hope someday we meet again to finish what we started." He darted out the back door and was quickly swallowed up by the night.

Emily had to physically restrain herself from vomiting. Leaning her head back against the wall, she took deep breaths, waiting for her anger and nausea to subside, then wiped her face and the touch of him from her.

Save for the boys, no one had seen what had happened. Thank God they'd come when they had or she surely would have been raped. The memory brought tears to her eyes, but she blinked them away. She wouldn't allow Rusty Doyle's evilness to touch her where it counted: in her heart.

Determined to block him from her memory she took several more deep breaths, smoothed down the folds of her dress, and returned to the party.

A few minutes later she found Jess.

"What took you so long?" he asked. "I searched the room but couldn't find you."

She felt light-headed at the prospect of what would have happened had Jess found her again with Doyle. It was likely he would have believed the worst. "I felt warm, so I stepped outside to get a breath of fresh air. Guess all that dancing took its toll."

He squeezed her waist. "You're not complaining, after how hard you and Frances worked to get me to dance, now, are you?"

She shook her head and smiled. "I never would have guessed that a man as big as you could be so light on his feet. You're very talented."

Leaning his head down, he whispered, "I'll be happy to show you just how talented I am later, babe, but right now our esteemed mayor is getting ready to talk."

"I think we've set enough tongues wagging for one day, don't you?" she reminded him. "I'd like to keep whatever's left of my reputation."

All traces of teasing gone, Jess gave her a pensive look. "Emily, there are some things—"

As the mayor began his speech, the crowd cheered enthusiastically, and Jess was unable to tell Emily all the things she needed to know, like how much he loved her, wanted to marry her, and would, as soon as he could get a divorce from his wife.

He was conscious of the fact that her reputation had been besmirched by their night in the line shack, and he didn't want her to suffer for what had been a glorious time between them.

He had never thought to love a woman again. Never believed he could trust again. But Emily had changed all that. He'd realized after making love to her that he wanted to go on making love to her for the rest of his life. He wanted to live all the rest of his days with her by his side. And he wanted no more secrets between them.

Emily was laughing at something Mayor Dandy said, and her smile jolted his heart like ten volts of electricity. She was beautiful and kind. All the attributes Frosty had expounded upon about her were true.

Looking across the crowded room, Jess found his foreman staring adoringly at Frances Ferguson, and he smiled. The woman was obviously equally as smitten, for she was looking at Frosty as if he were the only man in the room. The two lovebirds were likely to tie the knot before him, and Jess felt envious at the prospect. But he also felt great joy, for he loved them both and wanted to see them happy.

Emily tugged on his coat sleeve. "What are you grinning at? You haven't heard one word the mayor's said."

"I think Frosty and Frances are falling in love."

Her smile full of forbearance, Emily shook her head. "Are you always the last to know about matters of the heart, Mr. Murdock? Ye must be blind, mon," she quipped, using a dose of Mrs. Ferguson's Scottish brogue.

Jess laughed. "Aye. But I hae me eyes opened by a little spit o' a lass," he mimicked, adding, "How about meeting me in my office after everyone's gone to bed tonight? There's something I want to tell you." He wouldn't confess about Nora just yet. He knew how important fidelity was to Emily, and he feared the truth would destroy what had blossomed between them.

Not long ago he had overheard Emily talking to Frances, reassuring the older woman that her love for Frosty wasn't a betrayal of her love for her first husband.

She had stated unequivocally how important fidelity was between two people, how the sanctity of marriage could be severed only by the death of one's spouse and that Frances was free to love again.

Emily would hate him if she knew he was still married. Nora was still very much alive, as far as he knew.

But though he couldn't tell Emily about his wife, he intended to tell her just how much he loved her.

Emily's heart raced, beating in time to the kettledrum that was sounding out the news of Montana's new statehood. Jess was planning to confess his love for her, she just knew it, and nothing would keep her from hearing him out this night.

"I'll be there," she whispered.

The office was dark when Emily entered a few hours later. Only the flames from the burning fire cast any light into the shrouded room, and it took a moment for her eyes to adjust.

"Come over here to the sofa." Jess's soft but compelling voice came out of the darkness, and she followed it. "I hope you're naked beneath that robe," he said.

Her cheeks warmed, and she swallowed, feeling utterly wanton. "I am."

With a low growl, he reached for her and drew her down on his lap. "God, woman! You excite the hell out of me. I feel like an untried youth who's about to lose his virginity."

The writer's curiosity within her was strong, forcing her to ask, "When did you lose your virginity? I mean, how old were you, and who was the lucky woman?"

"Don't you know it's not polite to ask a man those kinds of questions?" He tweaked her nose. "Oh, yeah. I almost forgot. You're a writer, aren't you?"

She playfully punched him in the arm. "Don't try to change the subject. I can be awfully persistent when I put my mind to it." As if he didn't already know.

"I was fifteen. A very charming neighbor lady introduced me to the carnal pleasures while her husband was off selling pots and pans. She lured me to her house with the promise of milk and cookies, but she gave me other treats as well." He grinned at the memory, though there had been nothing funny about it at the time. His first experience had been awkward but damn exciting. Stella Thornton had bared her large, pendulous breasts, placed an experienced hand on his privates, and led him into manhood.

He'd heard that she'd eventually died of a venereal disease, which came as no surprise, considering her proclivity for anything in pants.

Emily's eyes widened. "You had sex with a married woman? That's awful! Why, you should be ashamed of yourself, Jess Murdock. The Bible cautions us against—"

Her words confirmed his worst fears. Unwilling to discuss a topic that was hitting a little too close to home, Jess covered her mouth with his to silence the lecture he knew would be forthcoming.

Emily soon lost herself in his kisses and caresses, and all thoughts of the Bible and adultery fled. "Oh, Jess," she confessed, snuggling in his arms like a contented kitten, "I could stay like this forever. I find such comfort and joy in your arms."

Holding her face between his hands, he looked deep into her lovely blue eyes and his heart constricted. "I love you, Emily Jean Bartlett. I think I have from the first moment I laid eyes on you, rolling around on the floor with Zach. Being with you, loving you, has made me whole and the happiest man alive."

Tears filled her eyes, and she threw her arms about his neck. "I love you, too, Jess. So much that it hurts."

He lowered her beneath him and proceeded to show her just how much his words meant. "You're truly beautiful," he whispered, opening her robe and baring her body to his view.

He trailed his tongue from her lips down her chest to her navel, lapped at the indention, then moved lower to sip at the bud of her femininity.

Emily's blood heated instantly, and she flooded with wet warmth, throbbing everywhere Jess's lips and hands touched. "Take me, Jess. Take me now," she insisted. "I can't wait."

He left her only long enough to remove his pants, then knelt before her, lifted her buttocks, and plunged into the hot depths, smothering her cries of passion with his mouth.

With frenzied pumping motions they reached the peak in a matter of moments, climaxing together. When they were sated and breathing normally again, Jess brushed back the damp, matted hairs from Emily's face.

"You're mine, Emily. Now and forever."

A lump caught in Emily's throat. She waited for him to propose, to ask the question that would bind them together for all eternity—"forever" meant marriage in her books—but the words didn't come, and she was disappointed.

Unwilling to spoil the treasured moment by saying something that she might regret later, Emily held her tongue and caressed his cheek with her hand.

Jess would propose in his own time and in his own way. She was sure of it. And until he did, she would be content to know that he loved her and wanted her with him forever.

Chapter Sixteen

EMILY PUT THE FINISHING TOUCHES ON THE TENTH chapter of Jess's biography, gathered up the manuscript pages into a neat pile, and smiled happily to herself. There was something about loving a man that gave her inspiration. The book was coming along quite well, and she'd soon be able to send it off to meet her publication deadline. Max would be ecstatic; she would be relieved.

Jess Murdock: Legend of the West was going to be a huge success. She could feel it in her bones. Wise Publishing would be saved, and she, Jess, and Zach would become a family and live happily ever after, just like the characters in her novels.

Emily sighed, realizing that she'd never been as happy as she was right now. Not even when she'd attained her lifelong dream of a writing career. Penning books for Wise Publishing didn't compare to the euphoric feeling of being in love.

Smiling blissfully, she hurried down the stairs and was about to enter the kitchen when Frosty burst through the front door, shouting for Jess. Alarmed at the anger she heard in his voice, she spun on her heel and went in that direction to investigate.

Jess emerged from his office, as did Mrs. Ferguson and Zach from the kitchen, to see what all the commotion was about. They descended on Frosty at the same time Emily did.

"We've lost over a hundred head of cattle, Jess," the old man announced breathlessly, his face red from running. "And Doyle's gone. Cleared out his gear and disappeared sometime last night while we was gone to the celebration. I suspect it was him all along that's been doing the rustling."

"Son of a bitch!" Jess shook his head, silently berating himself for his blindness and stupidity. He'd always disliked Doyle, had never fully trusted him. He should have known that something was up, especially after the way the bastard had behaved with Emily.

At the news, Emily's face paled as she recalled the cowboy's words of farewell: "Good-bye, sugar. It's been a real pleasure knowing you. . . ." Rusty had told her he was leaving last evening, but in her anger and revulsion she'd dismissed his good-bye. And she hadn't told Jess of his presence at the party, either. If she had, what had happened might have been prevented.

Hoping to rectify that error now, even at the expense of Jess's wrath, she cleared her throat nervously and said, "I—I saw Doyle at the party last night."

Jess turned to look at her, and his eyes widened in surprise. "You didn't say anything to me about him being there, Emily."

"I didn't want to upset you. He said if I tried to gain your attention to let you know he was there, he would harm Zach. I couldn't risk that, knowing what type of person he is."

Despite the fact that he was filled with rage at Doyle's threat to harm his son, Jess held his temper in check. "Did Doyle happen to say where he was going? Give any hint of where we could find him?" He suspected the bastard was headed to Canada, where there was a ready market for beef and eager buyers were likely to ignore altered brands. Profit usually outweighed principles, and Doyle knew it, having been around the cattle business long enough.

Emily shook her head. "No. But I don't think he's working alone." She explained about the man she had seen in the barn a few weeks back—the one who wore the distinctive pearl-handled pistol. "I was suspicious, but when I questioned Rusty about him he said it was one of your neighbors, a man by the name of Tim Little."

A knowing look crossed Frances's face. "So that's why you asked me about Tim Little."

"Doyle said Mr. Little came here to buy horses. Mrs. Ferguson confirmed that there was such a person, so I didn't think any more about it. I assumed he'd been telling me the truth."

"Tim Little doesn't wear a sidearm. He carries a repeating rifle. And Doyle rarely ever told the truth about anything," Jess stated.

Frosty nodded in agreement. "'Fraid that's so. The man's slimy as a snake. I shoulda figured it was him. Guess he fooled us all."

"There's more." Emily swallowed hard at Jess's savage expression and waited while he ushered everyone into the front room, except Zach, who was sent to his bedroom to study.

Watching as Jess paced impatiently back and forth across the room, Emily felt the knot in her stomach tighten. After seating herself on the sofa, she clutched the housekeeper's hand in her own and began her narrative. "When I first arrived here at the ranch I told you that I had been robbed of my money."

"That's right, lass, ye did," Mrs. Ferguson confirmed with a nod.

Jess remained silent.

"The man who robbed me had a pearl-handled gun similar to the one I saw the man in the barn wearing. His partner in crime, a man by the name of Slim, referred to him as El Lobo."

Frosty's mouth fell open, then a shrill whistle flew from his lips. "El Lobo! I haven't heard about that bastard in years. I thought he was dead and buried by now."

Jess's eyes turned into chips of blue ice. "Go on."

"I didn't see the man's face the day of the robbery. He wore a bandanna. But I heard him speak. His accent was definitely Spanish or Mexican."

"Did he hurt you?"

Emily shook her head. "No. He scared me, though. He made threats, ugly ones." Her cheeks crimsoned as the memories flooded back. "But he didn't act on any of them. There was a posse on his heels; he didn't want to waste the time."

"Goddamn! I bet Doyle's been using the line shack for his meetings with the Mexican bandit." Jess spoke his thoughts aloud, voicing the suspicions he'd had since seeing the rumpled bed the day he'd brought Emily there.

He turned to his foreman. "Have the men saddle up. We're going after the wily bastards."

Horrified at the prospect, Emily jumped to her feet. "You can't do that, Jess! They've got guns. They might kill you. The cows you lost aren't worth your life."

He looked at her as if she'd lost her mind. "I've got no life without those cows, woman. And I'll not run from a fight. That's not my way. You should know that better than anyone, after all the research you've done on me."

"Then I'll go with you. It's my fault that Doyle got away."

Jess shook his head in disbelief. "You can barely sit a horse, Emily. I practically had to tie you on Caesar's back when you rode home from the line shack the other day. Now quit wasting my time with these ridiculous suggestions. I've got to go."

A stricken look crossed the young woman's face, bringing all of Frances Ferguson's protective instincts to the forefront. "'Tis plain tae see that the lass is worried about ye, Jess. There's no need tae take offense or be rude tae her."

His anger over Doyle had made his words harsh, and Jess sought to make amends, drawing Emily into his arms. "I'm sorry, Emily. But you know what I've got to do. You mustn't worry. I'll be back before you know it. And while

I'm gone I'd like you to take care of Zach for me. Will you do that?"

Tears filled her eyes, and she nodded. "Of course. But how long will you be gone?"

"As long as it takes, babe." He kissed her gently on the lips, and then he was gone.

Emily wept softly into her hands, and Frances came forward to wrap a comforting arm about her. "Ye musna cry, lass. It willna do ye any good. 'Tis the way o' things out here. And if ye're going tae be staying, which I'm certain ye are, than ye've got tae learn tae make the best o' it. 'Buck up,' as my dear Frosty is so fond of saying."

"I could have stopped Doyle, Frances, but I didn't want Jess to know that he had assaulted me at the party."

The older woman gasped, and Emily sought to reassure her. "It was a kiss, nothing more, but he made me feel dirty. I didn't want Jess to confront him, so I kept the incident to myself. I should have said something. That makes me responsible if anything happens to Jess."

"Ye're a foolish girl, Emily Jean, tae be thinkin' like that. Under the circumstances, what ye did was probably wise. And nothing's going tae happen tae Jess or tae Frosty, fer that matter. They've been fighting the fight longer than ye've been born, and they know what they're about.

"Now let's go get us a cup of hot tea and see what the wee lad is up tae. He's been tae quiet, if ye ask me. And that never bodes well."

* * *

Zach was dozing fitfully when Emily checked on him half an hour later. She grew immediately concerned, for it wasn't like the rambunctious child to be sleeping in the middle of the day.

Standing by his bed, she noted that his face was flushed. She felt his cheek to discover that he was burning up with fever, and a feeling of dread consumed her.

At her gentle touch, Zach's eyes opened. They were brightly glazed. "I don't feel good, Miss Emily. My throat hurts, and I'm hot."

The child was still fully dressed down to his small stack-heeled boots. "Let's get you out of those clothes and into your pajamas so you can rest more comfortably, sweetheart." She helped him to undress, fetched his night-clothes, then handed him a glass of water. "Drink this, Zach. I want you to drink lots of water."

"How come? I'm not thirsty and my throat hurts."

His high fever would likely dehydrate him, but she doubted he'd understand such a complicated term. Her younger brother had suffered from throat infections, colds, and other childhood maladies, and Emily had always been instrumental in nursing him back to health. Her mother had been useless in stressful situations, especially when her children were involved.

"You just do what I say, all right? I'm going to ask Mrs. Ferguson to prepare some chicken broth for you to eat, for when you're feeling better. I'll be right back."

He reached out for her, clasping her hand in his small one. "I love you, Miss Emily. I want you to be my mommy. Will you?"

A lump formed in her throat, and she caressed his soft cheek. "I'd like that, Zach, but first I'll have to talk it over with your father. Okay?" She didn't know if Jess would find the idea quite as appealing as she did.

"Papa likes you. He told me so. I think he wants to kiss you sometime."

She smiled softly. "Well, that's just too bad, because I'm saving all my kisses for you, Zachary Murdock." She bussed him on the forehead, noting again how hot he felt, and hurried to fetch the housekeeper, who confirmed her worst fears a few minutes later.

Examining the young patient, Frances *tsk*ed several times, then declared, "The lad's got a putrid throat. I'm worried fer him. I dinna like the feel o' his skin. He's tae hot."

"When my brother ran a high fever the doctor said to stick him into a bathtub of tepid water. It helps to draw out the heat and bring down the fever." Knowing that high fevers could sometimes cause a body to convulse, Emily was determined to prevent that eventuality.

"I'll go fill the tub while ye ready the boy," Frances said.

Emily and Frances took turns bathing Zach over a period of several hours. His fever subsided for a time, but then shot right back up, and both women were at a loss as to what they should do.

"I could ride into town and fetch the doctor," Emily offered, her face a mask of worry as she stared at the sleeping child. If anything happened to Zach, she would never forgive herself. And neither would Jess, who had asked her specifically to care for his son.

Mrs. Ferguson's horrified expression said more clearly than words what she thought of Emily's ridiculous suggestion. "Jess was right about yer riding capabilities, lass. Ye're nae going anywhere on the back of a horse."

"Then I'll take the buckboard."

"In this snow? And as inexperienced with a team as ye are? No, Emily, and that's final. We'll do our best, and the good Lord will help us."

"But what if Zach takes a turn for the worse? What if he doesn't get better?"

"There's no sense fashing over that now. Let's nae borrow trouble till we hae tae. I say we sit tight and wait fer Jess tae return and for Zach tae improve."

But what if neither happened? That was Emily's greatest fear.

Jess had picked up Doyle's and the Mexican's tracks and had been on their trail for hours. As he'd suspected, they were headed to Canada.

Though the outlaws had a good head start, moving cattle in the snow wasn't an easy process, and he felt they'd catch up to them soon. No one was better at tracking than he, except perhaps for Frosty, who was fond of claiming that he could find animal tracks on water.

The snow was still deep from the last storm, making the going slow and arduous. But it also provided an excellent tool for trailing the bastards, for it made it almost impossible for the rustlers to conceal their tracks.

"The men are tired and hungry, Jess." Frosty pulled up the collar of his sheepskin jacket and tugged down the brim of his hat, trying his damnedest to thaw out his near frozen eyelashes and beard. The frigid wind had been blowing through his aged bones for hours. "We've been pushing hard since this morning. I think it's time we make camp for the night."

Jess gazed at the sky, which was dark and ominous, and he worried that they were in for another bout of nasty weather. If conditions worsened, they might never catch up to the rustlers. "There's still a couple of hours of daylight left. I want to push on. We can't afford to let those bastards get too far ahead of us. No telling who they're planning to hook up with. And if they put those cows on a railway car, we're done for."

"Won't do us much good if we're froze dead before we find them."

Jess took the old man's grumbling in stride. "Hope you ain't getting soft on me, old man. You used to sit in the saddle a hell of a lot longer than this. And you're the only one I hear complaining." A few of the hands chuckled at Jess's remark, and Frosty stiffened ramrod straight.

"I can ride as long as any man. Just don't see the sense in it when we're likely to catch up to them tomorrow."

Wearing the smile of Lucifer, Jess fingered the revolver at his side. "Guess I'm just anxious to hang me a couple of rustlers. Or maybe I'll shoot them and save myself the rope. Or maybe I'll just castrate the two of them for making lewd advances toward Emily."

Eighteen-year-old Billy Parsley, the youngest of the hands, shifted nervously in his saddle. "Uh, how you fixing to go about that, boss? I mean, are you going to do it the same way we castrate the bulls?" His baby face paled at the thought.

Jess and Frosty exchanged amused looks, then Jess assumed a fierce expression as he began spinning his tale. "I'm gonna get me a knife about yea big." He held his hands apart about eight inches, and the boy's eyes widened to the size of silver dollars. "Then I'm going to string up the bastards, like sides of beef hanging in a butcher store, and strip 'em naked. Then I'm gonna take that sharp, long-bladed knife and—" Before Jess could finish, Billy fainted and fell off his horse and into the snow with a soft thud.

Frosty chuckled. "A boy his age don't like to think about having his privates messed with."

The other cowboys laughed, except Jess, who merely shook his head in disgust and said, "Guess we'll be making camp here for the night."

Having consulted Frances's copy of *Dr. Chase's Recipes,* Emily and the housekeeper had tried various concoctions the doctor had recommended for sore throats.

One of them appeared to be working. Zach's fever had broken during the night, and he was resting more comfortably, much to Emily's great relief.

She had passed the night in a chair by his bed. This morning her back felt stiff and sore, as if she'd been riding horseback for days on end. Trying to ease the stiffness from it with the palm of her hand, she stared out the window toward the hills beyond and wondered where Jess was and if he was still alive.

A steady snow was falling, which she knew would make his journey treacherous and far more difficult. Knowing as well that Doyle and El Lobo were vicious men who would stop at nothing to get what they wanted, Emily's apprehension grew more acute with every passing hour.

"Mommy, I'm hungry."

At the sound of the child's voice, she spun from the window to find Zach sitting up in bed, looking quite well for someone who'd been out of his head with fever just a short time ago. Silently thanking the Lord for making children so resilient, she moved toward him.

"You're looking much better today, young man." She felt his forehead to find that he was cool. "I don't mind telling you, Zachary Murdock, that you had me and Mrs. Ferguson awfully worried."

"I'm hungry, Mommy. Can I have something to eat?"

He had called her "Mommy" again, which under the present circumstances Emily didn't think was a very good idea. Jess was likely to think she had overstepped her bounds and put the child up to it.

Sitting on the edge of the bed, she took Zach's small hand in her own. "Of course you can have something to eat, sweetheart. But I'm not sure it's a good idea if you call me Mommy. Your father may not like it."

He considered her words, then asked, "Do you mind?"

She shook her head. "No. Of course not. But—"

"Then I'm going to call you Mommy 'cause that's what I want you to be."

As Emily had discovered over the past couple of days while nursing Zach, being a mother entailed a lot more than bestowing sweet kisses and reading bedtime stories. There was a wealth of worry, of figuring out the best thing to do, when it came to taking care of a child.

She wondered if she would make a good parent, if she ever got the chance.

Emily also had her career to think about. She'd worked long and hard to establish herself as a writer, loved what she was doing, and wasn't sure she'd be able to toss it all away to devote herself to being a full-time wife and mother.

And she knew that both Jess and Zach deserved that kind of commitment. Especially Zach, who'd been deprived of having a mother, save for Mrs. Ferguson, these many years.

It was obvious the child longed for someone who could fill that void in his life. She'd seen the yearning in his eyes when they'd read stories of families, of mother's hugging their babies to their breasts and loving them, of children who had brothers and sisters to play with.

Zach needed all that and more, but Emily wasn't certain that she was the one who could give it to him. And even if she could, she wasn't certain that Jess had that role in mind for her.

The subject of marriage hadn't been broached, but Emily wasn't about to settle for anything less.

* * *

Jess stood in his stirrups to peer down at the valley below through his binoculars. The moon reflecting off the snow in the predawn darkness illuminated the surrounding area, and he could make out the quiet camp and his herd of cattle huddled nearby.

"We've got the bastards," he told his foreman. "Have the men fan out. We'll take them by surprise. The sleeping fools will never know what hit 'em. Don't aim to kill unless you have to."

"How many men you figure they got?" Frosty asked. There were eight hands from the Bar JM, counting Billy. But the old man would just as soon leave the boy behind, and he told Jess as much. "Billy's green as a grasshopper. Let's leave him out of the fracas."

Jess nodded in agreement. "There aren't many. I counted four, maybe five. The odds are even, and we've got the element of surprise on our side."

A grin split the old cowhand's face, then he spat a wad of chewing tobacco into the pristine snow, leaving an ugly brown glob to mark where he'd been. "Then what are we waiting for? Let's ride."

Following Jess's lead, the men of the Bar JM rode down upon the camp, guns blazing and whooping like a band of Comanche on the warpath.

"Holy shit!" Doyle shouted at the sight of the riders approaching. "It's Murdock! Mount up! Mount up!" But the warning came too late. Murdock's men were already descending upon them, leaving no room for Doyle to escape.

El Lobo's eyes narrowed, and his hatred spewed forth at the sight of Jess Murdock's approach. "We are outnumbered and outgunned, you stupid bastard!" he told Doyle while mounting his horse. "I will not wait to die with you."

Doyle panicked, and his voice turned pleading. "Don't leave me, Juan. What about the cows? You said you needed them."

The Mexican's laughter was sinister. "I need my life more, *amigo*. But do not worry. I will not let your death go unavenged. I will kill Murdock if it's the last thing I do."

Rusty Doyle watched his compatriot ride off into the darkness, his hope for riches and a life of ease gone, just as Jess leaped off his horse and tackled him to the ground.

"You filthy scum! I'm going to kill you for what you did." Jess's fist plowed into Doyle's stomach, then connected with his jaw. Blood spurted everywhere, and the cowhand begged for mercy.

"I needed the money, Jess," he tried to explain, covering his face against the vicious onslaught. "Surely you can understand how it is for a man. You have everything, while I have nothing."

"I'm not going to kill you for taking the cows, Doyle. I'm going to kill you for threatening my son and for what you tried to do to Emily. I should have done it that night in the barn." But he hadn't believed her cries of innocence, and he would bear that guilt for a long, long time.

Doyle shrank back at the pure animal rage he saw on the rancher's face. "Nothing happened, Jess. I swear. I never did nothing to Emily but kiss her."

Straddling the cowboy, Jess wrapped his large hands around his throat. "You just sealed your fate, you bastard.

I'm going to kill you for kissing her. Emily's mine; no man touches her but me."

"Jess!" Frosty shouted, yanking on the angry man's arm, fearful that he would make good on his threat to kill Doyle. "Leave him be. He ain't worth your trouble. And the law will take care of him."

"He's got a lot to answer for, Frosty." To Doyle he said, "Where's your Mex accomplice? Where's that bastard El Lobo?"

The man's face was starting to purple, and Frosty yanked harder. "Jess! Stop! You're killing him."

Finally the haze of red anger clouding his judgment receded, and Jess nodded, releasing Doyle to his foreman's custody. "Take the scum. I hope never to lay eyes on him again."

A short distance away hidden behind a stand of fir trees, Juan heard Murdock's claim about the pretty woman and knew exactly how he would gain his revenge.

He'd lost a great deal of money today because of Jess Murdock and a considerable amount of credibility with his buyers. It was only fair that Murdock should lose something of equal or greater value, too.

Juan Villalobos vowed to make it so.

Chapter Seventeen

THE BACK DOOR BANGED OPEN AND EMILY SPUN around from the stove, the pot of soup she was stirring for tonight's dinner completely forgotten. Jess stood in the door frame, covered in snow from head to toe, his eyelashes and brows frosted white. He looked weary and dirty, and he smelled of horses, but to Emily he was the answer to her prayers.

"Jess!" she screamed, rushing forward to wrap her arms about him. He laughed, hugged her, then set her from him.

"You're going to soak yourself, Emily. I'm covered with snow. And I don't smell too good at the moment."

"I don't care. I'm just so happy to have you home."

And Jess was happy to be home. He thought of how hard he and Frosty had ridden to get home to Emily and Frances.

Doyle and most of his compatriots, save for El Lobo, who had escaped, had been taken to the nearest town by Jess's men and deposited at the sheriff's office to await trial. Doyle would likely hang for his crime. Rustling, whether it be cattle or horses, was a hanging offense in Montana and elsewhere in the West.

But Jess didn't want to think about Doyle. He wanted to be with Emily, to kiss her, to wrap his arms around her and tell her how much he loved her. He wanted to put the events of the past few days behind him and look ahead to a future that bound them together.

"I guess I don't have to ask if you missed me." He grinned when her cheeks filled with color.

"Just a little. We were running low on firewood, and I had no desire to go out to the woodshed in this horrible weather and cut my own," she tossed back with a teasing grin, then her face sobered. "Zach was ill. But he's much better now."

Jess paused from pulling off his sheepskin jacket and gloves and looked up, his face a mask of worry. "What's the matter with him? Are you sure he's okay? I'll go up and check on him."

"Frances just brought him his lunch. He's doing fine. He had a sore throat and fever, but he's on the mend."

He sighed in relief. If anything had happened to Zach— Jess pushed the unthinkable notion away. "Thanks for taking such good care of him."

"I love him, almost as much as I love his father, so it was no trouble at all."

He pulled her onto his lap. "I love you, too, babe. And as soon as I get cleaned up properly, there's something important that I need to talk to you about." He intended to propose, to explain his past, to present their future.

Emily's heart raced at the prospect of what that might be. "All right."

A loud banging on the front door ensued just then, and Jess and Emily exchanged puzzled looks. "I wonder who that could be," she said. There hadn't been any visitors at the ranch while Jess had been gone, and Emily couldn't imagine why anyone would venture out in such horrible weather.

He shrugged and rose to his feet, taking her with him. "I doubt it's Frosty. He was as eager to see Frances as I was to see you." Glancing out the window, he found the snow still falling down. "Guess we'd better go see. Whoever it is, is likely frozen to their roots."

They walked to the door hand in hand, like young lovers strolling in the park. When they reached it, Jess pulled Emily into his arms and kissed her once again. "I sure as hell missed you, woman!"

She caressed his cheek. "And I you."

The banging grew more insistent, and they both laughed guiltily. Then Jess opened the door, and his eyes widened in surprise.

"Nora!"

"Hello, Jess. It's been a long time."

He blinked several times at the vision in green wool, unable to believe that his wife was standing before him. He'd nearly forgotten how beautiful she was, with her auburn hair and sparkling emerald eyes. But he hadn't forgotten her treachery, and his lips thinned in anger and disgust.

Emily noted the tension between the two and wisely kept her mouth shut, wondering if Jess would invite the woman in or let her freeze to death out in the storm.

After what he'd told her about his former wife, she hoped it was the latter. Especially after discovering that Nora Murdock was an extraordinarily beautiful woman. Emily felt downright dowdy standing next to her.

"Come in before you freeze to death," Jess offered, but there was no welcome in his voice. He slammed the door hard behind her.

The woman smiled at Emily, then held out her hand in introduction. "I'm Nora Murdock, Jess's wife."

Emily stiffened at how the woman referred to herself. She didn't know Nora Murdock, only what Jess had confided about her, and she usually prided herself on giving strangers the benefit of the doubt. But she couldn't stand by and allow this woman to refer to herself as Jess's wife, not after everything that she, Emily, and Jess had shared.

"I know it's none of my business, but don't you mean Jess's former wife? After all, I believe you are divorced."

Nora's smile grew calculating. She turned an amused expression on Jess, who had paled considerably at the young woman's question. "As far as I know, Jess and I are still very much married. It's true I've been gone for a number of years, but we never got around to ending our marriage. Isn't that right, Jess?"

Jess turned to find Emily's accusing glare burning into him like a white hot poker, and his heart sank. "Emily, I—" He halted in midsentence, deciding not to continue the personal discussion in front of Nora.

Adulterer! was the word that came to Emily's mind as she stood staring at Jess's wife, and she grew physically ill.

She had to escape, to get her thoughts together, to lick her wounds like an animal who'd been dealt a deadly blow. "If you'll both excuse me," she said, "I believe I shall adjourn to my room for a while. I have work to do."

Without thinking, Jess started to go after her, but Nora's mocking laughter held him back.

"Really, Jess! How ungallant of you not to have explained everything to the young woman. She's obviously in love with you and believed you to be honorable."

Grasping his wife's arm, he hauled her into the front room. "What the hell do you want, Nora? Haven't you wreaked enough havoc in my life? Why have you come back? Why now?"

Removing her coat and gloves, she moved to stand in front of the fire, holding out her hands to warm them. "That should be obvious. I've come for Zachary. He's my son, after all."

The moment he'd been fearing for years had finally arrived, but rather than the devastation he expected to feel, Jess felt only white hot anger. "You relinquished all rights to *my* son when you ran out on him years ago. Do you really think I would give him to you now?" He laughed bitterly, then poured himself a drink, not bothering to offer her one.

Nora stood her ground. "Zachary is as much my child as yours. I have as much right to see him, be with him, as you do. I am his mother."

He sneered. "You've never been a mother to Zach. A damn cow's got more maternal instinct than you do, Nora.

And I'll never allow you to have control of my son. I raised him, cared for him. We've built a life here."

She looked toward the open doorway where Emily had once stood. "And I see you've found a replacement for me."

"That's none of your business."

"I doubt the court will think so, Jess. Not after I tell them how you and that woman have been living here in sin, without the benefit of marriage. That's not a very good example to set for a small child, now, is it? I doubt the court will find you a very acceptable father."

With great effort, he held on to his temper. He didn't intend to give Nora any ammunition to use against him, should she make good on her threat to take him to court and demand custody. "Miss Bartlett is living here while she writes my biography. She's not my paramour, as you would believe, but an author of some note who's been assigned by her publisher to pen my memoirs."

"I don't believe you."

He shrugged, as if her opinion didn't matter at all. But her threat to take Zach had his stomach tied up in knots. "Ask anyone here on the ranch. They'll all confirm what I've told you."

Nora considered his words, wondered if they were true, and decided that she didn't really care. She had never really loved Jess Murdock, the man. But she had been terribly enamored of Jess Murdock, the Wild West legend— the dashing hero who had been unlike any of the other men of her acquaintance.

Strong, handsome, and considered the catch of the

century, Jess had been the stuff of dreams. Every woman under the age of eighty had wanted him, and Nora had made up her mind after their first meeting to have him.

But the fairy tale had been short-lived. She hadn't bargained on a child, hadn't realized just how stifling and dull marriage could be. Jess had turned out to be a solid family man, a homebody, not the devil-may-care cowboy she'd envisioned.

When she'd been offered the opportunity to leave for Europe with a gentleman friend and escape her drab existence, Nora had jumped at it. She'd been residing there these past five years, enjoying life to the fullest. But her circumstances had taken a turn for the worse, and now she needed help.

"Perhaps I jumped to conclusions," she finally admitted. "But that doesn't mean that I'm not entitled to visit my son while I'm here."

"And what do you propose to tell the child, Nora? That you ran out on him for purely selfish reasons? That you didn't want a child, didn't have any love in your heart for him?"

Jess's words had the power to wound, and she turned a stricken look on him. "I've always loved Zachary. Maybe I wasn't able to cope with motherhood five years ago, but I've changed. I deserve the chance that God intended me to have."

Jess tossed back his head and laughed, but there was no humor in it. "Where the hell did you learn to act? Your performance is quite credible. Unfortunately I know you too well."

Jess's instincts were correct. Nora didn't really want to play the role of mother again. But she was broke, and she believed Jess to be quite wealthy. She had come to Montana to see how much money he'd be willing to pay to obtain a divorce and to keep custody of his son. Judging by his vehement response to her threat to take the child away, she decided he'd be willing to pay quite a tidy sum.

"I'm not leaving until I see my son."

He glanced out the window to find the snowfall unrelenting and knew that his "wife" wouldn't be leaving anytime soon. The accumulation would make travel back to True Love nearly impossible. "You can remain here for the time being, but only because the weather is bad. I wouldn't turn an animal out into this storm, let alone a human being.

"As for Zach . . . I will need to prepare him for your visit. He believes you're dead."

"Dead?" She seemed horrified by the prospect. "You told him I was dead?"

"It seemed the kindest thing to do. Telling a small child that his mother didn't want him seemed cruel and—"

"I understand," she interrupted, unwilling to be reminded of her perfidy once again.

"Good. I'll have my housekeeper fetch you when your room is ready. In the meantime, wait here. I'll go up and see if Zach is feeling well enough for a visit. He's been feeling under the weather, and I don't want to upset him if he's still ill."

Nora nodded, watching Jess walk away and admiring the fact that he was still as handsome as ever. The years had made him even more distinguished, more appealing. And Nora hadn't had a man in her bed in a very long time.

Perhaps she'd been too hasty in her decision to take the money and run. Perhaps she would find something far more valuable than monetary gain in Montana. It was definitely worth considering.

As Nora pondered her options, Emily was in her room trying to decide what course of action she should take.

The inclement weather had made leaving the ranch impossible. And even if she wanted to run away, to forget all about Jess Murdock and his deceitful ways, she had a book to finish and a commitment to Wise Publishing.

She was trapped—by her sense of duty, her integrity, and her love for a married man.

The knock on the door had her bracing herself for the confrontation with Jess she knew would be forthcoming. Her first instinct was to cry, to rail at the heavens and curse the injustice that had been done to her; her second, to rush into Jess's arms and pretend that nothing had changed.

But it had. Everything had changed.

"Please open the door, Emily. I'd like to speak to you." Jess's voice was filled with as much anguish as she felt. She crossed to the door and opened it, then spun on her heel and seated herself on the edge of the bed, folding her arms across her chest.

"Emily, I came to explain—"

She didn't allow him to. "How could you have deceived me so? I would never have—" She couldn't bring herself to say the words. "Had I known you were still married, I would never have entered into a personal relationship with you."

He shut the door and came to stand before her. The sadness in her eyes made his gut wrench. "I never meant to hurt you, Emily. Please believe that. I was planning to explain everything, but Nora showed up unexpectedly and ruined it all."

"Yes, I guess having a wife show up would ruin things between a philanderer and his mistress." *God, am I really somebody's mistress?* It sounded so sordid, so unlike her.

"I don't love Nora, I love you. I would have ended our marriage long ago, but she disappeared without a trace when Zach was a baby, and I never had the opportunity to file for an annulment. In fact, I wasn't entirely certain that she was still alive."

"You should have told me, Jess. I had a right to know."

Kneeling before her, he took her hands in his. "I wanted to, Emily. I wanted to tell you everything. But I was afraid at first. I thought you would use the information against me. Then, when I got to know you better, had fallen in love with you, I thought you would hate me for . . ."

"For making love to me while you were still married to another woman?"

"I admit it was cowardly of me. And I truly regret not telling you everything from the beginning. I love you, Emily. I don't want to lose you. I want to marry you."

The words she had longed to hear now stabbed into her heart like a jagged-edged knife. "You already have a wife. How were you planning to get around that fact?"

"I'd already contacted the Pinkerton Agency and asked them to try to locate Nora. And I'd been making discreet inquiries with some of my former acquaintances in New York. Bill Cody is well connected there. I asked for his help."

The revelation came as a surprise. "So you were planning to find Nora and divorce her?"

He nodded. "I don't love her. I probably never did. I certainly never felt about her the way I feel about you."

The ice around Emily's heart began to melt. She'd been so hurt, so furious that Jess had duped her, but it was hard to stay angry with someone you loved, someone who humbled himself at your feet and begged for forgiveness.

"Nora is Zach's mother. That will never change, even if you divorce her."

Rising, he began to pace the room, his expression suddenly quite agitated. "Nora's threatening to take Zach away from me."

Emily fairly flew off the bed to land on her feet, her face a mask of concern. "Oh, Jess! You can't let that happen. Zach loves you. And this is the only home that child has ever known."

"Don't you think I know that? But she's going to institute a custody battle." He told her of Nora's suspicions concerning their relationship. "I lied and told her that you were merely my biographer, nothing more. I can't allow her to use our relationship against me."

"So, we're to pretend that we're merely business associates?" No one who saw them together was going to believe that. And Nora Murdock did not look naive.

"Nora has a purpose in coming here, and I don't believe it's solely to be reunited with our son. In time she will reveal it. Until then, we must be circumspect."

In time! Just how long was he planning to allow her to stay? Long enough for a reconciliation?

Nora was Zach's mother. And even after everything that had transpired between them, she was still Jess's legal wife, while Emily was merely his mistress. The thought had her temper flaring anew. "You needn't worry that I'm going to throw myself at you again, Jess Murdock. I do not believe in cavorting with a married man, no matter the circumstances."

"Emily." He held out his hands beseechingly, but she would have none of it.

"I have a job to do. When the book is finished, and if things are still not resolved between you and your *wife*, then I shall return to New York, sadder but wiser in my dealings with men."

Her unreasonable attitude galled Jess, and his temper ignited. "Women have been, and always will be, the bane of my existence." With that, he stormed out.

Emily plopped back down on the bed and allowed the tears she'd been holding back to flow. Tomorrow she would be strong once again. Right now she intended to wallow in a great deal of self-pity.

*　　*　　*

Jess went straight from Emily's room to Zach's. His distressing confrontation with Emily still had him reeling, and he wasn't looking forward to a similar discussion with his son. His selfish stupidity and mistrust had caused him to hurt the woman he loved most in the world. Now he feared doing the same thing to Zach.

Entering his son's bedroom, Jess found Zach at the window, staring wistfully out at the snow, no doubt eager to go outside and make snowmen. Zach was an active child who usually rebelled against constraint of any kind.

The child turned when he heard the door close, and his face lit. "Papa!" Zach rushed into his father's arms.

Jess hugged him tightly, and every fatherly instinct he possessed to protect his child came rushing to the forefront. "Emily tells me you've been sick, son. Are you feeling better now?"

The child nodded, then climbed back in bed and pulled the covers up to his chin. "Gran will yell at me if she finds me outta bed. I promised her that I would rest. You won't tell her that I was looking out the window, will you?" He gazed out the window again, and it was clear that keeping his promise to the housekeeper was extremely difficult. "I sure do want to go outside and play," he admitted.

Jess took a seat on the bed and ruffled his son's hair. "You'll be fine in a couple of days, then we'll go outside and make the biggest snowman in the state of Montana."

"Really?" Zach's face brightened instantly. "And can Emily come too? She likes to have fun. I sure do like her, don't you?"

Heaving a sigh, Jess was unsure of just how much to admit. "Yes, son, I do. But—"

"I want Emily to stay here and be my mommy. I told her that you wouldn't mind. Do you think she will?"

His heart aching at the yearning he saw on the little boy's face, Jess cursed inwardly and wished he had never laid eyes on Nora. Of course, then Zach wouldn't have been born, and he would have been deprived of the greatest joy God had seen fit to bestow upon him.

He engulfed the child's small hand in his own and searched his heart for just the right words. "Zach, there's something very important that I've got to tell you."

"About Emily?"

"No, Zach. About your real mother."

Confusion wrinkled the child's brow. "About how she died? I thought you said—"

"Your mother is alive, Zach. I lied when I told you that she had died. I wanted to spare your feelings, so you wouldn't be hurt when you found out that she had left of her own accord."

Zach took a moment to digest his father's words, then asked in a small voice, "How come she didn't want me? How come she left us?"

Jess pulled the boy onto his lap, wishing he could spare Zach the anguish he was feeling—the same anguish he had felt when Nora first abandoned them. "I don't know the answer to that, son. I've asked myself the same thing many times over, but I never could come up with an answer. Maybe she was scared. Having a child is not an easy thing."

"But you didn't run away, Papa. You stayed and hired Gran to help take care of me."

"Not all women are cut out to be mothers, son. Remember last spring when the piglets were born, and the sow wouldn't have anything to do with them?" Zach nodded, and Jess continued. "Well, that sow just didn't think she wanted to be a mother to those baby pigs. Sometimes nature plays tricks on animals, same as it does on people. I guess your mother was one of those people."

"We all took turns feeding the piglets and they survived."

"That's right, Zach. Life goes on. When one door closes another opens. Remember how Reverend Higgbotham is always telling us that?"

The child remained silent for a few moments, allowing Jess the opportunity to plunge ahead and reveal the real reason for his visit. "Your mother is downstairs, son. She wants to come up and meet you. But I told her that the decision would be yours and not hers. If you don't want to talk to her, you don't have to."

Zach started to tremble, and Jess hugged him tighter, wishing with all his heart that he could spare his son this difficult decision. "I told her that you'd been ill and might not be up to having visitors. Why don't you lie back down and think about it? She's going to stay at the ranch until the storm is over."

Despite his fear, Zach's curiosity to meet the mother he had never known overwhelmed him. "I guess I should meet her, since she came all the way here to see me."

Jess was inordinately proud of his son's courage and told him so. "I'll tell her to come up."

As Jess started to rise, Zach grasped his hand. "Nothing's going to change, is it, Papa? We're still going to live here at the ranch? She's not going to take me away from you?"

"No, son. Nothing and no one will ever take you from me. I promise you that." And it would be a promise Jess would keep, no matter what he had to do.

Chapter Eighteen

WHILE JESS, ZACH, AND NORA MET TOGETHER AS A family for the first time in five years, Emily took refuge in the kitchen with Frances Ferguson, wondering the entire time what was going on upstairs.

Frances had been absolutely furious at the news that Nora Murdock had returned to claim her son, and she was still spitting bullets over the recent turn of events. "I canna believe that Jess would allow that woman tae come into this house. 'Tis beyond all common decency that she would ask tae see Zach after everything she did tae those two poor souls.

"I remember when I first came tae work fer Jess. He was sad all o' the time, and it nearly broke my heart. At first, he'd thought some harm had come tae his wife. Then, when he realized she had left o' her own free will, he was devastated." Frances shook her head. "Those two lads have had their share of heartache because of that, that— I'll nae call her what I'm thinking, but a female dog bears the same name."

If she hadn't been so miserable, Emily would have smiled at the housekeeper's vehemence. Frances fancied herself to be a very proper woman, but her Scot's temper had definitely revealed itself since Nora's arrival.

"Do you think Jess was in love with his wife?" Emily had been obsessing over that point, even though he had assured her that he'd never been truly in love with Nora.

Frances shrugged, then set the copper kettle of water on the stove to boil. "I suppose he cared fer her, or he wouldna have married her tae begin wie. But he never said a word tae me about his feelings." Emily's face registered despair, and the older woman added, "Don't ye be thinking that he'll go back tae her, lass. Jess is tae smart fer that. And it's ye he loves now. Ye can be certain o' that."

Emily wished she possessed Mrs. Ferguson's confidence. She wasn't certain of anything at this point, besides the fact that she was still hopelessly in love with Jess. Considering the present circumstances, that wasn't an enviable position to find herself in.

Emily's uncertainty soon magnified when Nora Murdock strolled into the kitchen alone, looking as if she had every right to be there, as if she belonged.

"Hello again," she said to Emily. "Jess tells me that you're a published author who's come to write his life story." She turned to Frances and said in her most imperious voice, "I'd love a cup of hot tea."

The housekeeper was about to tell the bossy woman just what she could do with her demand for tea, but Emily shook her head in warning, then replied, "Yes, I am. I write for Wise Publishing in New York."

The woman's eyebrow arched. "I've heard of them. How is it that a woman can succeed in a profession usually reserved for a man?"

Seating herself at the table across from Zach's mother, Emily wondered how someone so lovely on the outside could be so ugly within. No one who had abandoned a loving child like Zach could be considered anything but ugly, in her opinion. "I'm stubborn, headstrong, and tenacious. I don't give up easily."

"Really?" Nora's smug smile held a great deal of confidence. "Well, neither do I. When I want something I go after it. It seems we have a lot in common."

Emily wondered if Nora had decided to "go after" Jess. She also worried that the woman knew there was more than an author-subject relationship between her and Jess. Emily decided to try to throw her off the track.

"You mentioned that we have a lot in common, Mrs. Murdock. Are you a writer, too?" Though the title "Mrs." stuck in her throat like a rotten grapefruit, Emily knew that if she were to be convincing in her role as Jess's biographer, she would have to play the role to the hilt.

At the question, Nora's high-pitched giggle filled the room. Whereupon Frances set the cup of tea on the table before her and mumbled, "That cat must have wandered in here again," not looking at the woman directly.

Nora's indignant expression made Emily swallow the laughter bubbling up her throat.

"I have no aspirations of working for a living, Miss Bartlett. I'm used to the finer things in life."

"*Hmph!*" came Frances Ferguson's loud response.

"If you don't mind my asking, Mrs. Murdock—writers are a curious lot, as I'm sure you know—where have you been these past five years?"

"In Europe, traveling about from one country to the next. I had a wonderful time. My com . . . companion"— she tripped over the word, and it was obvious that her traveling cohort was more than a friend—"and I saw many interesting and beautiful sights."

The heavy cast-iron skillet came down on the stove with a bang, and Emily nearly jumped out of her seat. Doing her best to ignore Frances, she said, "I'm sure nothing you saw in Europe could compare with Zach. He's such a wonderful child."

Realizing her mistake, Nora hesitated, and her cheeks filled with color. "Yes, of course. My son and I had a delightful chat." Actually, the rude child had spent most of their time together staring out the window. Nora hadn't found him to be wonderful at all, merely petulant and somewhat backward.

"He'll probably want you to go outside and build snowmen with him. Zach does love to play."

"Aye," Mrs. Ferguson said, picking up where Emily left off. "O' course, ye mustna stay outside too long. The lad's a wee bit lax in his bowel habits. I'm always finding meself having tae change his drawers when he messes them. And then there's that disgusting snake he keeps as a pet under his bed."

Her mouth falling open, Nora looked horrified at the prospect of snakes and other distressing childhood matters. "Zachary still wets himself?" she asked.

Not blinking an eye at the outrageous lies she was telling, Frances nodded. "Oh, aye! 'Tis been a trial these many years having tae change his clothes and the bed linens every night, I can tell ye that. I guess since ye're here now ye can take over the chore if ye like."

"I do not like!" Nora rose to her feet so quickly, she nearly upset the cup of tea in front of her. "Excuse me, but I feel a slight headache coming on. I'll just go up to my room and lie down for a while."

"'Tis my room ye'll be sleeping in, miss, and I'll just apologize in advance fer the unpleasant odor ye might encounter. Zach's fond o' sleeping wie me, ye see, and getting the smell out o' that mattress has been nearly impossible."

Paling whiter than Frances Ferguson's apron, Nora Murdock covered her mouth and rushed from the room and up the stairs. As soon as Emily and Frances heard the bedroom door slam shut, they burst into laughter.

"Did ye see her face, lass?" Frances held her sides, rocking back and forth, her eyes brimming with tears of merriment. "I thought she was going tae faint."

Emily grinned from ear to ear. "You're a wicked woman, Frances Ferguson, for letting her believe those awful things about Zach."

"Not as wicked as she is, and that's a fact. Let her have a taste of her own medicine, I say. I'm nae usually unkind tae anyone, but I've decided tae make an exception in this case."

Emily wiped her eyes. "I'm glad you did."

The housekeeper folded her arms across her bosom and with a determined gleam in her eyes said, "She willna stay long. Mark me words."

*   *   *

Emily went to Jess's office later that day on the pretext of asking him a few questions about the book.

She'd given a great deal of thought to his explanation about the circumstances surrounding his wife. She regretted her harsh words of this morning and had decided to give him the benefit of the doubt and make amends. She loved him too much to do otherwise.

Clutching the precious manuscript to her chest, she knocked softly on his door, then entered, pulling up short at the sight of Jess and his wife, heads bent close together, engaged in what appeared to be a heated conversation. Jess was frowning fiercely, Nora looked bereft, and Emily took consolation in both.

"Excuse me," she said when they turned to look at her, trying to tamp down the jealousy she felt at seeing the two together. "I thought Jess was alone."

"Come in, Emily. Nora and I were just discussing *my* son." He'd let the bitch know in no uncertain terms that he would never relinquish control of Zach.

Nora pasted on a smile, unwilling to let Emily know that there was trouble brewing between her and Jess. "Yes. Jess was just regaling me with some of Zach's adventures."

Nora's smile made her appear even lovelier, if that were possible, Emily thought with a great deal of dismay and a small amount of self-pity. "That's nice," she replied without enthusiasm.

"Our son seems to be quite a remarkable child," Nora said to her husband. "But you should do something about his wetting the bed. I don't think it's wise to let something like that go on for too long." She shivered at the distasteful notion, and Jess's brows wrinkled in confusion.

"I wasn't aware—"

"I have a few questions about the book, Jess," Emily interrupted quickly, not wishing to let either parent know that Frances had been fabricating stories about Zach. No doubt Jess would disapprove, and she didn't want the housekeeper to get into trouble. "I hope you can help me."

"I could probably give you some interesting insights into Jess's character, Miss Bartlett." Nora's secretive smile was somewhat seductive. "There are some things only a wife knows about her husband."

Her words implied a great deal of intimacy, and Emily's jealousy manifested into anger. "I wasn't aware that you had been married to Jess long enough to know anything of real importance about him," she retorted, unable to restrain herself despite the warning look in Jess's eyes.

"Sometimes quality outweighs quantity, Miss Bartlett." Jess's wife reached over and touched his arm in an intimate manner, and Emily wanted nothing more than to yank every one of the hussy's hairs out of her head.

"Jess and I had some rather remarkable times in the short span of time we were together, didn't we, darling?"

Noting the hostile look on Emily's face, and not liking the direction in which the discussion was heading, Jess rose to his feet. "If you'll excuse us, Nora, I believe Emily and I need to work on the book. She's on a tight deadline and needs to finish as soon as possible."

Was Jess hoping she would finish the book so she would leave, as she'd foolishly threatened to this morning? Emily wondered, her heart sinking.

Taking her dismissal in stride, Nora rose. "I shall go and visit with my son. We need to get a little better acquainted."

"Perhaps you should let him sit on your lap," Emily tossed out, and there was no shortage of venom in her voice.

Nora gazed down at her emerald green velvet skirt and cringed. "I—I'll keep that in mind."

Jess scratched his head in confusion. "Is there something going on here that I don't know about?" he asked after his wife had left the room. "I'm starting to feel like everyone's in on the joke but me."

Emily feigned innocence. "I'm sure I don't know what you mean."

Recognizing the stubborn set of the woman's chin, Jess knew it was useless to press the matter. "Did you need to ask me something?"

The cloying gardenia scent of Nora's perfume lingered behind, and Emily wrinkled her nose in disgust. "I never did care for gardenias. They remind me of funerals."

Jess smiled inwardly. "You needn't be jealous of Nora. She doesn't hold a candle to you, Emily Jean."

"Perhaps you need glasses. The woman is gorgeous."

"I prefer my woman dark haired, petite, and feisty as all get-out."

"Are you sure you don't love her, Jess? I mean, she's everything I'm not."

"Which is exactly the reason I prefer you." He drew her into his arms, slanting his mouth over hers in an all-consuming kiss. "You're all the woman I will ever need, Emily Jean Bartlett."

Just outside the partially opened door, Nora drew in her breath, eyes hardened in anger as she eavesdropped on their conversation.

Jess had lied to her about his relationship with Emily, just as she had suspected. He was in love with dowdy little Emily Jean Bartlett—a writer of dime novels, no less. The notion that he preferred the writer to her was outrageously pathetic and totally unacceptable.

Nora might not have wanted Jess Murdock for a husband, and she certainly didn't want a sniveling, bedwetting child, but she'd be damned before she'd turn them both over to another woman without a fight. That just wasn't Nora's way at all, as Emily Jean Bartlett would soon find out.

Juan Villalobos stared down at the ranch house from his position atop the rise and lit a cigarette. The smoke rings curled about his head, clouding the frigid afternoon air.

The outlaw had been biding his time until he could exact his revenge against the rancher. Jess Murdock had a lot to answer for as far as Juan was concerned.

The unrelenting snow had made his plan to kill Murdock difficult—hardly anyone had ventured out of the house in days—but Juan was a patient man. He hadn't survived as long as he had without being meticulous in his planning.

Many years ago, when he was just a small child in the poor farming village of Tecate, he had vowed that one day he would become a rich man, never to toil in the harsh sun as his father had. He would make his living off those who exploited the poor—the white Anglos, the rich Americanos.

Juan wasn't remorseful for the nefarious deeds he had executed. His mother had taught him as a young boy that the strongest always survived and the weak were made to serve the strong.

The men he had murdered—and they numbered many—had brought swift justice upon themselves with their foolish show of bravado. The women he'd raped had wanted him, for it was inconceivable to Juan that they would not. He was a handsome, virile man. The money he stole had supported him in style, and he always sent some to his parents back home to make their lives a little easier.

The cows Juan rustled from the rich American ranchers made his life of crime a little less dangerous. He was rarely caught stealing cattle, and it wasn't as if the wealthy Americanos would miss them; they had so many. Banks and stagecoaches were a far more difficult target. The money he plundered often came from people as poor as he once was, and the authorities were relentless in their pursuit to get it back.

He had made a lucrative success out of his life of crime. Business had been going extremely well until Jess Murdock had decided to play hero and rescue his stolen cattle, ruining everything. The buyers Juan had lined up in

Canada had been furious when he couldn't deliver the goods, had canceled their contract, and were now refusing to do any more business with him.

Jess Murdock had made his life very difficult and extremely unhappy. And Juan did not like to be unhappy. He considered himself to be a good-natured, gregarious man who enjoyed life to the fullest. Now Juan would have to pay the rich American rancher back in kind for all the trouble he had caused.

Soon the snow would stop, and the unsuspecting Americanos on the Bar JM would go about their normal routine. Very soon they would let their guard down, giving Juan the opportunity he had waited cold days and frigid nights to take.

Dinner the following evening was a torturous affair for Emily. Nora had dressed in a low-cut gown totally unsuitable for ranch life and had taken a seat at the head of the table, opposite her husband. She had proceeded to monopolize the entire conversation with details of her adventure in Europe.

The foolish woman had given no notice that she was giving offense, not only to Jess, who didn't seem at all pleased to hear what a wonderful time she'd had cavorting about the English and French countryside while married to him, but also to Zach, who was listening to his mother's commentary with nothing short of confusion and heartbreak written on his small face.

Emily's heart went out to the child. "Would you like some more potatoes and gravy, Zach?" she asked, hoping to distract him from his mother's unfeeling treatment. Didn't the stupid woman realize that the child would wonder why she had chosen Europe over him? Or didn't she care? Emily suspected the latter.

"The potatoes are very good, and you've hardly touched your dinner. You're not still feeling sick, are you, sweetheart?"

Zach shook his head. "No, Mommy . . . I mean, Emily." He darted a glance at his real mother.

Nora gasped in outrage, then shot Emily a venomous look. "My son is perfectly fine, Miss Bartlett. You needn't concern yourself with his welfare. I made sure that Zach was feeling all right before I suggested he join us for dinner this evening."

Before Emily could retort, Zach reached over and clasped her hand in a very grown-up fashion. "I'm feeling fine, Emily. I'm just not very hungry tonight. I guess my stomach's not as big as it used to be."

"I bet it's big enough for some of your Gran's pecan pie," she replied, squeezing his hand.

"I don't think it's wise to stuff children with sweets. I read somewhere that it's not at all good for their teeth. And sugar does make a body fat." Nora preened and postured, showing off her figure to its best advantage, implying that she didn't need to worry about such a thing happening to her.

"Zach's lost weight since being ill, Mrs. Murdock. I don't think it'll hurt him to put some of it back on. And his teeth are just fine. He brushes them religiously every night before bed."

"I realize that I may not be the foremost authority on children, Miss Bartlett, but I don't think that you are any better versed in the subject of child care. After all, you're not married, are you?" Nora didn't bother to hide her smirk, and Emily felt heat rise to her throat.

"No. But it takes more than a marriage certificate and a wedding band to make a wife and mother. As I'm sure you are well aware, Mrs. Murdock."

Jess remained silent, watching the exchange between the two women with interest. Nora's jealousy of Emily was somewhat amusing, if not confusing, considering she'd been the one to break off their relationship. But her threats about the custody hearing and Jess's relationship with Emily were not. Emily's protective attitude toward Zach was not at all surprising. She loved his son like her own child and would make a wonderful mother when the time came.

Though he was furious that Nora had intruded in his life, and had disrupted his happy home with Emily, Jess was relieved that he could now institute divorce proceedings and get rid of her.

Unfortunately, that time would not come at all if Nora didn't agree to a divorce. Jess opted for a less confrontational approach, in the hope of placating his so-called wife until he could figure out a way to get rid of her once and for all. "Ladies," he said, smiling apologetically at the woman of his heart, "I don't think arguing about what's best for Zach in front of him is doing anyone, least of all Zach, any good.

"I'm sure you both have his best interests at heart, so let's leave it at that and try to finish our dinner in peace.

Mrs. Ferguson has outdone herself tonight with the pot roast."

Noting the cautious look Jess flashed her, Emily smiled apologetically at Nora, though it was done with a great deal of difficulty. "I'm sorry if I gave offense, Mrs. Murdock. It was not my intention. I was merely concerned about Zach."

Nodding in acceptance, the woman sipped her wine and replied in a most condescending manner, "I realize that you, being of the working class, Miss Bartlett, have not had the benefit of a proper social background, so I accept your apology."

Rather than take the insult as it was meant, Emily threw back her head and laughed, gaining shocked looks from both Nora and Jess and a pleased-as-punch smile from the youngest Murdock. "My mother and father would be terribly insulted to hear you say that, Mrs. Murdock. You see, Marian and Louis Bartlett consider themselves to be part of the social elite of New York City. And, well, my mother would be beside herself with mortification to hear that you thought my social graces were lacking. The poor dear worked terribly hard to make sure that I was up to snuff, so to speak."

Nora's mouth hung open for a moment, then she snapped it shut. "You're part of the New York Bartletts? Why, your family is quite wealthy and extremely well connected. Why on earth are you working for wages?" She couldn't imagine anyone giving up a life of ease to toil like a common laborer. The Bartletts were rich, disgustingly so. Why would Emily Bartlett prefer working to wealth? Montana to New York City? Both choices were simply preposterous.

A smug smile curling her lips, Emily pushed back her chair and stood. "Because I can and choose to do so, Mrs. Murdock. Now, if you'll excuse me, I believe I have several hours of work left to do on the book before I can retire for the evening."

"I'm tired, too, Emily," Zach said, following her lead. "Would you tuck me in bed tonight?"

Emily smiled warmly at the child and held out her hand. "Of course, sweetheart." Although she hated the thought of leaving Jess in Nora's conniving clutches, Emily left the room with Zach in tow.

When they reached his room, Zach climbed on the bed and motioned for Emily to sit down. "Can you stay a minute, Emily? I know you've got lots of work to do, but I sure do miss you. We haven't been together much lately."

"I know, Zach, but I thought you should have a chance to get to know your mother without outside interference."

He nodded, not looking at all pleased about the situation. "That's what I figured. But she's not as much fun as you."

The last thing Emily wanted to do was come between mother and child. That wouldn't be fair to either. "Now, Zach. I'm sure—"

"I asked my real mommy to play soldiers with me, the way you do, but she said that ladies don't sit on the floor."

Emily bit the inside of her cheek. "She's probably right, sweetheart. It's not really very ladylike."

"Then I asked her to read me a story, but she said that it would do me more good to read it myself, so I wouldn't grow up to be stupid and dependent on others."

Her eyes narrowing, she caressed his cheek. "Nora's not very experienced with children, Zach. I'm sure that in time—"

"I know she's my real mommy, but I don't like her much. She's not any fun, and she doesn't really love me. Not like Papa does, or Gran, or even you."

Emily wrapped her arms about the small boy. Children were awfully perceptive. Nora was not a warm person. Obviously her reserved demeanor had come through loud and clear to Zach. But Emily needed to make the child understand that love between him and his mother would come in time. It had to. For Zach's sake.

"Sweetheart, you mustn't think such things," she tried to explain, but Zach would not be mollified or persuaded to think otherwise. Heaving a sigh, Emily tucked him under his covers, kissed his cheek, and decided to go back downstairs and have a talk with Nora.

Perhaps if she explained how the child felt, Nora might be able to rectify matters before permanent damage was done.

Emily hoped it wasn't already too late.

Chapter Nineteen

NORA HAD PURPOSELY DRESSED FOR SEDUCTION THIS evening and was elated when Emily announced her intention to retire. She and Jess were finally alone, and it would only be a matter of time before she had him back in her bed where he belonged.

Patting the space on the sofa next to her, she said, "Come join me, darling. We finally have a few minutes to ourselves without children or authors hovering about."

Jess heard the blatant invitation in her voice and wondered what game his wife was playing now. Nora had gone to a great deal of trouble to dress provocatively tonight. It was obvious she thought she could waltz back into his life after all these years as if nothing had happened and pick up where they'd left off.

At one time perhaps that might have been true. But now, after Emily—being with her, loving her—he realized that all other women paled in comparison. And Nora did not possess the sweetness and caring that was so much a part of Emily's kind personality.

"I prefer to stand." He poured himself a drink before crossing to the window. "Looks like the snow has finally stopped." Maybe now Nora would finally state her reasons for being here and leave.

She came up behind him and wrapped her arms about his waist. "I've missed you, Jess. We used to be so together."

He turned, and she clasped her arms about his neck, pressing into him. "I know you still want me as badly as I want you."

"You're wrong, Nora," he said in a voice filled with disgust. "Nothing could be further from the truth."

"Kiss me, then tell me you don't want me, Jess. I saw the way you looked at me tonight, with hunger in your eyes."

Removing her arms from around his neck, he shook his head and almost felt pity for the woman she had become. "You are a beautiful woman, Nora. But only on the outside. Inside there's nothing but selfishness and immaturity. You made your bed five years ago. Now you must lie in it."

Nora wasn't accustomed to begging, but Jess made her long for how it used to be between them. He was a skilled lover, unlike any she'd had since, and she'd been without a man for a long time. So she made an exception. "I'm not asking for anything permanent. Just a night of lovemaking. We used to be so good together, darling."

"I'm not interested. Perhaps you shouldn't have been so quick to leave your European friend."

"François meant nothing to me. He was merely a means to an end."

"Someone to help you escape your unpleasant life?" He sneered. "I'd hoped you'd changed over the years, Nora, that maybe you had actually come here because of Zach. But you didn't, did you?"

At his accusatory tone, she became agitated, wringing her hands nervously. "I—I came because I'm completely broke. François grew tired of me and left me stranded in Vienna. It was only by the grace of a certain benefactor that I was able to secure passage back to America."

"So you whored for your passage, is that it?"

She shrugged. "I did what I had to to survive."

"And I suppose you gave little or no thought to those you hurt along the way."

"I never meant to hurt you or Zachary, Jess. Please believe me. I loved you as much as I can love anyone. But I should never have married you or anyone else. I'm just not cut out for that kind of staid life."

Jess dropped into the leather wing chair by the fireplace, toying with the stem of his snifter. "What is it you want from me, Nora? That is, aside from satisfying your carnal lust, which I have no desire to do."

She downed the remainder of her wine in one gulp, and her face grew flushed. "I want money," she said without batting an eyelash.

"Money?" His laughter was sardonic. "You came here to ask for money? I should have known." The only difference between Nora and a whore was the price of her services.

"Surely you've got lots stashed away after your glorious days with the Wild West show. I'm only asking for a portion of it. It's a small price to pay to finalize our marriage."

To that, he would have to agree. "Let me get this straight—you want money in exchange for a divorce?"

"It's obvious that it's the only thing I have left to bargain with, Jess. And it's not much to give so that you can keep your son and marry the woman of your dreams." Then she added with a sneer, "Though your choice of mate leaves something to be desired."

His look turned lethal. "Leave Emily out of your twisted demands."

"I could make things very unpleasant for you both, if you don't do as I ask. I know people in New York who'd be willing to spread a little gossip about you and Miss Bartlett. I doubt that would be too good for her professional reputation, if you get my meaning."

"You conniving bitch!"

"Careful, darling. It wouldn't do to make me angry. I'm sure you don't want me to petition the courts for custody of little Zachary. I'd win, you know. I've done a bit of research on the subject of child custody cases and found that in almost every instance the court ruled in favor of the mother. A child always belongs with his mother." She smiled smugly.

"You really are a bitch, Nora. To think that I actually fancied myself in love with you at one time."

She laughed at that. "You loved an illusion, Jess, the same as me. The reality of who we are is much more difficult to deal with. I married the dashing hero, you the beautiful socialite. We didn't delve too deeply below the surface and therefore never noticed that we had little in common and were nothing alike."

"Thank God for that!"

"You may call me names and think what you will, but that doesn't change the fact that I want money, and lots of it, before I agree to end our marriage."

"How much?"

"Ten thousand dollars. I figure that's a small price to pay for your happiness, don't you? And the money will keep me in the style to which I have grown accustomed until I can secure another benefactor. At my age that's not an easy feat, despite my beauty and figure."

Jess poured himself another glass of brandy. He had the money to pay her—he'd been saving it for Zach's education—but the thought of handing it over to the woman who had caused him so much grief infuriated him. Still, if the money would get her out of his and Zach's life forever, he would pay it and consider it a worthwhile investment in their future.

"How do you know that I won't just kill you with my bare hands, Nora? It would be an easy enough thing to do." He took a menacing step toward her, but she stepped back.

"Though you might be tempted, you will think of your son first. You always have."

"As you have not." He tossed down the liquor and wiped his mouth on his shirtsleeve, then threw the glass into the fireplace, watching it shatter into a hundred tiny pieces, the way she had shattered his tranquillity at one time. And his heart, if he were truthful.

"The money is in the bank at True Love. I will have to make out a draft. But only after I'm assured that you have filed the necessary divorce papers."

Her smile was gloating. "I've already done that. They're in my room. All that's required is my signature and yours. Once the papers are filed with the court, you will be a free man."

And a poorer one. But any amount of money would be worth getting rid of Nora once and for all. Zach's future would be assured, and the termination of his marriage would allow him and Emily to marry and make a real home for Zach.

"Bring the papers to my office first thing in the morning. After they're signed, I will give you the bank draft and have one of my men drive you back to town. I don't ever want to see you again. Is that clear? You're to have no more dealings with my son."

"As if I would want to." She laughed at the absurdity of the threat. "It's obvious that I'm not cut out for motherhood. Why should I pretend otherwise?"

Emily shrank back from the doorway, appalled and disgusted by what she'd just heard. She hadn't meant to eavesdrop, but when she'd overheard Jess and Nora arguing she couldn't pull herself away.

To think she had come down to talk Nora into becoming a better mother to Zach. What a joke! The woman had no love for anyone but herself. That had been made abundantly clear by her blackmailing of Jess, by her condescending opinion of marriage and motherhood.

Noting that their conversation was at an end, Emily backed toward the stairs. Jess had suffered enough humiliation for one evening and might not appreciate her knowing what had transpired between him and his wife.

When he was ready to tell her, he would. In the meantime she would do everything in her power to make up for Nora's treachery and callousness, even if it meant sacrificing the literary career that she'd worked long and hard to establish—the thing she loved, other than Jess Murdock and his son, above all else.

As the buggy transporting Nora pulled away from the ranch house, Jess cleared the condensation from his office window with the heel of his hand and watched another chapter of his life come to a close.

On his desk were the papers that would soon make him a free man. Tomorrow he would ride into town and file them with the court clerk.

Today he intended to spend the day with his son and would endeavor to explain why the woman who had given Zach birth had come back into his life, then just as suddenly disappeared again.

The boy would no doubt be hurt and confused by the events of the past few days, and Jess was not looking forward to performing the necessary explanation.

The only saving grace to it all was that Nora was finally out of their lives for good and would never bother them again.

* * *

As Jess thought those prophetic words, the man who intended to make them a reality watched the buggy advance down the road from his hiding place and smiled evilly.

Juan Villalobos had been waiting patiently for his chance, and now it had come. Murdock's woman—the lovely señorita he had robbed so many weeks ago—was in the buggy. He had seen her leave the house bundled up in a hooded red wool cloak. The driver, a young boy who reeked of inexperience, would not present much of an obstacle to his plan.

Señor Murdock was sure to be surprised and saddened when Juan deprived him of the woman, as Murdock had deprived him of his livelihood.

Revenge would be sweet, as would the kisses of the lovely señorita before he shot her dead.

At the ranch house, Jess had just finished explaining the details of his mother's leaving to Zach. Emily had joined him, and together they had tried to make sense of all that had happened.

"I'm not sad, Papa, so don't worry about me," Zach confessed, sounding very grown-up for a five-year-old. "I didn't think my real mommy would stay because she dressed fancy, and I don't think she would have liked being around the horses and cows too much."

At the young boy's perceptiveness, Emily and Jess exchanged startled looks. Then Jess ruffled his son's hair and in a voice choked with love and pride said, "You're a fine son, Zach. I'm very proud of you."

Watching the two together, Emily felt tears clog her throat. The fact that Jess loved his son more than life itself was written on his face, displayed in every gentle gesture and spoken word. He was a wonderful father to Zach. And it was more apparent than ever why the accidental death of Rory Connors had devastated him so.

Jess Murdock was a kind and gentle human being. He had done his best to protect his son from life's harsh realities and from a mother who didn't want him. And though Jess would no doubt take the guilt over the little boy's death to his grave, he had given so much of himself to those who lived and had made amends for his error. He truly was the stuff of heroes, Emily thought proudly, turning her attention back to the pair.

Zach grinned, hugged his father about the neck, then whispered so Emily couldn't hear, "When are you going to ask Miss Emily to be my mommy, Papa? I've been waiting a long time, and I think she has, too."

Jess threw back his head and laughed, then looked over at Emily, who was staring at them both with a loving expression. "I guess I'll go take care of that right now, son. Thanks for reminding me."

Frosty Adams was having similar thoughts as he entered the kitchen. The woman of his heart was readying the pies that would be served with Thursday's Thanksgiving dinner.

Frances looked up when a blast of cold air hit her, and she shook her head in admonishment. "Hurry up and close the door, old mon. 'Tis freezing, I am."

He walked up behind her and circled her waist with his hands, and his warm breath on her neck made goose bumps rise up everywhere. "Maybe I could warm you up, Fanny darlin'."

The woman blushed to the roots of her hair. The old man was impertinent, but she adored him anyway. "I'm expecting Zach tae come in here at any moment, Frosty Adams, so don't ye be carrying on now." She continued to roll out the piecrust, while Frosty wondered how he was going to approach her with the all-important question he'd been wanting to ask.

With a great deal of hemming and hawing and shuffling of feet, he finally found his courage. "I've come to speak to you about something very important, Fan. Do you think them pies could wait for a few minutes?"

Frances was about to remark that the dough would dry out and be useless if she didn't tend to it right away, but the earnest look on Frosty's face made her swallow her words. She had her suspicions why he'd come, and her heart fluttered in her chest like a young girl's. "I guess I can spare a few moments, if it's important."

Clearing his throat nervously, Frosty slicked back his hair with the palm of his hand before beginning. "I guess I don't have to be telling you how much I care for you, Fanny. I think by now that you know my intentions are honorable."

Wiping the flour from her hands, she nodded. "I do."

"Then it should come as no surprise that I want to marry you, Frances. I want you to be my wife."

She crossed her arms over her chest and leveled a straightforward look at him. "And do ye want me tae be yer wife because ye're lonely and need a cook and house-keeper, Frosty Adams? Or is there another reason?" She held her breath, waiting for the declaration. Frosty had spoken of marriage, but not of love. And she would marry no man without it.

It took a few moments for the old man to decipher her words. When he figured out finally what she was getting at, he grinned and drew her into his arms. "I'm crazy in love with you, old gal. I thought for sure you knew that." He kissed her then, and Frances's toes curled.

"Will you do me the very great honor of marrying me, Frances Ferguson?" he asked, his heart pounding and filled with love for this woman.

A smile lit Frances's eyes and tipped the corners of her mouth. "I will, ye darling mon. I surely will."

In the office, Jess was pacing back and forth while Emily waited patiently on the sofa. She was nearing completion of the book, had only a few more pages to edit, and she was anxious to go upstairs and finish so she could take it into town and mail it off to Max. She knew he was waiting on pins and needles for it; his last telegram had been absolutely frantic.

Emily needed to be working, not sitting in Jess's office waiting for him to unburden himself about Nora, if that was his intention. She knew everything she wanted to about the selfish woman.

"My son has just reminded me of something, Emily," he said, pausing in front of the sofa and holding out his hands to help her rise.

"Zach?" Emily's eyes widened in confusion. "What on earth could he—"

"He says I've been taking too long to ask you to marry me. And I think he's absolutely right. I'd like to rectify that now, if you'll let me."

Her breath caught in her throat, and tears filled her eyes at the declaration. After everything that had occurred the past few days, she hadn't been expecting a proposal. "Oh, Jess."

He bent down on one knee and took her hand in his, kissing it gallantly before saying, "Emily Jean Bartlett, I love you more than life itself, and I want to marry you and make you mine forever." He rose and kissed her softly on the lips. "Will you be my wife, Emily?"

Throwing her arms about his neck, she knocked him backward onto the sofa and smothered him with kisses. "Yes! Yes! Yes! I'll marry you. Oh, Jess, I love you so much it hurts."

"And I love you. And perhaps later, after everyone has gone to bed, you'll allow me to show you just how much." He kissed her again so passionately that Emily feared her bones would melt.

"I can't think of anything I'd like better."

"Tomorrow we'll go into town and take care of ending this farce of a marriage to Nora. We'll also make plans with Reverend Higgbotham to perform a wedding ceremony. I'll leave all of the arrangements up to you."

She bounced off the sofa, filled with excitement and unbridled happiness. "I'll need to stop at the post office and mail off my manuscript, too."

His eyes widened. "The book's done?"

"Yes. I've just been going over it to make sure it's perfect."

"Can I read it?"

Her heart warmed, and she nodded shyly. "I wasn't sure you'd want to, so I didn't ask. But yes, I'd be honored if you'd read it and give me your opinion."

"I'll read it right now. It'll take my mind off ravishing that sweet little body of yours and keep me occupied until this evening." His sexy smile had her heart beating double time, and she wondered how she'd keep herself from dwelling on their planned rendezvous.

"You will be honest in your opinion of the book, won't you?" Even though it would hurt to hear that he disliked it, Emily wanted honesty rather than sugar-coated words of praise. And she knew there was still time to fix anything problematic, if need be.

"From here on out, there'll be no more evasion or duplicity between us. On that you have my word." He grinned. "But you needn't worry. I'm sure I'm going to like it. After all, it's about me, isn't it?" He tweaked her nose, and his heart felt whole and at peace for the first time in a very long while.

Screaming, Nora clutched the arm of the frightened young man next to her as the outlaw approached the buggy. Hysteria bubbled up her throat as he pointed the menacing revolver at them.

"I have been waiting a very long time for this, señorita. Now get down off the buggy. You should remember that it isn't wise to keep Juan waiting."

The woman shook her head vehemently, and the hood covering her lush auburn hair fell to her shoulders. Juan's eyes widened in surprise when he realized that this was not the same woman from the stagecoach holdup. The knowledge filled him with anger and disappointment, until she said:

"It's obvious that you don't know who I am, sir. I'm Mrs. Jess Murdock, and my husband will pay handsomely to have me released."

Billy Parsley nodded, his voice shaky, though he was doing his best to remain brave. "She's telling the truth. This here lady's married to Jess Murdock of the Bar JM." He didn't bother to point out that their marriage was to be of short duration, according to what Frosty had told him.

The outlaw's grin grew calculating. "Is that a fact? So you are Señor Murdock's wife? That is even better."

Noting the satisfaction in the man's eyes, Nora paled. "Please let me go. I have a train to catch." And a bank draft for $10,000 to deposit.

He waved the gun at them again. "I'm afraid I can't do that, Señora Murdock. You see, I have a score to settle with your husband, and you will provide me with the means to do just that."

Realizing her foolish mistake immediately, Nora knew it would do little good to retract her false statements now. She decided on another tack.

The outlaw was a handsome man, despite his filthy attire and evil looks. She was a beautiful woman who had conquered more than one beast in her lifetime. Knowing that womanly wiles were often quite effective when dealing with the weaker sex, she licked her lips provocatively and said, "I'm sure we can work something out, sir." After alighting from the buggy, she moved toward him, swaying her hips suggestively, while Billy looked on wide-eyed.

"I'm not without experience." She pressed her hand to his chest. "And in exchange for my release, I would be willing to . . ." She smiled coyly, and the outlaw laughed in her face, making Nora stiffen.

"You are a *puta*. It appears that Jess Murdock married himself a whore. That is almost justice in itself." He laughed at the irony of it. "But I'm afraid not quite enough." Grabbing her arm, he pulled her into his chest.

At that moment, an outraged Billy Parsley reached for his gun, but El Lobo was quicker and answered the threat with a bullet. Billy fell off the buggy and into the dirt.

Nora screamed at the sight of all the blood and beat on the outlaw's chest ineffectively. "You bastard! How could you shoot that innocent boy?"

Crushing his mouth to hers, he kissed her into submission, then said, "First I will take what you have offered, *puta.* You are well endowed." He fondled her breasts. "And I am a man who has not lain with a woman in a very long time."

Nora's eyes filled with fear even as her heart beat in anticipation. "I will lie with you willingly, but please do not kill me. I beg you."

He caressed her cheek as if contemplating her words, then said, his tone almost apologetic, "I am sorry, pretty one, but I must. Juan Villalobos always keeps his word."

Nora Murdock would relive those words over and over again during the next brutal hour until the final moment of her death.

Chapter Twenty

ABSORBED IN EMILY'S WELL-WRITTEN NARRATIVE OF his life, Jess didn't hear the study door open or see the frantic look on his foreman's face, until the old man started stomping his feet impatiently to gain his attention.

"Sorry to interrupt, boss, but I'm worried about Billy. He's not returned from taking Mrs. Murdock to town, and he shoulda been back by now." Frosty rubbed the back of his neck in agitation.

Jess glanced out the window to see that the sun had set some time ago, and his brows drew together in a frown. Billy should have been back hours ago. Setting aside his biography, he asked, "Did he say he was staying in town for any reason?" It wasn't unusual for the cowboys to visit one of the whorehouses when the opportunity arose. And Billy was young and still sowing his oats.

Frosty shook his head. "Nope. And he wouldn't have stayed without permission. I taught that boy right. Told him to hightail back to the ranch as soon as the deed was done."

Frosty had taken young Billy under his wing when the boy had first come to the ranch looking for work. He'd been green as a grasshopper, and the Bar JM's foreman had attempted to guide him in his ranch work and in the ethics of cowpunching.

Jess knew that the old man wasn't one to raise an alarm without reason, unless he had a strong gut feeling. Frosty's instincts had saved his hide a time or two, so he wasn't about to take his concerns lightly. "Take a few of the men and ride into town. I wouldn't put it past Nora to have seduced the kid. But I want to make sure he's all right."

"I hope to hell you're right and the boy's just sowing his oats. The alternative ain't something I can stomach."

But it was the alternative that had Frosty pacing the upstairs hallway several hours later, while he waited to hear if Billy Parsley was going to survive the bullet wound to his chest.

About midway to town Frosty had found Billy's half-frozen body lying facedown in the snow. The bullet wound had bled profusely, but the cold snow had served to stanch the flow of blood to a trickle and had prevented him from bleeding to death.

Nora Murdock's dead, naked body had been discovered about fifty yards away. They would have missed it in the dark were it not for the reticule they'd found lying nearby, which contained a bank draft for $10,000. That had prompted them to look further, for Frosty knew that Jess's avaricious wife would not have left without her money.

The bedroom door opened and Emily came out, carrying a basin of blood-soaked bandages. "How's the boy, Miss Emily?" Frosty asked. "Is he going to make it?"

Nodding, she smiled wearily. "Mrs. Ferguson was able to get the bullet out, and Billy is resting comfortably. We'll send for the doctor in the morning just to make certain we didn't overlook anything." Frances was worried about infection setting in, but Emily spared the old man that.

Wiping something that looked suspiciously like tears from his eyes, Frosty said, "There but for the grace of God he coulda ended up like . . ." He nodded in the direction of the barn, where Nora's shrouded body lay, unwilling to speak the dead woman's name.

They'd all agreed that Zach would be spared the news of his mother's death for now. The child had had enough to deal with of late, and it would serve no purpose to cause him additional pain. Emily was extremely grateful that Jess had made such a difficult but wise decision.

"Billy was lucky you found him in time, Frosty. If it hadn't been for your worrying about him, he probably wouldn't be here right now."

He rubbed his chin whiskers. "I'm a strong believer in fate, Miss Emily. I believe that all things happen for a reason. Good and bad." She knew he was referring to Nora Murdock's death, though he didn't say so.

"You and Jess'll soon be able to put all of this unpleasantness behind you. Zach will be needing both a mother and a father."

Her eyes widened. "Did Jess tell you that he had

asked me to marry him?" She hadn't thought he'd told anyone as yet.

Frosty chuckled. "Didn't have to. A man my age knows these things." With a wink he disappeared into the room, and Emily continued on her way down the stairs.

Much later, when everyone had reassured themselves that Billy was going to make it and had retired to their rooms for the night, Emily snuggled in Jess's arms, listening to the crackling of the fire and his steady heartbeat. They hadn't made love as they'd originally intended, but had taken solace in the warmth of each other's love.

"I'm sorry about Nora, Jess. Even though I wasn't fond of her, I wouldn't have wished her to end up as she did."

Jess heaved a sigh. He'd had mixed feelings about Nora's death. Sadness, surely. No living creature should have had to endure what Nora had gone through. Vicious bite marks and bruises had covered most of her body.

But Jess had also felt relief upon hearing the news. Nora's death had made him free. She wouldn't be able to cause him or Zach any more grief. And because of those feelings, he felt a large measure of guilt.

"I guess we'll know more about what happened when Billy awakes, but by then whoever did the murder will be long gone."

"Promise me that whatever you find out from Billy, you won't go after the murderer." She knew it was a useless plea, as it had been the last time she'd made it. Emily had seen the look of murderous rage in his eyes when Billy had been brought back half-dead. She had also seen resignation on his face when he'd viewed his dead wife's body, as if he'd somehow expected her to come to such a horrific end.

"You know I can't make you that promise, Emily. A man's got to protect his own. If we allow outlaws to murder at will without suffering the consequences of a hangman's rope, then we're inviting chaos and unrest into our midst."

His intractable expression said his mind was made up. "I won't allow that. I can't. I've got you and Zach to think about."

She pressed her body closer, eager to change the disturbing subject of his leaving. "Did you finish reading the book?"

He smiled into the darkness. "Yes, and it's wonderful. I was touched and awed by how your words made me seem so much larger than life, but still retained a sense of the common man that I am. Thank you." He pressed his lips to her forehead.

"I want everyone who reads that book to see you as I do, admire you for the wonderful man you are. You're my hero, Jess Murdock. I want everyone to know that. I want you to be everybody's hero."

"I don't need hero worship, Emily. As long as you and Zach love me, that's all that matters."

"I doubt Max will share your sentiments. He's looking for some big sales to take him out of debt. I hope and pray that *Jess Murdock: Legend of the West* will do just that."

He toyed with the strands of her hair, curling them around his finger. "How would you feel about making love to a legend?"

"I think I'd rather make love to the man." Reaching down, she pressed her palm against his maleness and felt him harden instantly. "Do legends always react like that?"

"Two can play that game, E. J. Bartlett." Reaching down, he pulled up her nightdress and began massaging her woman's mound, while at the same time he untied the ribbons that held her gown together and pressed his mouth to her breasts.

In a matter of moments Emily guided him to her, opening herself to receive him.

Jess plunged into her, covering her mouth with his own to smother her cries of passion. Together they lost themselves in their love and need for each other, blocking out the horrors of the day and the uncertainties of tomorrow.

There was much to be thankful for Thanksgiving Day.

The doctor arrived early that morning and pronounced that Billy was well on his way to recovery. He marveled at the excellent job Frances Ferguson had done in removing the bullet and had even offered her a position as his office nurse, much to her delight and Frosty's disgust. When she graciously declined, he had offered to transport Nora's body into town and deposit it with the undertaker to spare Jess and his son any more grief.

Upon learning of Billy's injuries, Zach had asked a few probing questions, but Jess had been able to sidestep them with the explanation that Billy had been wounded on his return trip to the ranch by an unknown assailant. The answer had placated the inquisitive child, much to everyone's relief.

When Jess questioned Billy about the shooting and murder of his wife and discovered that the outlaw El Lobo had been the cause of Nora's death, Jess's rage had known no bounds.

"I'll get that bastard if it's the last thing I do," he'd vowed emphatically, and Emily's blood had run cold.

Even now, seated at the kitchen table, enjoying the delicious meal of roast turkey, stuffing, and sweet potatoes that Mrs. Ferguson had lovingly prepared for the holiday feast, Emily sensed that Jess was still distracted by his need for vengeance, though he spoke nothing of it in front of his son.

"You've outdone yourself this year, Frances," he remarked, heeding Emily's pleading looks and trying not to spoil the day. "I'm as stuffed as that tom once was."

Several of the cowboys who'd been invited to partake of the special meal nodded, agreeing wholeheartedly; then Webb Parker said, "Only my mama makes better stuffing, Mrs. F.," before helping himself to another portion.

The older woman smiled. "'Tis kind of ye tae say so. But I canna take all o' the credit for the meal. The lass here helped me to prepare those flaky rolls ye're eatin', as well as that fancy French soup ye was so fond of."

"Mighty tasty, ma'am," the cowboy remarked. It was a far cry from the comments he'd made previously about

Emily's cooking, and the young woman smiled in remembrance.

When the meal was finally done, and the coffee and pies had been served, Frosty tapped his glass with a spoon and cleared his throat. "I've got an important announcement to make."

"It ain't hard to figure out what that'll be," Stinky said. "You two have been cooing like lovebirds for weeks. But I ain't a sore loser."

Frances's cheeks filled with color, while Frosty shot his co-worker a look of pure triumph. "Me and Fan is fixin' to get hitched. We want all of you to come to the wedding. Even you, Stinky," he added with a good-natured grin.

A loud chorus of shouts, whistles, and catcalls went up, and Frosty's face turned the color of cranberry sauce.

"Why, Mr. Adams, I do believe ye're blushin'," Frances remarked with a chuckle, feeling giddy with joy.

Jess raised his glass and toasted the happy couple, then announced his own intention to marry Emily, whereby Zach jumped up from the table and threw himself at Emily, hugging her fiercely.

"This is the best Thanksgiving I've ever had," he announced, making everyone laugh.

Wiping tears of joy from her eyes, Emily exchanged a meaningful look with her husband-to-be, then leaned over and kissed Frances on the cheek. "I'm so happy for both of us."

"Aye, lass. Who woulda thought these foolish men would finally come tae their senses? Nae I, that's fer certain."

"So when's your wedding going to take place, Jess?" Frosty asked, grinning from ear to ear. "Guess you'll be wanting to tie the knot as soon as possible."

Jess reached over and squeezed Emily's hand. "I was thinking that Christmas Eve would be a nice time to share our joy. No doubt the good reverend would be thrilled to have his church filled to capacity that evening, seeing as how Emily and I are such oddities around here."

Emily laughed and made a lighthearted comment, but inside fear had taken hold of her heart as uncertainty wrapped itself around it.

What if Jess rode after El Lobo and did not return?

What if she never again had the chance to gaze upon his smiling face, as she was now, to be held in his arms, to hear him say how much he loved her?

What if he left her a widow, before she had a chance to become his bride?

Emily's fears continued to multiply over the next ten days. Jess and Frosty had ridden out to hunt El Lobo the day after the Thanksgiving holiday, leaving the remainder of the men at the ranch to look after the women, in case the outlaw decided to return.

Billy had nearly recovered from his injury and was once again living out in the bunkhouse, complaining daily that he hadn't been allowed to go after the man who had shot him.

Frances, who was normally stalwart about men and their missions of revenge, had been unusually high-strung and nervous. Though the women had tried to keep themselves occupied with various chores, and baking for the upcoming Christmas holidays had consumed a great deal of their time, their thoughts were never far from the men whose faces they feared they might never see again.

Licking sugar and cinnamon from her fingertips, the housekeeper heaved a sigh. "I'm worried about the old mon, Emily. I don't know what I'll do if he ends up—" She stopped in midsentence, unable to finish her gruesome thought.

Emily looked up from the Christmas stocking she was sewing for Zach but couldn't offer any words of encouragement. They'd had no word from Jess or Frosty as to how the hunt for El Lobo was going or when they would return, and she was just as worried as Frances.

Even Reverend Higgbotham and his wife's visit to the ranch a few days ago to discuss plans for the wedding hadn't been enough to take her mind off her fear. It had actually made things worse, for it had pointed out once again the very real possibility that Jess might not make it back for the wedding.

"I guess we'll have to leave things in God's hands this time, Frances. I begged Jess not to go, but I was wasting my breath, as usual."

*Tsk*ing several times, the older woman shook her head in disgust. "'Tis a man thing, that's fer sure, lass. We women aren't likely tae understand the why of it, but there's no saying we've got tae suffer in silence. I, fer one, am going tae give Frosty Adams a piece o' me mind when he gets home."

They exchanged a look that said "if he gets home," but neither voiced the fear, and Frances mercifully changed the subject.

"Have ye had word about the book from that mon in New York City? Does he say when it'll be ready fer sale?"

Emily had had a lengthy letter from Max just two days before. He'd been very complimentary about the book and had rushed it into production. Expecting it to be on the shelves before Christmas, Max had revealed that preorders were brisk, even better than he had originally anticipated.

Max felt confident that Jess's book was going to save Wise Publishing from financial ruin, but he'd taken Emily to task over her written announcement that she would be retiring from publishing to take up the reins of wife and mother.

Emily had given her career decision a great deal of thought before writing to Max of her intention to quit. In light of all that had happened, Nora's death in particular, she realized that life was too short and filled with uncertainties—Jess's unexpected manhunt was proof of that—and she wanted to devote all of her days and nights to making a real home for Jess and Zach. They deserved no less.

Writing took a great deal of energy and time—time she could better spend being a wife and mother. Zach needed a full-time mother—Nora had never been there for him—and Jess deserved someone who would remain by his side and give one hundred percent of her energy to their marriage and to the success of the ranch.

It would be too difficult, she had finally decided, to split herself in two and have separate careers.

Emily hadn't mentioned her decision to Jess. She would tell him after they were married. But she owed it to Max to be honest and forthright with him, as he'd always been with her.

Her publisher would need time to find a replacement for her, and she had already decided that she would allow him to use the "E.J. Bartlett" pseudonym to continue selling books under that name.

Someone else would be writing those books, using her hard-earned reputation, but as long as she was assured that the author chosen would produce quality work, she could live with that decision.

"Emily? Are ye all right, lass? Ye seem tae be a million miles away."

Frances's hand on her shoulder made Emily refocus her attention on the older woman's question, and she smiled apologetically. "I was just thinking about the book. And to answer your question: Max says that *Jess Murdock: Legend of the West* will be on sale before Christmas." It wouldn't be an easy feat, but if anyone could accomplish it, Max could.

Frances's face lit for the first time in days. "I can hardly wait tae read it. And will ye sign a copy fer me, lass? I never had a signed copy of a book before."

"Of course I will. And you should be very proud that you're able to read it, Frances. It's commendable that you put such effort into learning to read and write. I bet your sister was surprised when she received your first letter."

Wiping tears from her eyes with her apron, Frances replied in a voice filled with emotion. "I canna tell ye what a thrill it was fer me to get her letter and be able tae read it. Fiona and I were so close growing up, but the years and the miles had separated us. Now, thanks tae ye, lass, we'll be able tae grow close once again. I feel truly blessed."

Emily stood, wrapping her arms about the woman. She'd grown close to Frances, loved her dearly, and wanted only the best for her.

"I was only the instrument of your learning, Frances. You did all the work and therefore deserve all the credit. You've learned to read. You can now correspond with your sister. And you've won the man of your dreams. Not bad for a few months' work."

The housekeeper chuckled. "By God, but the old mon would get a kick if he knew I was blubbering over him, now, wouldn't he?"

Emily smiled. "I suspect that Jess and Frosty have much more on their minds at the moment than worrying about a couple of worrywarts like us."

"The bastard can't be that far ahead." Frosty squatted down to examine the fresh tracks and horse droppings. He picked up the stool and smelled it, then rolled it between his fingers, trying to determine how long it had been since it had been deposited. "I'd wager he's less than two hours' ride ahead of us."

Frowning, Jess scratched the ten days' growth of beard that itched like the very devil. "I'm not going to stop until I catch up to him, old man. So if you don't think you can keep up, then hightail it back home now. I plan to kill that Mex bastard today and be done with it." He was anxious to get home to Emily and Zach and to begin his new life.

"If I didn't know how tired and ornery you were, Jess, I'd pull you down off that horse and beat the living crap outta you. But I won't. I want to catch El Lobo just as much as, if not more than, you do. Billy was nearly killed. Do you think I've forgotten that?"

Jess shook his head, then smiled at the feisty cowboy's irate temper, an indication that his teasing remarks had worked. "Guess your blood's heated up sufficiently, old man. We'd better make tracks."

Mounting up, Frosty harrumped loudly. "Don't know why that sweet Emily would want to saddle herself with the likes of you. I'm gonna tell her when I get home just what a pain in the ass you are. She'll probably have a change of heart and break the engagement."

"Then I'll have to tell Frances that you talk in your sleep and snore loud enough to wake the dead. She'll probably think twice about marrying up with you."

Frosty grinned, and there was a devilish gleam in his eye when he said, "And what makes you think that the old gal doesn't already know it?"

Two hours later they came upon El Lobo's camp. Spotting his horse, then the man himself, they knew the time for confrontation was at hand.

He was bent over the campfire, intent on roasting a rabbit for his supper, and it was obvious to Jess and Frosty that Juan Villalobos wasn't expecting company. They split up and surrounded the camp.

Juan's horse soon sensed their presence and snickered, bringing the Mexican to his feet, gun drawn. "What is it? What do you hear, my old friend?"

The outlaw walked the perimeter of the camp, nervously, cautiously, peering into the treeline, and when he was satisfied that no one was about, he holstered his gun and squatted before the fire to attend to his rabbit once again.

Silent as a catamount, Jess crept closer and made his way forward. Frosty, on the opposite side of the campsite, stood hidden behind a copse of pines and waited patiently for his signal.

But Frosty's horse wasn't as patient and whinnied loudly, alerting the outlaw to his presence. El Lobo drew his gun. Instantly Jess lunged forward from behind the large boulder, tackling him to the ground.

The man grunted, then smiled in his cocky way. "Murdock! I have been waiting for you. Are you so anxious to die? As anxious as that *puta* wife of yours was to lie with me?"

"Shut up, you filthy bastard!" Jess punched the outlaw in the mouth to silence him, pummeling him viciously, but the man was as strong as Jess and fought back hard, landing several blows to Jess's midsection and face.

Jess struggled to gain control of the gun, but El Lobo resisted. Without warning it went off, and the bullet ricocheted off the tree that Frosty was using for cover.

"Holy shit!" The old man jumped back, deciding it was safer to enter the melee than stand on the sidelines and risk taking a bullet, despite Jess's warnings to the contrary.

"Reach for sky, El Lobo, you thievin' bastard," Frosty ordered, holding a bead on the man. "I got him covered, Jess. You can get off him now."

Jess rolled to his feet, his lip bloodied and his cheekbone bruised, but the outlaw looked much worse. Both eyes had been blackened, and blood was streaming out of the man's nose.

The old man chuckled. "Looks like you did a respectable job of beating the crap outta the bastard."

Suddenly the outlaw lunged for his gun, which lay only inches away, scooped it up, and fired at Frosty, hitting him in the hand. The old man dropped his weapon with a cry of pain.

In the space of a heartbeat Jess cleared leather and aimed his gun at El Lobo's head, firing and hitting him between the eyes. The outlaw fell to the ground, dead.

Standing over him, Jess kicked the inert body, then, satisfied that he was dead, he hurried to help his injured friend.

"Jesus, old man! Why don't you listen to me for a change? I told you to stay hidden behind the trees."

"Like some old woman? What fun would that have been? Besides, I ain't hurt all that bad."

After removing the bandanna from around his neck, Jess wrapped it around Frosty's hand. The tip of one of his fingers had been shot off, but other than that the old man looked fine.

Jess breathed a sigh of relief. He couldn't have lived with himself if anything had happened to Frosty—he loved the old geezer like a father—and Frances would have shot him herself if he'd allowed anything to happen to her fiancé. She'd told him as much before he'd left.

"You fixin' to take this outlaw back to True Love with us?"

Jess stared at the lifeless, worthless piece of offal and shook his head. "No. We don't need filth like him dirtying up the town. We'll bury him here, then we'll go home."

Chapter Twenty-one

WITH THE SAFE RETURN OF JESS AND FROSTY, ALL thoughts at the ranch turned to Christmas and the upcoming nuptials of Emily and Jess and Frances and Frosty.

Emily couldn't think of anyone she'd rather share her special day with and had told Frances as much, finally convincing the hardheaded woman when she'd put up a fuss that she wasn't intruding at all and that two weddings were better than one.

It had been decided that a double ceremony would be performed on Christmas Eve and that Emily and Frances would forgo the traditional wedding reception in favor of a nice quiet family gathering at home. Emily had telegraphed the news to her parents but didn't hold out much hope that they would attend.

Upon learning of their decision to hold the wedding at the ranch, Reverend Higgbotham had been vastly disappointed, for he had been calculating just how many parishioners he could cram into his church for each separate wedding and had already made grandiose plans for the gala receptions at the church hall.

But both Emily and Frances had been adamant, and as everyone knew, it was useless to argue with a bride-to-be, much less two.

In town, the women had just completed final fittings of their wedding attire and were crossing the muddy street to enter the mercantile.

Emily had promised Zach his own batch of walnut fudge, and Frances needed extra flour and sugar to complete her decorated sugar cookies. Frosty and Jess, who had gone to the tonsorial parlor, were to meet them in less than an hour to escort them back to the ranch.

"Oh, look at the lovely Christmas ornaments, Frances! My parents had similar ones when we were children." A twinge of nostalgia and loneliness filled Emily as she gazed upon them, and she drew a deep sigh of longing. She wondered what her family would be doing this holiday season, how her brothers and sister fared, if they had put up the tree yet or finished their Christmas shopping.

"You'll find none finer, I'll grant you that," Flossie Camden said, interrupting Emily's reverie. "Them delicate globes come all the way from Europe. How many would you like me to wrap up for you, Miss Bartlett?"

"They're frightfully expensive, Frances," Emily whispered to her companion, admiring the beautiful emerald and gold colors, the rich crimson and sparkling silver. Chewing her lower lip in indecision, she said finally, "Perhaps if I just bought one."

"Let's pitch our money together and buy several,"

Frances suggested. "I havena had anything pretty tae spend my earnings on in a right good while, and this seems like a worthwhile purchase. After all, we'll be wanting the tree tae look extra special this year, won't we?"

Emily nodded enthusiastically, hugging the woman about the waist. "I can't wait to put them on the tree."

"You needn't worry about your money here, Miss Bartlett," Flossie said. "Seeing as how you'll be hitching up with Jess soon, you can charge everything to his account."

"Oh, I couldn't do that, Mrs. Camden. I wouldn't feel right about it."

"Stuff and nonsense. It's a wife's duty to spend her husband's money. I'm always telling Frank that, and he's not found a suitable argument these last twenty-five years." She chuckled.

"Be that as it may, I won't spend Jess's money without his permission. Frances will purchase the ornaments, and we'll settle up between ourselves later." Max owed her money for the book and would pay her as soon as his profits began rolling in, which she hoped would be soon. She still needed to purchase Christmas presents and a groom's gift for Jess.

At the rear of the store, the women soon became engrossed in a various assortment of things and failed to notice when a nattily dressed gentleman entered the establishment a few minutes later.

He wore a black beaver hat and a gray tweed overcoat that matched his eyes. His impatience was evident by the way he paced back and forth in front of the counter in an effort to gain the proprietress's attention.

Taking her time, Flossie carefully wrapped the delicate ornaments in tissue paper, ignoring the man until she had completed her task. Finally she looked up and pasted on her most welcoming smile. "Need some help, mister?"

Maxwell Wise bit his lip, trying to keep his temper in check. The woman would never survive in New York, he decided. "Yes. I'm looking for some information. Would you happen to know where I could hire someone to take me out to the Bar JM ranch? I'm looking for a woman by the name of Emily Jean Bartlett. I believe she's residing there." Before the proprietress could reply, a woman's excited scream filled the air, and Max's eyes widened.

Emily came rushing to the front of the store as if her corset were on fire. "Max! Max!" She threw her arms about his waist, hugging him till her arms ached. At his startled look, she laughed. Since he'd seen her last, her hair had grown considerably and now almost reached her shoulders. "It's me—Emily. Don't you recognize me? I haven't been gone that long."

Max held his hand over his heart. "You nearly caused me to die of fright, Emily Jean Bartlett. My God! Do you greet everyone this effusively?" He shook his head, then smiled warmly. "I'm happy to see you, too, young woman."

"But what are you doing here?"

His eyebrow arched imperiously. "As if you didn't know. After I received your last letter there was no way I could stay put in New York and allow you to make the biggest mistake of your life."

Frances came forward just then, her lips thinned in anger. "If ye're referring tae Emily's marriage tae Jess Murdock, then ye're sadly mistaken. Jess is as fine a mon as ever walked the earth, and any woman would be proud tae be his wife."

Startled by the strange woman's outburst, Max looked at Emily, who was quick to explain, "This is my very dear friend Frances Ferguson, Jess's housekeeper. I believe I wrote you about her, Max."

He held out his hand in greeting. "It's you who are mistaken, Mrs. Ferguson. I've not come because of Emily's wedding, but because she has threatened to—"

Just then the door flew open and Jess and Frosty entered, causing Max to halt what he was saying and utter instead, "Good grief! This place is worse than the rail station in New York City. Is there nowhere we can go to talk?"

Emily flashed him a grin. "Jess! Frosty! Come over and meet my good friend and publisher Maxwell Wise. He's come all the way from New York to attend our weddings." Max started to protest, but she shot him a pleading look, then completed the introductions.

"Well, don't that beat all," Flossie interjected, shaking her head. "You're the man who's printing up all the books about Jess's life story."

"That's correct. In fact, I've brought some copies with me, if you'd like to sell them in your business establishment."

The woman's face flushed with excitement. "I surely would. I'll set up a display of Jess's books in the window.

Everyone in town is sure to want one. I hope you brought plenty with you."

He smiled as only a businessman calculating his good fortune could smile. "Madam, I've already shipped several crates to Mr. Murdock's ranch. When they arrive, you'll be restocked, so sell as many as you have and take orders for the rest."

Emily listened to the exchange, but her mind was on the complications Max's arrival would likely create. She hadn't yet told Jess about her decision to quit writing, and she knew Max well enough to realize that he wouldn't hold his tongue for long.

Emily hoped she'd be able to discuss her decision with Jess before Max cornered him, so she suggested that everyone return to the ranch to resume the reunion there.

Unfortunately, the first thing out of Max's mouth once they had settled into the Bar JM's parlor was the subject of Emily's retirement from writing.

"I just don't understand how you can ask this talented young woman to give up her career for you, Jess. I was taken aback when I received her letter informing me that she intended to go into retirement and give up her E. J. Bartlett pseudonym. Anyone who's read those books knows that no one can write them as well as Emily."

The revelation took Jess completely by surprise. Nearly dropping the cup of hot coffee he held, he turned to look at his fiancée, who was turning three shades of purple. "I'm afraid that you have me at a loss, Max. Emily and I have never discussed her foolhardy plan to quit writing."

Max heaved an audible sigh of relief, then all eyes turned on Emily, who swallowed with some difficulty. "I can explain," she said timidly.

Frances cast her a pitying look before bustling out of the room to get dinner started.

"I hope so, Emily Jean, because I have no intention of accepting your resignation," Max informed her in that no-nonsense tone she was so familiar with. "There's no earthly reason why you can't pen your manuscripts from here and mail them in, just as you've done with Jess's book. It's a simple solution, really."

"Emily, why didn't you tell me that you were intending to give up your career for me? Had I known, I would have thought twice about asking you to marry me."

Emily's distress turned quickly to ire. "In case everyone has forgotten, you included, Jess Murdock, this is my life we're talking about, and therefore should be my decision. I realize that both of you think you're protecting me, but I am quite capable of knowing what it is I want out of life."

At a loss to understand what had prompted Emily's sudden change of heart, Jess said, "But you love writing. You told me as much many times."

"But I love you and Zach more. I want to be a good wife and mother, Jess. I don't want to take away from those important roles to play another. I've had my career as a writer, now I want the other."

Jess crossed the room and took her in his arms. "Can't you see that you can have both, Emily? I would never ask you to give up something that's so important to you.

You've worked hard to establish yourself. You shouldn't just cast it all away."

"But writing consumes a great deal of my time. It wouldn't be fair to have it interfere with our family life."

"It doesn't have to, Emily Jean," Max interrupted. "You've always wanted to write novels other than penny dreadfuls, and I see this as the perfect opportunity.

"You've just proven that you're capable of so much more. *Jess Murdock: Legend of the West* is a creative masterpiece. I'm very proud to publish it. And I'd be just as proud to publish one of those romantic novels you're always talking about writing, or a work of nonfiction, or whatever else you can come up with. Of course, if you decide to continue with the E. J. Bartlett series, I'd be delighted as well."

She chewed her lower lip. "I don't know. . . ."

"You wouldn't be working for wages anymore, Emily Jean. I would pay you an advance against royalties, and you could take as long as you like—within reason—to get your books to me."

It was all too much for the young woman to take in. Feeling light-headed, Emily was grateful to have Jess's arm about her. "I'm not sure what I should do. I had already resigned myself to quitting, and I'm not altogether sure that I even want to consider what you've proposed." Though it would be a wonderful opportunity, that little voice inside her head reminded her, to have her own name on a novel, to prove to the world, to herself, that Emily Jean Bartlett had finally succeeded.

"I didn't mean to overwhelm you, my dear. Take

some time to think about it," Max advised. "Jess has invited me to stay a few days and attend the wedding, so I don't need an answer right away."

Jess turned her in his arms and gazed into eyes filled with uncertainty. "Emily, Zach and I don't mind sharing you and your talent with the rest of the world. I'd feel guilty as hell if you gave up your career for me. And Zach's already mentioned that he wants to help you write a book for children."

Her eyes widened, then filled with tears. "He has?"

Jess kissed her nose. "Think about all we've said, babe, before you decide to retire. You're far too young, and I was thinking that it might not be a bad thing for me to be living off all those earnings you're likely to make."

Max's booming laughter filled the room, and Emily finally joined in, then said, "I never would have guessed that you were marrying me for my money, Jess Murdock, considering the fact that I haven't had two nickels to rub together since arriving at your ranch."

"Speaking of money . . ." Max withdrew an envelope from the breast pocket of his jacket and held it out to Emily. "Here's half of what I owe you. I'll have the other half as soon as I return to New York."

Emily peeked inside, and her mouth dropped open. There was twice the normal amount that she usually got paid. "I think you made a mistake, Max."

The older man shook his head. "Your old salary was for writing dime novels. Jess's book is far bigger than that. I thought it required a bit more compensation to show my appreciation for all of your hard work. Consider it a wedding present."

"But the bills . . ."

"Almost all paid for," he answered proudly, and Emily was even more astounded.

"Oh, Max, I'm so happy for you."

"I couldn't have done it without you, Emily. And there's another little surprise that I've been keeping."

"Another surprise? Good heavens! I'm not sure I can take any more. You and Jess have quite overwhelmed me."

Max grinned. "Not even if I were to tell you that *Jess Murdock: Legend of the West* is poised to make the bestseller list? My contact at *The Bookman* says it should be listed in the next issue of the 'Books on Demand' column."

Emily screamed, held her flushed face in her hands, then promptly fainted in Jess's arms.

The Murdock household was a beehive of activity as everyone rushed about making ready for the upcoming wedding reception, which would be held the following evening.

Frances and Emily had been cooking up a storm in the kitchen, preparing all of the food for the small gathering, whose guests would include the cowhands of the Bar JM, their dates, a few of Jess's closest neighbors, Max, and the immediate family.

Two turkeys had been roasted and a ham baked, along with various side dishes and breads. The housekeeper had outdone herself with the preparation of a traditional two-tiered wedding cake, frosted with white confectioner's icing.

Even Clara Higgbotham had entered into the frenzied activities by sending over three dozen petit fours, just in case extra guests happened to show up. Frances had remarked with a chuckle that it was likely Clara would be one of those who did; the woman hated missing out on any social event.

Max had lent Frosty and Jess a hand with the cutting of the Christmas tree, claiming he hadn't had such fun since he was a child Zach's age. Zach, who'd accompanied the men on their trek into the woods, had grown quite fond of the older gentleman and had taken to calling him Uncle Max, much to Max's great delight.

In the parlor Emily was just putting the finishing touches on the nine-foot fir tree. The ornaments she and Frances had purchased looked incredibly lovely as they sparkled in the afternoon sunshine. The greenery and candles decorating the room and the rest of the house lent a festive and fragrant air to the holiday and marital festivities. And she'd even managed to talk Jess and Frosty into decorating the large fir tree in the front yard with cranberry-and-popcorn strings and a large silver star at the top.

Emily sighed in wonderment. "Doesn't it look beautiful, Frances? I couldn't have picked out a more perfect tree if I'd chosen it myself."

"Aye, lass. I havena seen a prettier one," the older woman said, wiping a tear from her eye with the corner of her apron. "I know I'm being a foolish old woman, but I'm just so happy tae be marrying Frosty."

Emily knew just how her friend felt, for she had to pinch herself from time to time just to make sure that her marriage to Jess wasn't all a dream.

She and Jess had spoken at length about Max's proposal that she continue writing, and they had finally decided that Emily would maintain her literary career, despite her previous reservations to the contrary.

Jess had convinced her that she would be able to manage both a career and a family and that he and Zach would be there to help if things got too overwhelming for her. He had fallen in love with a writer, he'd said, and a writer was what she should be.

Hugging Frances about the waist, Emily replied, "I feel the same way. Everything's just about perfect."

"Just about?" The woman's smile faded. "Good Lord! What is it we've forgotten, lass? I've made so many lists I'm going cross-eyed."

Emily smiled, despite the great void in her heart. Only one thing could make the occasion truly perfect, but she had no intention of burdening her friend with that now, not when Frances was so jubilant.

There'd been no word from her parents, no joy at her upcoming nuptials, no offer of congratulations or words of "I love you," and it broke her heart.

She'd learned long ago that wishing for something didn't necessarily make it come true. That happened only in fairy tales. And as much as she longed to be reunited with her family, she knew that wasn't likely to happen, not after all the time and unpleasantness that had passed between them.

As if the older woman could read her mind, Frances caressed Emily's cheek. "Ye mustna give up on them, lass.

Ye'll see them again. Mark my words. I havena lived this long not tae know o' such things."

"If only my father were here to give me away." She heaved a dispirited sigh. "I know it's selfish to wish for that after everything I've been given."

"'Tisna selfish at all, lass. But ye've got Max tae walk ye down the aisle. When one door closes, another always opens. 'Tis a true enough saying."

"You're right, of course. And I am marrying the most wonderful man in the world."

"Did I hear my name mentioned?" Jess walked in, grinning like the Cheshire cat, and Emily could see that her remark had inflated his ego to gargantuan proportions.

"You've already got a swelled head, Jess Murdock. I'll not add to it by singing your praises any further."

Frances chuckled, then excused herself, allowing the affianced couple a bit more privacy.

Jess crossed the room in three strides and scooped Emily into his arms. "Have I told you lately how much I love you?"

Emily smiled and shook her head. "Not nearly enough."

He kissed her passionately, and she felt her bones start to dissolve. A moment later she pulled back when she realized her resolve to avoid intimacy with Jess until their wedding night was starting to dissolve as well. "Shame on you, Jess Murdock! You promised to behave yourself. What if Max or Zach had walked in on us?"

He shrugged, and his grin remained naughty. "So? I intend to make an honest woman out of you tomorrow."

"You know it's bad luck to see the bride before the wedding." She lowered her voice. "I thought we agreed that we'd wait to . . . to . . . wait until after the ceremony."

"I must have been drunk when I promised that. Won't you release me from it? I need you, babe."

Emily could feel the evidence of that need pressing into her leg and wasn't at all surprised, for she felt her own desire as keenly. But she had no intention of giving in; she wanted a proper wedding night. "You'll have me come tomorrow night. Just be patient."

He cupped her breast, felt her nipple harden. "And can you wait? I think you're as impatient as I am."

She spun out of his arms and was across the room before he knew what was happening. "It's all a matter of self-control," she lied, hoping he wouldn't attempt to prove her wrong. "And it's not as if we haven't been together."

"I'm tempted to come over there and prove that you're lying through your teeth, Emily Jean Bartlett. If I recall, you're quite good at it." At the look of alarm on her face, he smiled. "But I won't. I've waited for you my whole life. I guess one more day won't matter."

Emily's eyes filled with tears. "Oh, Jess. Just when I think I can resist you, you go and say something sweet, making me crumble all to pieces inside."

"Just be sure you're completely whole by tomorrow night, babe. I want every little bit of you."

Watching him walk out the door, Emily felt her heart constrict and she burst into tears.

Being a bride-to-be was hell!

Chapter Twenty-two

BEING A BRIDE WAS HEAVEN, EMILY DECIDED AS SHE slipped lower into the copper bathtub of steaming water and sipped champagne from the crystal flute that Jess had purchased especially for their wedding night.

Both weddings had gone off without a hitch. Jess and Frosty had looked dashing in their black suits and string ties, Max had been the perfect substitute father to give her away, and Zach had been well behaved and adorable in his role of ring bearer.

Everything had been storybook perfect. And in a few minutes it was going to get even better. Smiling in anticipation, she leaned her head back against the rim of the tub and wondered when her husband would return with the second bottle of wine. She was going to enjoy being married, Emily decided, closing her eyes.

"If you don't stop looking so darn sexy, I'm going to put an end to your bath right now, woman."

Relaxed and feeling almost lethargic, Emily opened her eyes with an effort and found a shirtless and incredibly appealing Jess perched on the edge of the tub, holding another bottle of champagne.

"I'm having the most delightful time."

"You'd be having a better one if you'd get out of that damn tub. You're going to be as wrinkled as a prune if you don't."

Emily's grin was decidedly crooked, owing to the amount of champagne she had consumed. "Does that mean you won't want to make love to me?" Feigning disappointment, she added, "And I was so looking forward to consummating our marriage." With a shrug of her shoulders, she reached for the soap and handed it to him. "In that case would you mind soaping my back?"

Setting aside the champagne, he took the scented lavender soap and knelt by the tub. "I can't promise to keep my hands strictly to your back." His grin was wicked, but hers was downright lurid.

"I'd be awfully disappointed if you did."

Kissing her gently on the lips, Jess used both his hands as a washcloth, soaping them thoroughly, then gliding them over her back and shoulders until she moaned in ecstasy.

"That feels positively decadent," she admitted, closing her eyes once again. "Mmmmm. I'm not sure how much of this exquisite torture I can take." And it was exquisite, Emily thought as his hands moved to fondle her sensitive breasts.

"Your wish is my command, ma'am," he said huskily, rolling her rigid nipples between his fingers until her eyes popped open and she groaned aloud, then whispered his name on a sigh.

He kissed her again, saying, "I love you, Emily," then took the soap and spread her thighs to continue his intimate ministrations.

Intense heat suffused every inch of Emily's body as Jess thumbed the bud of her femininity while his tongue caressed her mouth. The pleasurable pain quickly became too intense, and she cried out for release.

"Take me, Jess. Now!"

As if she weighed no more than a feather, he scooped her out of the water and carried her to the large bed, laying her gently atop the coverlet. "You are the most beautiful, the most perfect, woman in the world, Mrs. Murdock," he whispered before covering her mouth and her body with his own.

With his every passionate thrust, Emily soared to heights she'd only just imagined, feeling as if she were floating above herself. As they reached the final pinnacle and climaxed together, she felt Jess's seed go deep inside her and knew that now she was truly his, forever and for all eternity.

"I love you, Jess. I always have and I always will."

By the light of the fire, he saw tears falling down her cheeks and kissed them away. "I love you, too," he whispered, rolling to his side and taking her with him.

With a soft smile, she caressed his cheek. "And will you love me when I'm old and gray and run to fat?" She had a sneaking suspicion that she'd be the latter soon, though not from overeating, and her joy knew no bounds. But she wouldn't tell him yet, not until she was sure.

Smiling into the darkness, Jess replied, "You talk too much, woman," then he smothered whatever else she was going to say and proceeded to show her again just how much he loved her and always would.

The Murdock and Adams families, along with Max, had just sat down to a sumptuous Christmas feast of roast goose with all the trimmings when a loud banging ensued at the front door.

Emily and Jess exchanged startled looks, then Emily said, "I wonder who that could be?"

"'Tis fer sure we're nae going tae find out sitting here." Frances looked radiantly happy and well pleased with life at the moment, which might have had something to do with the way her husband's chest was puffed out in pride. Emily feared Frosty would pop all the buttons off the new blue gingham shirt Frances had made him for Christmas.

The banging continued, and Max finally asked, "Is anyone going to answer the door?"

"Maybe Santa Claus has come back," Zach offered hopefully.

Everyone laughed, then they pushed back their chairs and hurried to see who had come calling on Christmas Day.

"I hope it's not the Reverend and Clara. I don't think I'm up for a visit from them quite yet," Emily said, recalling the long-winded, officious sermon the cleric had delivered during the ceremony last evening.

Jess laughed. "The man was in his element, wasn't he?" He yanked open the door to find a group of strangers standing there.

With a gasp, Emily stared wide-eyed at the family she'd thought never to lay eyes on again, then promptly fainted dead away.

When Emily opened her eyes a few moments later, it was to find herself on the parlor sofa with her mother hovering over her like an avenging angel, patting her hand to revive her. Marian Bartlett was giving Jess a tongue-lashing for some supposed offense, and she didn't seem at all as incompetent or flighty as Emily had remembered.

"Has my daughter been sick, Mr. Murdock? You should have written if that were the case. I would have called in a specialist or hired a nurse to administer twenty-four-hour care."

Jess looked as if he didn't quite know what to say, and Emily felt extremely sorry for him and almost smiled. Her mother's forthright manner took some getting used to.

"No, ma'am," he tried to explain, shaking his head. "Emily's been just fine. I think the shock of seeing you was just too much for her."

Hoping to rescue him, Emily finally sat up. "I'm fine, Mother. Truly." She squeezed the older woman's hand, noting how little she had aged in the past three years. "I'm so happy to see you." She gazed across the room to where her father was standing with Max, who was smoking a cigarette.

"Hello, Father. You're looking well."

Louis Bartlett grunted, but there were tears of joy in his eyes when he looked upon his oldest daughter. "Your telegram took us by surprise, Emily. We were very grateful to Mr. Wise for filling us in on the details of your marriage to Mr. Murdock."

Standing by the fireplace, Max looked suitably guilty. Emily would always be grateful to him for the hand he'd played in bringing her family to her.

Marian caressed her daughter's cheek. "I'm so happy we were able to make the journey, dear, even if we are a bit late for the actual ceremony. Your father and I have missed you dreadfully, Emily Jean."

Looking about the room, Emily frowned when she didn't spy her brothers and sister. "Where did Elaine, Herbert, and Harry run off to? I can't wait to see them again."

"Hmph!" A look of disapproval crossed her mother's face. "That bossy Scottish woman herded them all into the kitchen to feed them. She said your father and I were quite enough to deal with at the moment." Her face softening, Marian smiled ruefully. "I suppose she's right."

Bless Frances's heart, Emily thought. The considerate woman always knew just the right thing to say and do.

"Guess you heard that Emily's new book is a huge success," Max said to no one in particular, winking at Emily in conspiratorial fashion.

Louis nodded, unable to conceal the pride in his voice. "It was the talk of New York when we left. It's going to take some getting used to having a daughter who's a celebrity."

"We're very proud of you, dear," her mother assured her. "All of us are extremely proud. Your father has already purchased a hundred copies of the book to hand out to his friends and business associates."

"Really, Father?" Emily's eyes filled with tears, Max's with dollar signs.

Louis came forward, taking the seat on the sofa next to his daughter. "Your mother and I have been stupid these past few years, Emily." He clasped her hand in his. "I hope you can find it in your heart to forgive us for being so narrow-minded. We thought we were doing the right thing, but we know now that were wrong and selfish."

Throwing her arms about him, Emily kissed him, then turned to her mother. "There's nothing to forgive. I love you both very much. I'm so happy that we're all going to be together again as a family. I've missed that most of all."

Turning to look at her husband, Emily said, "Jess and I are both thrilled that you've come for a visit, aren't we, Jess?"

Noting the pure joy on his wife's face, Jess could only smile and nod, but he wondered where he was going to bunk five extra people. The house was already packed to capacity, and the Bartletts didn't look like the type of people who slept on the floor.

Later, when things had settled down and the Christmas dinner had finally been eaten, Jess and Emily found a quiet moment in his study, where he expressed his concerns.

Emily laughed. "You're turning into a bigger worry-wart than me, husband dear. I thought that was the wife's role."

He took her in his arms. "I know how important it is to have your family here, Emily Jean. I just want everything to be perfect for you."

"It already is." She circled his waist with her arms. "Having you in my life has made it perfect. And now I've got something to tell you that I hope will make yours the same way."

"You're not working on another book already, are you? We've hardly found time to celebrate the present one."

She giggled and shook her head. "The project I'm working on is far more exciting than a book, but it's going to take a bit longer to produce—say, about nine months."

"Nine mo—" Confusion turned quickly to joy, and his eyes widened as he lifted her off the ground and swung her around, grinning from ear to ear. "You're going to have a baby?"

"I'm not positive, mind you, but I've got all the symptoms. I was going to wait to tell you until I was sure, but I just couldn't. I hope you're as happy as I am."

"Happy? Woman, I'm stunned, overjoyed, downright speechless."

Her smile was radiant. "Merry Christmas, Jess."

"Merry Christmas, babe." Then he kissed her passionately and patted her stomach, amending, "Babes."

Her eyes filled with tears of happiness, Emily knew that she had finally found her hero.

AUTHOR NOTE

Just as my heroine, Emily Jean, was wont to take literary license with the truth—we authors really do lie for a living!—so I have taken a wee bit myself.

Though book publishing had become a fully developed industry by the second half of the nineteenth century, the advent of the best-seller list did not actually take place until February of 1895, with the first issue of *The Bookman*, a literary magazine whose column "Books in Demand" featured the best-sellers of the day.

The list was compiled from bookstore sales in sixteen cities across the United States, much the same way publishers compile their lists today.

It is interesting to note that many of the characteristics that exist today in publishing—editors acquiring manuscripts, best-seller lists, and so forth—existed during the nineteenth century, though probably on a much smaller scale.

I hope you enjoyed *True Love* and your foray into the trials and tribulations of a dime novelist.

Emily Jean Bartlett was a woman this author could definitely identify with.

— *Millie Criswell*

FALL IN LOVE WITH AWARD-WINNING AUTHOR MILLIE CRISWELL

Flowers of the West Trilogy

- **WILD HEATHER**
(0-446-60-171-3, $5.99 USA) ($6.99 CAN)
- **SWEET LAUREL**
(0-446-60-172-1, $5.99 USA) ($6.99 CAN)
- **PRIM ROSE**
(0-446-60-323-6, $5.99 USA) ($6.99 CAN)

The Lawmen Trilogy

- **DESPERATE**
(0-446-60-415-1, $5.99 USA) ($6.99 CAN)
- **DANGEROUS**
(0-446-60-497-6, $5.99 USA) ($6.99 CAN)
- **DEFIANT**
(0-446-60-498-4, $5.99 USA) ($6.99 CAN)

AVAILABLE AT A BOOKSTORE NEAR YOU FROM
WARNER BOOKS

1016